PRAISE FOR

YOUR FINAL SUNSET

"A kaleidoscope of grief, longing, and the surreal, *Your Final Sunset* reads like an elegy to the forgotten and the forsaken."

— Stuart Conover, *Horror Tree* and *JournalStone Network* EIC

"A tight bundle of dynamite."

— Alex Woodroe, *Tenebrous Press* EIC, author of *Whisperwood*

ALSO BY

SJ TOWNEND

Sick Girl Screams

Content warnings are available at the end of this book. Please consult this list for any particular subject matter you may be sensitive to.

YOUR FINAL SUNSET

SJ TOWNEND

CONTENTS

I Have Seen Seven Bad Things.. 1

Tonight, the Moon is Not Quite Complete............................. 13

To Cherish 33

Love Letters 55

The Haze-On Lady 61

Gurgle 81

Like Sardines.. 93

Bonus Kiosk 101

Emily's Journey 131

Empty Nest... 139

Everyone, Monsters 151

He Has Not Seen a Bird 171

Be Kind to Your Children: They Choose Your Nursing Home.......... 187

This Echo Chamber Life... 205

I Vomited Every Hour for Three Days After You Ended Things...... 219

Niche P*rn 225

Garden Path.. 239

Neglect Takes the Form of the Recovery Position 261

Five Knuckle Shuffle... 275

Afterword.. 295

About the Author 297

Content Warnings.. 298

Credits.. 299

I HAVE SEEN SEVEN BAD THINGS

Daddy, escorted home by the police on a grim January evening.

At the top of the stairs, dressed in my pyjamas with Teddy squeezed tight in my arms, I sit, knees huddled to chest, and witness it all.

No arrest has been made, according to the sombre policeman, but this doesn't stop my mother from exploding with fury after she hurries my father in and shuts the front door. Daddy must sleep on the sofa tonight. After the lounge door closes, I hear the clunk of cupboards and drawers in the kitchen. My mother passes me on her way up the stairs, one of her glass bottles under her arm, and instructs me to go back to bed. I do as I am told.

From under my Ninja Turtles duvet, in the dark, through the thin plasterboard floor and walls of our council house, I listen: Daddy's snores, Mummy crying herself to sleep.

In the morning, my father still wiped out in the sitting room, my mother gives me one of her awkward hugs, kisses me on the forehead, then crouches down to meet me at eye level. "I love you, Boo, but I've got to leave," she says, her face puffy, her breath wine-sour. Over her arm, her half-zipped bag spews bundled clothing. I plead for her to take me with her. I don't want to stay with Daddy. Both our eyes fill with tears. "We'll stay in touch, I promise, Sweet-pea, but you must stay with Daddy. Your father understands you better than I ever will. Now, be a darling, go and wake him up."

I ignore my mother's instruction and follow her down the hallway, and stand a few feet behind her as she searches for her car keys. She finds them, then reaches for the front door handle. My fingertip runs faster and faster round the loop of my teddy-bear's snout, the place where the fur fabric is most worn. My mother turns, speaks, "Stop doing that to your bear, Michael. Please," then leaves.

For a while, my mother picks me up on Saturdays for ice cream and the occasional trip to the swings, but her visits dwindle to the annual birthday card in the post as the years pass by.

2. The drawing on the whiteboard at school: a stickman with fingers and thumbs in places they shouldn't be. The caption underneath, scrawled in the handwriting of a rushed nine-year-old child: *"Michael Andrews and his family are all weirdos."*

I cry, deny it, rush for the wiper, and scrub the sick image away before the supply teacher we've been told we've got today arrives; but as Jenny Brown sticks her tongue out at me, and flicks her pigtails back, she exposes the lobe and the canal of her right ear.

Something flutters in my stomach.

The board a blank canvas again, I toss the wiper on the teacher's desk, thrust my hands into my trouser pockets, and slope back to my plastic chair at the side of the room where I sit down next to Miles "Cheesy" Johnson.

The supply teacher arrives.

The class settles.

The teacher instructs us all to copy today's date from the board into our workbooks, but all I can think about is Jenny Brown's earlobe. For the first time, I wonder if there is, perhaps, some truth in the graffiti I cleared from the board.

3. Judy's face.

A single-parent household now, Dad unable to afford a sitter, he tells me to stay in my room; a woman named Judy is coming for dinner and I am not invited.

"Eleven-year-olds should be able to entertain themselves for a few hours," he says, and presses a warm paper bag with the blue Greggs logo on its side into my hands.

Later, in the night, I take a peep into Dad's room through a gap in the door, drawn there by a sound similar to a wet fish being reeled onto land. Judy is perched on the edge of the bed, and Dad is standing, fully clothed, by her side, his clumsy hands all over her face.

He shouts, "Get out."

Judy screams. She shuffles up her belongings and pushes past me to make her way downstairs.

Despite the nightmare qualities of the scene I've witnessed— Judy's too wide eyes, my father's fingers plumbing up her mouth and nostrils, his head and eyes rolling back in some sort of lost, ecstatic trance, back in my own room after Judy has gone and Dad has returned to bed—with a grin on my face, I take deep joy in playing the scene out, again and again, in my mind.

In the morning, Father doesn't seem cross or disappointed, tells me he's sorry I caught him up to his 'old tricks.' "It never feels as good with the same person a second time anyway, kiddo," he says as he pours me a bowl of the weekend cereal, even though it's Wednesday.

I never see Judy again.

I sit my GCSE exams a few years later. Father is out on the drink, up to 'old tricks,' as he so often is, when I receive my seven failed grades in the mail.

4. Midnight, my greying father in a dive-bar cubicle, his thumbs up some lad's nose.

After a long shift in the warehouse, I find myself at Cheetah's, a Gentleman's Club full of anything but. I come here now and again to let off steam. The beer is cheap and the dance floor is always busy, even in the small hours of the morning. Not much choice of venue this side of the town centre.

Three pints down, I have the urgency to piss.

There he is, my father, in the stalls with a redhead. If I'd have known he'd be here, I would have gone somewhere else.

I pause, hidden behind the door jamb of the Men's, and try to interpret what the heck is going on. The redhead, a slim lad perhaps a few years older than me, has his arms around my father's waist. Dad's hands are cupped around the young lad's face, intimately so. But they do not kiss.

Instead, Dad's pinkies caterpillar in and out of the redhead's ears, his thumbs, the redhead's nose. My father's body shudders as the face between his hands laughs.

Still unaware of my lurking presence, Dad pulls the young lad's face closer to his, breath-close, then worms his index finger under the lad's left eyelid.

The redhead grunts and yanks Dad's roving fingers out and away from the holes of his face. My father staggers back, apparently far more drunk than me. "That is not what we agreed to," the lad says.

Dad stutters, apologises, but his spidering fingers lurch for the poor lad's face again. The redhead slaps him, rightly so. "Security," the redhead shouts above the thrum of resonating bassline, and while doing so, his eye catches mine, "And it's extra for voyeurism."

As father sees me, I cannot tell you which one of us looks more surprised.

"Shit, son, I'm sorry," he says.

"You owe me thirty," the redhead is addressing my father. Dad reaches into his pocket and passes him a bunch of crumpled notes. The lad takes them and spits on my father's shoes before slipping out past me, swallowed in the queue for the crowded bar. Dad sways to his left, attempts to take a swig from an empty plastic pint glass that had been balancing on the hand dryer.

"Let's get you out of here, Dad."

ଊଛ୫ଓ

At home, I help him undress and get him into bed. Dad slurs as he tries to explain something to me. "We're hexed, son. Me, my father, my grandfather—the whole damned line of us Andrews. We've all been cursed to fuck."

I pass him a glass of water and let him ramble on.

"And your mother, she knew it'd pass on to you, too. Mothers always know."

"That's why she left me with you?" I find myself drawn into his deluded story, although he's beyond answering questions; just one long drunken soliloquy to come, until he passes out, I expect.

"At first, it was just an itch, something I could push down and ignore. But then this need, this curse, became an obsession. The relief when I slide my fingers into someone's face-holes, dear God—" He stares into the space between us, his palms turned up, his fingers spread out, each hand an upturned crab. Said crabs shake in time, emphasising the cadence of his words. "This curse, son—as the wheel turns, it develops, becomes an insatiable condition. My body crawls with agony when I'm not plumbed in."

"Dad, you're oversharing nonsense. Too much to drink again. Get some sleep." I don't dare tell him about my own sick fetish. The one that's been growing within me, extrapolating towards my fingers and toes, like a seed's roots stretching out through dirt, probing, un-furling, since I first saw Jenny Brown's ear-hole in Year 4.

Dad apologises profusely, his tongue thick with alcohol, then passes out.

With gaffer tape initially, then with the four coiled bike locks I retrieve from the garage, out of shame and out of love, I tether Dad to his bed.

Sometime mid-morning, he wakes screaming, shifting in his sheets, writhing like Renton without the gear, the stench of beer drip-ping from his pores. I apologise, "Look, Dad, I'm sorry." I have no choice but to tape his mouth shut too, before I go to work.

5. The contents of the bag.

I move with urgency. Father has been alone for six hours and will be in pain, begging for release. Of course, I'll never untie him. He's well past the point of no return. To liberate him entirely from his sweat-stained bed would be insanity, could put innocent people at risk.

The heavy bag I carry bashes against my leg as I walk, its contents squelching like my sodden trainers through the puddles.

The rain descends in almost horizontal wet grey hyphens. I swear the wetness whispers 'hurry' as my feet pound the pavement back to the apartment Dad and I share. I arrive, wade through the knee-high grass of our front lawn, unlock the door, go inside, and kick off my shoes. *Clunk clunk clunk.* The headboard of Father's bed bashes against his bedroom wall.

Still exulting from my date earlier with Aisha, despite how things evolved, I dump the bag on the kitchen counter and sniff my fingers. The scent of her mucus and waxes lingers on the pads of my damp thumbs. After we'd kissed, I'd asked her permission, had said it was sort of a kink. I had to try, with real flesh. My urges have been growing stronger.

I'd slid my finger in her ear, just for a second, then her nostril. On the edge of a pleasure greater than orgasm, an indescribable need had driven me to it.

But this curse, it's not a sexual thing, not carnal. It's primal: intrinsic and all-consuming. My yearning to plumb and plug grows weightier by the day. God knows what will happen in time. At least I don't have a child who'll catch me mid-action and keep me restrained in shame. I can control it, anyway. I'll always ask for consent. I'm not weak like Father.

Aisha had laughed at first, before she'd asked me to stop. "It's not doing anything for me," she'd said, before tugging her hijab back on.

Irritated, but in control of myself, I'd told her it wasn't going to work out between us, had grabbed my stuff and left. I'd marched in the rain to the butcher's after leaving her house, to fulfil Dad's request.

I peek into the carrier bag, pegging my nose as the odour hits my olfactory system. Inside, ogling back up at me: the severed pig's head.

I'll have to settle myself the same way father does tonight. In the morning, I'll hit Tinder again, try to find a new source for a new day.

6. Father's face as he plumbs.

Until now, I've pacified Father with cold slices of meats, latex substitute body parts. Last month he'd even been able to get his fix from a pair of old, warmed leather gloves. But these substitutions no longer seem to be enough. His body has become weaker without a daily pure flesh fix, and his urges have grown stronger. I've researched it, our condition. It seems, in the dark corners of the web, there are others like us out there, scattered across the globe. I promised myself, while leafing through microfiche slides in the library, to reach out and connect with the others, see if there is a cure.

I carry the butcher's bag up to his room. "Release," he wails, his voice reedy, like his limbs. Ensuring his waist and ankles are still restrained accordingly, with the correct combination of numbers I will never reveal to him, I unlock his bound wrists as old sunken eyes implore me to bring the bag and its contents closer to where he lies.

I let him plumb his fingers into the meaty sockets, the snout, the whiskery ear canals, the stale, raw swine maw. His own tongue pokes out, lolls from side to side. His frantic, desperate fingers and thumbs explore the dead flesh. Father's head tilts, his eyes closed. He purrs in an ecstasy I now fear I nearly understand.

To watch him pleasure himself this way unleashes something in me.

Surely, I'm too early on in this sick downhill trajectory to need to join in with him, to abuse the hog's head in such a filthy way? The stench of the aged meat repulses me. The putrified odour turns my stomach. But the white hair which pokes out from my father's nostrils has quite the opposite effect. I learn fast: to observe is too much for me to bear. I can't help myself. I'm not as strong as I'd thought.

"I'm so sorry," I say, although my father is so momentarily oblivious; I'm unsure if he hears. He's in a faraway place, dancing with fairies, or demons, as his near-skeletal fingers pump in and out, revelling in the hogshead which rests, milky-eyed, upon his lap.

I sit on the bed beside him and slide my finger into Father's ear canal. I push it through layers of wax, like a stick in a toffee apple, until I reach the tympanic membrane. Bliss.

We both recline together, in another level of pleasure, my fingers probing and plumbing more into my father's skull-holes, and his, digging deeper into the skull-holes of the pig, pulverising pork into mince.

Father has a sudden moment of lucidity, becomes aware of what I'm doing to him. He screams. He withdraws his fingertips from the pig and plugs all ten of his jellied, blood-covered exploratory worms into my mouth and nose.

Connected like a twin-human ouroboros, a mass of wigwagging wet skin, bone, and hair, I wonder, in my own brief moments of lucidity, if I can get my big toe in my father's mouth.

For minutes, an hour perhaps, side-by-side on the bed, we writhe and sweat and probe each other's faces, limiting the other's oxygen supply, the macerated pig's head between us, staring up at the ceiling, perhaps feeling left out like the third person in an unsuccessful three-way.

♋

We embrace our Magnum Opus. I am not sure when I come to realise father is no longer breathing, his body already stiff from the outside in, and that I too am no longer present in my mortal body. Like a reverse claustrophobia, I am both suddenly unfolded from my shell, inside and out, then out, out, all at once.

Time is of no relevance now, as our once-entwined bodies separate out into sentient nothingness, somewhere up here in an ethereal plain.

Below, the emptied, twisted double-headed knot of what was us lies hard and yellow, bracketing a minced pig's head, splayed out on vermillion, sodden sheets.

Father and I, or the cursed apparitions of us both, snake our way, like oil in water, towards the other mass of curling and furling energy. So this, I think to myself, my last independent thought, is what lurks beneath the veil.

Together, we wisp up, and join with the single, timeless point of entanglement; a singularity of darkness. We become everywhere and nowhere all at once, with no beginning and no end: true release.

7. What lies beneath now, cold and solid.

Now, we inhabit no human bodies. We all move as one. Between us are infinite fingers and toes and thumbs, a pulsating, tendrilled ball of invisible force.

We call ourselves the Brotherhood and glide alongside man, although we'll never reveal our true form—it would drive the oblivious to insanity. Instead, we hide in plain sight, between the atoms of the air, in the blind spot when you drive, in your sense of déjà-vu.

Within the God particle we lurk, in the low frequencies of electromagnetic force. As one and as nothing, we swim in all the domains of science and religion no man will ever truly have the capacity to understand.

In this moment, we drift into the neo-natal clinic as a tired nurse loses focus, and there, we plant seeds of erotic asphyxiation in the souls of the sexually lost. Then we float to Mayhill Retirement Home once the old folk have gone to bed. We do what we have grown to love, that thing that brings release.

Beneath our collective now, as you read this story, an old girl rasps in her sleep.

Working as one, we pull the pillow into position, shifting the sheet of cotton one fractal thread at a time, then each of us, anchored to a thin white hair, help tip her head a little too far to the right, and anchor it there with our urges.

With all her orifices smothered, we release her from her opiated sleep and help her avoid the need to wake.

ℂℂℂ

We have seen seven bad things and we will see an eternity more.

TONIGHT, THE MOON IS NOT QUITE COMPLETE

It had been her, and if not her, then the spit of her: hair of titian waves, skin lit as if by moonlight, Celtic emeralds for eyes. *No, it couldn't have been her,* he thinks, and tries to return his focus to the theremin wand in the space between his hands, *as that would be impossible, impossible.*

Tonight, now, it is his gig, his time, his chance to shine from his up-lit spot on the stage in an otherwise dark hall. But now he's seen her, this woman who is like her but not quite like her, all he can think about is finishing his performance and stepping down into the crowd to search.

This same game of cat and mouse continues, month in, month out, as if he and she are trapped in a repeating loop of unrequited searching, a nightmare. But even though he wants to, he can't step down into the crowd now. Not now. He has to perform.

A hundred faces stare up at him. They are a hundred faces he cares not for, but they are also a hundred faces who have paid money, good money, to see his show, and a large part of this cash, he hopes, will become his. He needs this money to pay his way, if he survives the morrow.

The theremin, all polished steel and electromagnetic fields, beckons back his nimble hands. He makes wings, lifts his arms either side of his machine, and does as he has done before, does what he is good at, the one thing he is sure he is good at. He plays his theremin. Carving the air with his hands, he chops it into shapes, sculpts with it her cheeks, her patrician nose, the chin. He models the face of his long-dead mother into sounds some might call music all out of nothing but drunk-thick air. With each flick of his wrists, corresponding sounds are heard as he throws the contours of her face out into the ether.

The song of his mother's face is the melody they have all come for. It is the tune they've all heard before, the song that makes him able to attract such a crowd. *An overnight internet sensation,* they said, *you simply must see him play in the flesh, there is nothing quite like it. Such a sound from something never touched.*

Each part of her face is construed into sliding semibreves and minims. Eyes, lips, nose, cheeks, lips, eyes, nose. With wizarding thumbs, he depicts her brows. He plays on. Each feature of his mother's visage hangs, out of sight, in the air, and then dissipates, disintegrates, as if it were not really there. And it was not really there, not in the physical world anyway. Not in any dimension you or I might recognise. Some say he has magician's fingers, which, as they undulate and outline his mother's facial parts, release a little magic into the world.

Left hand oscillating back and forth, right hand descending, he shapes the waves of her hair. He crimps the invisible gaseous molecules and motes of dust held up within, and with his actions, each curl brings an eerie tone through the speakers either side of him on the stage. In his mind, a tear rolls down her cheek. He paints it in the space in front of him with his index finger, and lets the speakers cry out with depression.

The audience are taken with this emotion. Their hearts throb harder with the beauty of the sound. He lifts his arms higher, and then again, shapes his mother's almond eyes, twills out each long dark lash, and the crowd are lifted out from the sad place he had placed them in as the key of the oscillations change from minor to major. Resonating reverberations. Both melancholia and joy become entwined. His hands play on. Music from the electromagnetic whine of the theremin sprinkles an acoustic, near-sentient gift, like dappled sunlight through a forest canopy, onto and over the crowd.

He continues to play the face of his mother, the shape of the face of the mother he remembers, putting into each fingertip sweep and dot his heart and soul, yet all the while his own eyes continue their quest in searching for her in the crowd.

The hundred non-descript faces are brought to tears, but he wants his set to be over, for it to be finished, because he wants to find her this time: the visitor who never stays to say hello. He wishes to follow her off into the night and cup her face in his hands and ask her who she is, this woman who is but is not quite his mother.

Will it be like all the other times she has come to watch him perform and he has tried to find her afterwards, close, but no cigar? More than likely. But he is desperate to find her and from his accumulation of hopelessness, he manages to sift free a glimmer of hope.

There she goes again. He sees her, sees the light and dark of her long curls. She moves, skits from location to location, pocket to pocket, a human-shaped firefly dancing amongst the crowd. He spots her in the audience again, standing by a tall man with thick-frame glasses. He's certain it's her. But again, she flits. *Is it her? Was it her?* How can it be her—his mother died thirty years ago.

He scans the crowd and sees the faces of all those who are not her, not this entrancing apparition of familiarity. They're just strangers he cares nothing for, strangers swaying like willows in a spring breeze. They move in unison, under the control of the sounds he orchestrates while air-plucking, while searching, searching. *She's gone.* His mood sinks. *No, no,* he thinks, *I'm certain now, she is not there. Not anymore.* And the sadness this brings to his soul drifts like weightless ghosts into his music.

⚭

He plays his next song, from his solo space up on the stage. He is the closing act, the 'headliner', although he has never understood why people come. *I'm just a man, a man who drinks; a single, aging man with a theremin.*

He feels the sounds he generates are the sounds one might manifest if one were in a place without any sound at all, if one were caged alone in silence for an eternity. From nowhere, one might begin to hear a theremin wail. And it would make one feel more alone, he believes. He finds the noise he makes to be haunting, the last sort of sound he would wish to hear if he were alone.

And he is alone, in a way, always has been, since his parents died many years ago.

His father.

On the morning of Pa's thirty-seventh, something red opened up inside of Pa. His father collapsed and died, no warning. He, then a boy, had found his mother, a shade of ash, down on the kitchen floor, furled over Pa's warm corpse.

His mother.

She too died truly that day, but trudged through two more years, tending and caring for the boy now a man, until she chose to release her feelings by opening up her wrists on the morning of her thirty-seventh.

The man who makes the music now, then a boy, was left to be raised by strangers. He is now thirty-six. He is certain, knows, he will not make thirty-seven. Feels it in his chest—more so this night, with his birthday in the morning. He has daily tried to numb the pressure, the beginnings of problems, pains, with alcohol. Has tried repeatedly with drink to take the edges off the beginnings of his end.

But he does not want to die, not yet, for perhaps the grass is not always greener. Although he supposes he does not have a lot to live for. Although this may be the thoughts of the writer, as she scribes this poor man's tale. Or perhaps it is the thoughts of the reader, inflicting on a fictional character their own inner fears and concerns. Such is the way. So much is hidden in literature and so much is hidden in music, between the shapes the words and notes make.

But the musician on stage is sure he will not wake tomorrow morning, the first day of his own thirty-seventh year, as both his parents were lost on the morning of their thirty-seventh—some things are written in the stars, cast there in unreadable symbols.

In a matter of hours, he will fall asleep and not wake up. Something red, or something of a shade blacker than black perhaps, will open up inside of him, something beyond his control. And nothing feels in his control: the rise and the fall of the tides, the pain he feels building within his heart, the ever-increasing rent on his beachside property, whether she comes to watch him perform, whether she—this woman who is the carbon copy of his mother but then again not—stays until the end tonight or leaves part way through. Nothing much is in his control, of this, he is well aware. He does not really even know for definite if tonight will indeed be his final sunset. *But there is one thing I can control,* he thinks. He can control the sounds his hands release as they mark out the face of the dead in the air around his theremin.

This, he can control.

He must play on: it is all he knows, and he has bills to pay. Who doesn't? And if he does not die in the night, before the morning, he will still need to pay his rent soon. His beach house does not come cheap, and he craves the desolation of his abode, could not bear to live in shared accommodation with others. If he cannot pay his rent and gets evicted from his beachside home, he would miss the solitude of the sky-water horizon, the unabated company of gulls, the occasional basking seal. People, other people, they would not tolerate the ways of a drunken artist.

So each month, he plays at the clubhouse in the bay, along from the bay in which his house, which opens up to the sea, is on, and there, he shapes out the face of his father, then he carves out the face of his mother, and the crowd embrace the music. Sometimes he'll open up to requests, if energised by a new moon: the audience will hold up photographs, pass them to the stage, of people they have lost, people they wish to be considered, and he will take one or two of these images, and sculpt songs for them with the air between his fingers and palms. *It is as if they are there,* they say, *for a moment.*

And what good does it do, he thinks.

⁂

"I will not return, so tonight will be my last performance as I don't have much time left," he says each time before he performs, as he clutches his hand to his expectant, anxious chest, and the manager, each time, replies: "You will return, this is your reason, to perform, you have all the time in the world. The voice you bring, it is the voice of all souls gone, lost to a fog, crying as if they do not know how to return."

❦

He plays his last song, a request from a man a little older than himself who had passed forward a photo of a child. With a melody, more angelic than a well-played harp, he brings the grieving father and the entire audience to tears, enough tears to make an ocean of the floor. And it is a deep enough ocean in which to fully lose the woman he is searching for in the crowd, as he performs.

She has gone.

❦

The crowd depart and he is left alone. He drifts backstage in order to collect his things as bar staff and security clear up the venue. He tries to warm himself with more whisky and some positive thoughts. *She came to see my final performance,* he thinks, but it does nothing but sadden him furthermore, because she, as usual, did not hang around.

He contemplates his lonely, possibly final walk home on the eve of his thirty-seventh. It is a short yet challenging walk, back to his house on the beach. Once home, if he makes it, he will pour a thick glass of whisky, toast once more to all he has lost to the waves, to the knife-grey ocean, to whatever is left of the moon. The sea, vast and inexhaustible, is a staple in his life, perhaps the only rock, other than his whisky.

As he tidies away equipment, places cables and parts back into their correct housing, he catches a curl of brine scent which makes him crave hard the salt of ocean air. He needs to be near water. *Water.* Is the sea calling him home? But the whisky has gone straight through him, tickling and softening his insides on its way. He must make one last trip to the gents before setting off.

ೞ

Back across the stage, through the empty space which was packed to the rafters just half an hour earlier, through the door at the back of the room, he travels to the bathroom. He relieves himself, then stands in front of the sink. After washing his hands, he bends forwards, over the sink in front of the mirror, and splashes cool, cool water on his face. Still, the smell of the ocean. He is alone in the bathroom; the only sound, now the patrons have all left, is the rising burble of the drain. *It is a hard place to find,* he thinks, staggering slightly, *a place between intoxication and sobriety, for the short walk home to be smooth.* He splashes more cold water on his face then straightens his spine and catches his tired self in the mirror.

And her.

There she is. Behind him: soft almond eyes, hair a little longer than he remembers his mother's hair, skin a few shades out, but cheekbones, jaw, lips he feels he knows, had once known. *It is as if,* he thinks, *a selection of my mother's genetic traits have been distorted, blended, undone and reformed, to create something similar; alive, but not quite right.*

Familiarity, yet this woman who visits often when he plays here is both her and not her. Something more than her. He feels recognition. An attraction, yet also a simultaneous sense of repulsion.

Heart thumping hard, he clutches his palm against his chest. *This is it. This pumppump will be my last.*

He turns. Of course, the lady in the mirror is no longer there—was she ever? He closes his eyes, rubs them, then opens them again.

She is back.

"May I come home with you?" she asks and he feels as if she has unzipped something, as if something has come undone in his mind, something he is both happy to entertain and also unhappy to sustain.

Slowly, he nods his head.

If this is how the fabric of reality is to unzip, so be it, he thinks, *and I have more than enough whisky for two at home.*

"Sure."

And this cannot be Mother, he thinks, *because she looks no older than me, and if it were Mother she'd look far older. There would be white hair and lines deep enough for one to lose one's sane self within. I have not lost it yet. I have not tumbled all the way down the hole. She is just familiar.* He tries to reassure himself: *she is just familiar, not my family.*

⚯

At home, he escorts her through to the kitchen and drinks a large whisky, measured in thumbs and fingers, three of those, and so does she. Then he shows her around and apologises for the mess. "Hadn't been expecting visitors," he mutters. Has he ever had visitors? She nods, and when she speaks there is a sweetness to her voice reminiscent of childhood lullabies. But it is not the voice he remembers his mother having. *There is overlap*, he thinks. *This woman is a tracing, a silhouette of something cherished and long gone.*

"May I stay over?" she asks. He is taken somewhat aback.

"Of course." He rummages in the chest against the wall for blankets, soft bedding, something with which to prepare a warm nest for himself. He will sleep in the living room tonight. The living room, a room in which little true living has been graced during his time in the property, he thinks. He is not dead though, not yet—his body is still warm to touch, unlike hers, which he notices is icy, when she steps towards him and places her hand on top of his and looks him in the eye and thanks him with sincerity for accommodating a stranger.

This woman, this woman who is but is not someone he recognises, is as much a stranger to him he supposes as a stranger one might pass by on the street. A cold stranger. Yet also, she feels a *little bit* like home.

And in all of his homes, he sleeps with a knife beneath his pillow. *I will fetch my blade later,* he thinks. *I will sleep with it under this cushion here, the head end of my makeshift living room bed. There is no rush to retrieve it, not yet.*

"You may have my bed," he says. "My bedroom is much warmer than it is in here." And she smiles with a demi-smile, a mixture of joy and sorrow, of equal measures guilt and elation or pain and relief. She stares at him with this slight smile. Stares, stares, her smile like a smile from a mother of twins, one baby alive and the other perhaps not. Or perhaps it is a smile like the mother of Jesus. *Yes, Mary of Nazareth,* he thinks and takes a step back from the woman in his house as he recalls the iconography of the stained glass church window which had gaped at him throughout the funeral of his own mother many years ago. A little unsettled by this woman's presence, he suddenly wishes he could offer her a room outside instead, in a stable or a barn, somewhere separate from his own place of safety.

She lifts her cold palm to his cheek. A sense of calm, numbness even, washes over him. His mother, albeit with more warmth, used to touch him this way. With softness. Before his father died. Before the red and the black ripped their family apart. "It's okay, child," she says, although now, up close, she looks no older than him, younger, maybe. "You may rest by my side, share your bed with me."

He nods. Despite the chill of her touch, he likes the way her hand feels on his cheek; it is not a sexual feeling. He senses there is nothing expected, nothing to fear. Not yet.

CREND

It is late, but he feels restless, like he has to be a better host, so he suggests they wander down to the beach to wish goodnight to the moon. He passes her his sheepskin jacket to keep out the bite of the near-midnight air. "If you insist," she says and slips on the coat.

"The whisky tastes sweeter there," he says as he opens the front door.

She follows. They meander down to the beach, her carrying two glasses, and him a half full bottle of whisky and a lamp. When they arrive, he follows her lead and kicks off his shoes although since leaving the house, not a word has been shared between them. He is not really one for small talk; what purpose is there in bashing gums about the weather, when one is stood underneath the beauty of the stars, the night sky, drunk beside the sea? *Nature says it all,* he thinks, *but perhaps I should break the silence now.* So instead of small talk, he decides to talk about all he really knows. He speaks about his work.

"The theremin," he tells her, with his tongue in his cheek and just an inch of whisky left in his bottle, "was used at the turn of the millennia by scientists to send music deep into space. They put on a concert for potential extra-terrestrials via an interstellar radio message."

She smiles, although he can't see her clearly with the beach only lit by the light of the moon and his old gas lamp. "I know," she says. She points to the moon, waxing gibbous. "I know many things, and nothing is as it seems, and what a facade, to make so much effort exploring the outer limits when so little is known about what goes on inside and within. The desert, the rainforest, the hadal zone, one's own mind and soul—none of these places have yet been fully explored."

He is muddled by this, and believes it may be the whisky doing the muddling, as does the writer, portraying the events which are about to occur. He ponders as she continues to point at the moon. They are silent for a moment, both staring up at the sky. The relentless crashing of wave upon wave, a cycle slowly moving forward, slowly moving back, is deafening.

"I'm not sure what you mean," he says eventually, his words almost lost within the pattern of the dark water which pummels the shore. He speaks so quietly he is not even sure he has spoken so repeats himself to be sure. Louder yet stranger, his own words sound alien.

"The moon, for example," she says, and points again at the night sky, "is here and also here." Her arm drops. She points to the white, rippling disc, the moon's reflection, its partner, on the shifting skin of the sea. He thinks of earlier in the washroom at the venue, the reflection of this woman in the mirror, how one was a copy of the other, one real, one not, and neither actually his mother.

"The moon," she continues, "is not what it seems."

He knocks back the last of his drink. The alcohol burn does nothing to help him understand.

"You see it as a celestial body, a sphere of rock, orbiting another sphere of rock, shining back old light from a distant sun, controlling the ebb and flow of the tide," and he is not sure if she is making a statement or asking a question, or if she'll still be here in the morning, "but it is in fact a hole."

She leads him back to the house, his hand in hers feeling quite like a dream.

Will there be two sets of footprints in the sand come morning, he thinks, and she answers him, "Yes, yes, my child." But he is sure this time that he had not said this aloud and he thinks of the painting his mother had hung on the wall in her bedroom, a gift from an over-bearing god-botherer shortly after his father passed.

An image. Two sets of prints in the sand. Then one set of prints in the sand, and a message of hope, about how sometimes, when it appears that one set of prints has disappeared, it is not because some-one has been deserted but because that someone is being carried. And he knows this memory should make him feel better, but it has quite the opposite effect.

At home, he pours another drink for himself, offers her a top-up, which she declines, and she pats the side of the sofa. He slops down at her side. "Tell me," she says to the drunken man, "why do you drink so?"

He does not have a clear-cut answer, or a sharp mind, and he has not ever thought *why*, only *how* and *when*, but he knows the answer is somewhere hidden in his childhood. In loss, in grief, in the sensation he won't make it past thirty-six and may not wake in the morning to see any footprints in the sand.

He tells her of his fear, his curse: he will not make it through the night, *it is written in his stars,* he whispers, and she is silent for a moment.

"You say this is a given," she speaks eventually, "but remember, not everything is as it seems." And she lowers the top of her shirt to reveal the skin above her breasts. She asks him to lay on his hand. "Go ahead, close your eyes," she says. And he does as he is asked. His hand finds its place, he closes his tired eyes, and this is when he feels a shift.

"You say your certain demise is written in the stars like there is some use-by date stamped on your breathing corpse. Well," she says, and he pulls his hand away as if he has scalded himself on a hot stove, "Feel it. I have infinity etched into my soul."

Too much.

He does not remember after this. He falls asleep, and while asleep, in a safer place of dream, she stands over him, pushes up her sleeves, and without the laying of hands on flesh, she plays him, his body at rest on the sofa, like a silent theremin.

With movements of her hands, flicks of her wrists, she binds him, touch-free, with invisible ribbons, ties him up as a spider with a fly would do, and writes over him with inexplicable air-weave code countless unknown symbols.

☙❧

In the morning, he rises from the sofa, rubs his eyes, pours coffee, tops up his mug with a dash of bourbon, and recalls it is his birthday. He has awoken. He has made it through.

He searches the house. She is gone.

And there is nothing coming undone within him this morning, only a pounding headache he knows will be relieved by more of the same from the night before. A soft catatonia ripples through him. *Another day,* he thinks, *another day.*

He dresses and heads out down to the beach, in search of pairs of footprints, to confirm the dream he thought he'd had, was perhaps still in. He finds two sets, leading down to and back from the shoreline. *She had been here,* he thinks, and then knowing she had been real, he feels a pang in his chest. Loneliness. She is nowhere. Not in his house or at the beach. Now, she is nowhere to be seen.

☙❧

Of course, he drinks today, all day—this day is no day different to any other. He drinks and cries, cries out for his mother, waits for the numbness the bottom of the bottle brings, but it doesn't come. He continues to drink and cry until sometime mid-afternoon. It is then he hears the crash of the waves calling. *Water.* He needs to be on the shore.

Will she come again? he thinks, he hopes, as he has further questions. *Perhaps if I create with my hands and the electromagnetic force field of my instrument, an invisible form once more of Mother's face, or a face that bears some resemblance but is not quite the same, then maybe she will return.* So he does so. He carts his theremin, small generator, and amplifier to the beach, and sits in the same spot they had visited the night before.

His hands, encouraged by the abyss in his sad heart, weave the sea air. He curls and flattens breeze into hair and lips, the curve and plain and dip of her décolletage. Mother. Not quite Mother. Nothing. She does not come. *Perhaps the whisky is making a shambles of my precision,* he worries. Although he cannot yet feel the effect of the drink, does not feel drunk despite another swig, a glug, and then another.

He plays the Song of Mother over and over. He plays to the gulls who swoop at dusk hopeful for a catch, to the seals who bask on the rocks a great stretch of water away, to the water as it hugs and retracts from the shore. *But am I casting a true image of her face?* he wonders. *Is this a true likeness?* He questions his own palms and inspects his fingertips. Has the vision he holds of her in his mind, over time, become distorted, like an echo of an echo of an echo?

He plays until the sun begins to drop into its final position, as it descends towards a soft armchair of purples and crimsons on the horizon, just above the water. There it sinks, and as it kisses the water, *water,* the woman returns.

He spots her walking across the bay. The beach is his and hers alone.

He stops playing and his speakers fall silent. She is carrying something in her arms. She stops and kneels and releases whatever she has been carrying across the beach, a collection of things, all sizes. She arranges them around herself, until she is garlanded by a circle of dark bumps on the sand, right on the water's edge, and then she sits down in the middle.

He wants to go closer so he starts to pack up his equipment as his heart yearns to ask her who she is, or what she is, this creature who is familiar yet not. Is she a passing face that smiles blankly in a crowd, never to be seen again? Or is she the face of all things power-ful, all things recognised, combined? He is not sure.

She looks up, the last of the light enough for him to see her eyes glinting, and she speaks to him, "Stay, play on, play someone else. Why not play your father? That has always been one of my favour-ites," and he feels he has no choice, so he begins. But his father's face is not clear in his mind. All that he can capture from memory is the image of Pa furled in the kitchen, a bump, broken inside. He does his best and depicts with hands and air and swooping ethereal music what little of the shape of his father he can remember. "Good enough," she says. "That'll do. Play on."

He plays and he watches her by the last of the light of the day as she too waves her arms, stiff, then soft, both welcoming and repul-sive. She bends forwards, a sort of reiki, he supposes, and one of the still things which surrounds her shuffles, becomes a moving shadow, and scurries away into the dunes. He is taken aback and drops hands. Once more his speakers fall silent. But she commands him to play on. "Your father," she says, "or something that is not quite." His attention returns to his hands, as his heart thrums hard with red. And the day is not out; there is still time for something inside him to break, he worries.

And as if she has read his thoughts, "Nothing inside you will break," she says, and he knows she speaks the truth, but he is sure the seam in the fabric of his reality is coming unstitched.

She places her hands on another mound of darkness and moves them in time, in dimension with his. But the thing in front of the woman does not move this time, does not up and scuttle away. He watches as she tries again, whatever she is doing. He watches and sees her shake her head. "This one cannot be helped," she says, loud enough for him to hear, although he is sure she is talking to herself. "We give to those who can be helped, and take back from those who can't."

Her posture changes. She arches her back and lifts her hands up as if stretching to pull the last of the light from the sky. Up from the heap, the body—is it an animal?—shoots forked light, like lightning. Is it some part of the electromagnetic spectrum with which he is unfamiliar? The white light travels up and into her raised palms like distance into a retractable measuring tape, like the reeling in of a fishing line. *She is taking something from it,* he thinks. She shudders and then stands and kicks the spent vessel into the sea, then works her way around the rest of her circle, never touching anything with her hands. Some of the lumps, she kicks into the sea, others flap or swim away.

He wants to ask her what she's doing, but she again commands him to play, so play he does. He plays again and again the shape of his mother, her face in his mind clearer than Pa's. He plays until the last wisp of purple-orange daylight diminishes, and the moon, now full, or fully open if it is in fact just a hole, appears. The woman, with her raised hands, appears to focus all of her attention and energy onto the final sick beast at her side. This last mass is the largest of her macabre collection.

He sees now, its outline, now it's the last mound at her side.

It's a seal pup.

Over the noise he himself is generating, he hears it click and whistle and bark in distress. *Is it missing its mother,* he thinks, *or is its mother the reason it is lying here injured,* and he can't help but think this same thing about himself, as if he were there, in the place of the seal, being played upon by another, teased between a place of safety and the alternative by something that, in his mind, should be, or should have been, infallible.

She dances her hands around the young beast. It lifts its head and flops itself back towards the sea, and in, in, and away it goes.

From half-dead to half-alive or vice-versa—he cannot be sure—*this woman turns things, creatures*, he thinks. And now, under the light of the moon, he is certain: this is not his mother, this collector and donator of force. Not any of the good parts of his mother, anyhow. *Perhaps I have been playing her incorrectly.*

Enough madness, enough. He refuses to play anymore and places his tired palm against his own chest and feels the throbbing there. A strong beat. A consistent metronome. "What did you do to the pup?" he asks.

"The pup was injured, but salvageable, so I have given it the only gift I know how. I cannot play great music, cannot create sweet art, and I cannot heal its injuries or take away its pain. But I have given it a gift from my heart, the gift of eternal existence."

"And what gift did you give to me?" he says, his voice low.

She stands, steps out onto the sea, and glides forwards over its rippling surface, one soft footstep after another. He watches her, unable to ask his question again, and waits for an answer. She moves until she reaches the reflection of the moon. Here, she stretches her arms above her head, gives a bend to her knee, jumps up streamlined, and dives down through the white quivering circle on the water's skin. And through this moment, he sees her actions reflected in the night sky, her reflection also diving, but upwards, towards the heavens, towards the hole in the sky which is the moon. She vanishes through both moons in unison, as if the glassy surface of the sea is in fact a mirror.

She is gone.

It is as if she was not ever really there in the first place. And it is just him on the beach now, alone.

All is not as it seems, he thinks and swigs down the last of his whisky, although he realises, despite trying his very hardest, he hasn't felt drunk all day. He tosses the bottle then packs his equipment at speed, throwing everything back into the large case, and then he stumbles back up the path towards his house.

⊂⊃⊂⊃

Days pass, years. He no longer plays and he no longer drinks. Alcohol now does nothing to numb the loneliness which stabs at him from within. He no longer dares to weave the faces of the lost to himself or to a crowd and he no longer lives by the sea.

But he thinks he sees parts of her often, in the faces of others. Occasionally, he sees the best bits of her, but more often than not, he captures sight of the worst. But it is never her, never *quite* her.

And now he is old, so old he has outlived everyone he has ever played for, anyone he has ever loved, and anyone, any stranger, who has ever passed him by and caught his eye in a fleeting moment of inexplicable connection in the street. He is now so old, the lines on his face, the cragged seams that will hold his muddled grasp of reality together for an eternity, are deep. Deep enough to lose one's self in, entirely.

To Cherish

He was desperate to know where the nearly-babies came from, and the girl with the long, tangled plaits and the chipped front tooth said she knew. The girl, his neighbour, had been right about all the other things they'd discussed in the dark in the shared outdoor space between their neglected homes, like how the sun would never come out again, so he figured he had no reason not to believe her about the location of the babes.

Since way before the start of dark summer, the wood-skinned babes had appeared as glowing crops around the countryside, drawing people close with their infantile siren cry. Finding one of these bundles of half-alive joy had been all the boy had thought about since his mother had brought hers home: something to hold, something to cherish. An obsession.

☙❧

"Everyone has been paired up. The whole village has disappeared, must've found their babes and nested up. A done deal," the boy said to the girl.

"Everyone has received one, it appears, except for us," the snaggle-toothed girl replied. "Is it because we aren't good enough?"

"I have no idea," he said. He shrugged. But in his heart he felt she might once again be right.

The cobbled streets, usually flooded with the aroma of freshly baked bread and the choral mumblings of ale-addled farmers and a-throng with bustling villagers, had been empty, felt deserted for days. The bakers and the inn were now closed and Mr Nevis, the postman with the oiled ginger curls who whistled his own familiar yet songless tune, had stopped delivering post a month back. Mr Nevis had been the last person the boy had spoken to in any depth other than his mother who was now lost, and his neighbour, the snaggle-toothed girl.

"Come," the girl said. "Let's get moving." She shone her torch on the cart by her feet. A circle of light highlighted the wooden slat box she'd spent the morning harnessing to a set of old casters "If we find a birthing spot, we can pull more babes back in this."

"Makes sense," said the boy.

"I'm sure the map will take us straight to the source."

He wondered what she'd be like as a mother, this girl he'd known for all eleven years of his life, his neighbour. At only a year and a month older than him, he wasn't sure she'd be any good at caring for something so small, so helpless, especially with the shortage of sunshine and the many challenges that brought, and he certainly felt he wasn't ready for parenthood, but he didn't feel he had a choice. She'd cope as well as he would, as well as they could.

"We've got to find them," he said. "They'll be orphaned without us. No one will save them and activate them, because everyone in the village is already busy, present yet vacant, with a babe or two of their own."

To be an orphan meant no parents, no grown-up to tuck you in at night and kiss you on the forehead and slice up an apple into neat segments. The boy had found cutting up and preparing his own food a challenge, especially by candlelight. The sharp knife his mother had never let him use before she'd disappeared into her room with her nearly-babe had hurt when his fingers had slipped and received its wrath when he'd tried to prepare his own fruit a few days ago. And the fruit had tasted bad. Of something awful. Mold. He'd spat it out into the clogged sink.

Orphaned was exactly how he was feeling. Unheld and unseen. The boy crossed his arms across his chest, gave himself a gentle hug and sighed. The warmth of his exhalation hung in the otherwise silent black air between the two children for a moment. He wanted to ask the girl if she felt the same—unloved, unlovable—but decided to change the subject. She could change her mind about all of it, their desperate quest, if he became emotional. She might judge his ability to become a father and decide to venture on alone. "Do you think they're airlifted in from somewhere? And if so, by who?" he said. "And why?"

"Does it really matter how they get here?" The girl's words came quick and hard, each an angry blow to the boy's confidence. "Once you hold one in your arms, and it softens into you, you'll not care for anything else."

The thought of this brought a smile to the boy's lips, but the girl did not see because her torch was not pointing the right way; for several months, their village had been smothered by a blanket of darkness. "Temporary total eclipse," the postman had suggested the last time the boy had answered the front door to him. "The moon has stopped, paused for a rest dead-on in front of the sun." But the postman had also suggested that the boy should try to cut his own fruit and that at age ten the boy should be totally independent of his mother and had said that he wouldn't help him prepare food unless the boy let him in and let him get into his bed. The boy had felt this was wrong, had felt scared and had thus refused to answer the door to the postman again. Eventually, the postman had stopped knocking. The boy presumed the postman must have found a nearly-babe of his own to cherish.

But the boy wanted to express his happiness to the snaggle-toothed girl, at how full of joy he was at the thought of having a nearly-babe of his own to love, so he reached out in the dark and took her free hand, and guided it towards his balled cheeks. "You're excited," she said, a statement, not a question. "Me too." Then she pulled her hand away and reached down for the cart rope which lay on the ground by her feet. "Come on. The sooner we find the crop of babes, the sooner we can hold them."

"But," the boy shifted his weight from left foot to right, "seriously, don't you ever even consider where they come from?"

"Oh I don't know. Maybe someone from another village just turns up with a truckload. Maybe they just spring up like flowers from the ground. Your guess is as good as mine. But we have a map, so I guess we just call it a blessing and be grateful. Part of me thought we'd missed the boat." She shone her torch on his shoes and then pointed it in the direction they were already heading. "Come," she said and set off.

"Coming." He marched after her. Adrenaline sharked through his veins at the thought of what they might find.

The boy wiped sweat from his brow as he pushed onwards as fast as his legs would carry him. It was an effort to match her speed. The journey seemed long and the path was steep and they stomped in silence through the dark of the day. The boy was glad when after at least an hour of walking, the girl's pace began to slow slightly. After another ten minutes or so of moving at an amble, the girl stopped, first catching her breath before speaking. "If we do find the nearly-babies—*when* we find them—we take as many as we can manage and give them all the love we have. *All* of our love. Are you *sure* you're in?"

"I guess," he mumbled. "I mean, I'd like to think that's what will happen. I have so much love to give, and no one else to give it too right now—"

The girl replied curtly, "Good," and strode forwards again with a renewed zest. Her feet made a pit pat sound on the firm mud and grass and the wheels of the cart started to screech and clunk with each rotation. He followed the girl, unsure as to whether he should offer to tow the empty cart up the dirt track away from the girl's father's hay barn where they'd met, or let her struggle onwards. "W-would—"

She stopped again and, this time, turned around and stepped closer to the boy. With the torch in her hand, she illuminated her face as if about to whisper a ghost story around a campfire. She groaned. "What is it? Spit it out."

"Doesn't matter."

"Listen. They probably die, the babies, if you don't give them enough love. You know that, right?" she said. "The nearly-babes might die. If they're unloved, not held when they cry after they've been activated, we will have nothing left to hold and feed. And we can't let them die. We will be such excellent parents, or at least I know *I* will. We can't let anyone else get there first."

"There's nothing I'd like more than to hold one, nurture it for as long as it'll let me," the boy said. He bunched his fists into his pockets. He could just about make out the outline of a pebble by his foot under the light of the girl's torch. He kicked it away from the path.

"I can't remember what it feels like to hold another breathing thing close. My mother hasn't touched me for weeks. I haven't seen another soul other than you in months." He sighed, a tear in his eye, and pulled his hands from his pockets to reach out to her for comfort.

The girl dropped the rope of the cart and flashed the beam in his eyes then batted his arms away. "You and me both, bud. But don't go getting any ideas. Keep your greasy mitts off me." With her torchless hand, she pointed to her upper middle cracked tooth then moved in closer to confront the boy, so close he could smell the lack of care on her breath. He held his breath and turned his face from hers. "This was how my father showed me love before him and my mother left with their new ones. Good riddance to bad parents, I say. Neither of them had time for me anyway, especially after their nearly-babies arrived. My father didn't even take his beloved bottle of whisky with him."

The girl knocked into the cart as she spoke, and the cart began to trundle back down the slope. The boy stopped it with the side of his shin. He held in a yelp as the jagged wooden corner scraped against his leg.

"I know," he replied. "And I'm sorry. If it's any consolation, I haven't seen my mother since she got hers either. She hasn't even spoken to me. She took her nearly-babe from the delivery man before I could even see it, let alone hold it, and now the only sound she makes is with her fist against her bedroom wall. She bangs and bangs on the wall until I slide her in bread and milk."

"Sucks to be you."

"I remember it crying, once, the baby. Screeching. It woke me on the fourth or fifth night after it arrived. It howled for ages, and then it stopped. There was peace for a moment until Mother screamed. I haven't heard it cry since and ever since, Mother hasn't left her bedroom."

"Oh, the sound of a nearly-baby's crying is the worst. I guess."

"Yes. Yes, it is."

The pair continued to walk.

CR℘SO

"I think we're at the final crossroads," the girl said. She waved the beam of light ahead of them. The weak light bounced back: a black outline of the tree they used to hang a rope swing from and play, before the darkness came, a sentinel oak bent like an old maid with a dowager's hump. "Yes, this is it. We're close."

The girl stopped and pulled out a folded sheet from the pocket of her dungaree dress. With three shakes, the map was open. She directed the torch beam onto the tatty paper and traced the route they'd need to take with her fingertip.

"The map," he asked. "You say the storekeeper gave it to you then ran back upstairs?"

"Correct. He'd said he was out of stock, said he was tired, and asked if I was certain it was what I wanted, a nearly-baby," the girl said. "I visited his store every day for a fortnight, travelled there by torchlight, stubbed my toes on the journey more times than I care to remember."

"Paid off though, I guess," the boy said.

"I kept visiting, asking if he was expecting any more in. He must've grown tired of me bothering him. I'd ring the bell and each time he'd come down the stairs. No lights at all. No idea if he even had any clothes on or not. His stale smell filled the shop floor."

"Gross."

"He snapped at me, every time I called, said I'd wake his baby if I carried on ringing the bell. But I guess you're right. My persistence did pay off."

"Because he gave you the directions."

"Yep."

"And here we are," the boy said.

"And here we are." The girl passed the torch to the boy "Here, hold this. I think I know where to go now." She folded up the map and slid it back in her pocket. The torch flickered and dimmed in the boy's hand. "Dammit. It's running out." She took the torch back and pulled out new batteries from the satchel she wore over her body and replaced them. "Last lot," she said.

"Oh," the boy replied. "Guess we better get moving."

"Onwards. Into the woods."

They walked for another mile or so, around and through fields, until they reached the edge of the forest.

"Is it odd to not feel scared?" the boy said. "Or not as scared as I did when I came here once last year, before the sun went? In the dark, the forest feels the same as anywhere else."

"What you can't see can't scare you."

"You think? It's so quiet, as if all the wildlife has gone too," he said.

"Probably has. Nothing grows well without sunlight."

The boy shuddered. "Well, it's certainly colder," he replied.

She agreed. Wrapped in perpetual darkness, the woods were no different to the rest of the village in which they resided. Bathed in black, they could not tell, really, with their eyes where the field ended and where the thickness of trees began. Only with their hands and feet, it became apparent. "Come closer, so you don't stumble. The ground's uneven here, covered with some sort of bracken and there are lots of twisted roots," she said. She dropped the tow rope of the cart and linked her arm through his. "We'll leave the cart here."

They didn't have to walk far until they heard the melody. "The babies are near," she said. "What a song. If all the black keys on the upright piano in the school hall were played in turn, softly, in an order never attempted before, it wouldn't match the beauty of this music."

"It's… enchanting," he whispered.

The girl stopped and squeezed the boy into her side a little closer. "But they never sing as sweetly again as they do before you hold them for the first time," she said. "Molly told me so. Before her father bought her one from the black market and she stopped coming to school."

Hand in hand, the two children crept towards the music, until a cluster of emerald eyes winking through the blanket of blackness brought them both to a standstill. "Have you ever seen such a beautiful shade of green?" she said and dropped the boy's hand. He was lost for words. She shone the torch beam onto the collection of babes and the melody escalated into high-pitched screams. "Crikey," she said. "Sorry." The boy pushed her torch to angle its beam towards the forest floor. The melody became pleasant again so the girl and the boy edged towards the thumb print swirl of blinking green lights.

"Like wood," he said. His sentence came out incomplete.

"Yes, they are. Their skin, it's like knotted, polished timber—until you activate them."

The volume of the nearly-babies increased as the girl passed the torch to the boy. "Here, take it," she said. He took the flashlight and she crouched down and lifted a singing babe up in her arms.

"You're so cold. There, there, my darling." She whispered into where an ear might form.

The boy placed the torch on the forest floor and followed suit, taking hold of the babe nearest him. "There, there."

"This is unreal," she said quietly. "I never thought I'd get my own, and here we are. There are four, five including the one you're holding. All mine."

"Ours," he said.

"Yes. You can take one, the other four need me."

He ran his fingertips over the nearly-babe's hard outer casing. Its green eye-lights twinkled like the stars the two children used to lie on the roof of the barn and gaze at.

"A true blessing. Those who wait the longest receive the most," she whispered to the boy, and to the babe in her arms, she whispered, "I'm going to activate you now, my darling." She placed and held her forefinger over each green eye of the babe in the crook of her arm until the eyes no longer glowed. If it weren't for the dim circle of yellow the flashlight yielded, the girl and the babe would have sunken into the darkness of the wood completely. "Go ahead," she said, "activate yours too." The boy did as instructed. The girl held her babe close to her chest and then gathered up the others. Two were strewn, still immobile, on the forest floor and one was propped upright against a tree trunk. She held each close and activated it with her fingertip, then kissed each on where its forehead would develop.

As the last pair of green eye-lights went out, the sweet harmony stopped. The sound of their own breathing and the occasional crunch of leaf litter underfoot as they moved was all the two children could hear.

The boy picked up the torch from the ground, careful to support the fragile head of his baby as he did so.

"I feel like a God," the girl said.

"A creator," the boy said. "They're so small. My heart might pop."

"The four of them together, I never knew I could feel so joyful," she said. "But my, they're weighty for their size. But I daren't put them down." The girl rose up and together, they walked back out of the forest towards where they'd left the cart.

"Let's leave the cart. Unless you want to use it?" she said. "We should head back to the barn and rest there until we've enough energy to take them back to our homes."

The wood-like skin of his babe had already started to soften, become more flesh-like. Undulating fronds where he presumed arm buds might swell tickled against his skin. "No. I don't want to use the cart. I never want to put this one down."

"I feel them softening," she said. "They're gaining in weight too, already. I want to place them on my skin. Need to. But not here, not in the forest. It's too cold."

"Here," he said. He stretched out his arm. "Let me take one or two of yours. I can carry more weight. Just until we get back to the barn."

Before he had the chance to touch one of the four babies in her arms, she snarled. The boy gasped. "Back off. Not a chance. These are mine. My babies. I got the map. So I get the lion's share."

"Sure," the boy said, recoiling. "I'm sorry." He lifted his t-shirt up and placed his own baby against the skin of his chest. Instinct told him to do this. *Much easier to do with one than four,* he thought. He couldn't hold in the gasp of pure joy he felt as his wooden-skinned thing began to moisten, soften off as it touched the smooth flesh of his chest. "One will be enough for me," he said. *Surely, one will be enough,* he thought. He'd never felt such ecstasy. Pure, unfettered adoration for another thing. How could he want for anything more?

"Spring meadows, lemon balm." The girl inhaled her catch deeply and swayed with the scent. One of the young in her arms wriggled, then whimpered loudly. *Not a nice noise at all,* the boy thought. The girl was taken aback and stumbled slightly. It was the first sound any of the babies had made since their sweet melody had stopped. A flashback to the brick-laden bag of kittens her uncle had made her carry to the river several years ago. "That was… different," she said.

"Yes, different," the boy replied.

"We must get going," the girl said, and with four babies, each softening slightly in her arms, each moulding and contorting its wet willow limbs inwards and around her waist and chest to find its special place with its new mother, each finding her flesh through gaps in her clothing, she turned to exit the forest. "Come on, I need you to shine the way." One of her yield released another uncomfortable murmur. She drew in a sharp breath then cooed. The soothing nature of her voice calmed the fidgeting bundle in her arms. She cooed all the walk back.

ॐ

"Please, let me in," the boy rapped on the front door of the girl's house. He'd lost track of how many days it'd been since their journey into the woods. He must have closed his eyes for a split second, exhausted from caring for his baby, and his babe, strapped to his chest with its own limb buds, had started to cry. He knocked again, harder. He needed to get into the warmth of the girl's house so he could unswaddle the baby in order to begin the tedious stroking ritual the little one demanded. Anything to make the noise stop. And then once calm, ready, with her moral support, he would show her his discovery. He reached down and felt his leg tenderly. He'd tripped on his way, in the dark, to the girl's house, despite its proximity to his. The graze on his knee burnt.

Caring for the baby was hard enough, compounded by the lack of light. Whilst he had been out on his journey into the woods with his neighbour, his mother must have taken the last of the candles into her room before taking up private residence there again. The boy had reached breaking point, alone in the dark with the fresh wood-baby, so he left his house to the sound of his mother banging the wall of her bedroom. This was her demand for food, but there was nothing left in the kitchen to give her and he had spiked his hand hard on a broken glass jar while rummaging in the back of the larder. *She can fend for herself for a while*, he thought. His own stomach churned in hunger.

His decision to head over to the girl's house had not come easy—he was a little afraid of how she would react to his neediness—but he wanted to know what he had witnessed was normal, and he wanted to find out the best way to cope. And the girl next door always had answers.

"Get in." The girl opened the door. A row of candles on a plinth in her hallway flickered and rippled with the draft as she did so. He squinted at the brightness of her entrance room. After his eyes had adjusted, on seeing the bags under the girl's eyes, accentuated by the shadowing effects of the dim lighting, he greeted her then said, "You look how I feel."

"Exhausted?" she replied. "I haven't slept for days, not since we got back from the barn."

"Same." The boy followed the girl through. Despite the weariness he felt, despite questioning his own sanity at times, to be in her presence, in the presence of another not made from softened wood or cursed with the piercing cry of a banshee, was what he needed. And to be in a room with light again, after so long in the darkness of his own abode, felt at least a little better, although for some reason, the girl's words from their journey to retrieve the nearly-babes sprung into his head: *What you can't see can't hurt you.*

He told himself he was being silly. *What a silly little boy I am. Of course it's safer here, in the light. There's nothing here that can hurt me.* He exhaled audibly. The girl's house was surely safe. She looked tired, drained even, but she wasn't a threat to him. She waved him through to her living room where he sank into a wicker-cup chair.

"Here. Breakfast." The girl passed him a muffin. "It's stale but it's sustenance. The weight has fallen off you."

"Thank you. And same. I see your collarbone." He took a bite. His empty stomach curled with the arrival of solid food. Slowly. He would need to eat it slowly in order to not vomit. He placed the cake down on a table at his side and began the laborious process of untying his baby from his chest.

"They don't come away easily, do they?" she said and lifted her shirt. Myriad leather-like digits and limbs probed and hustled for skin space on the girl's bruised-blue torso. She stroked what he considered might be the spine of one of her babes and she cooed weakly. "There, there," she said. He turned away, unable to watch.

"No." He prised what he presumed were the lips of his nearly-babe from a raised mole on his stomach with the firm slip of his pinky and began to peel the rest of the baby from his chest. The girl strode around the room, in a repeating circuit, caressing each of her young ones in turn.

"I want you to watch something," he said. "I need to know if this is happening to you too."

"Go ahead," she said. She turned to face the boy then continued to rock in rhythm with her own gentle cooing and hushing.

The boy laid his baby down flat on the edge of the rug which lay in between him and the girl then perched on the edge of his seat. His nearly-babe began to whimper, then cry, then scream. The boy gripped the arms of his chair tightly. "I want to pick it up again. I've an overwhelming urge to tend to it, make it feel loved, safe, but I'm empty inside. Tired out. Every part of me aches. The lack of sleep, the constant soothing, it's too much." He spoke louder as the sound of his baby amplified.

"Make it stop," she shouted. Several of her babes, all strapped around her waist and sides, all in awkward positions, burst into tears. The boy's babe screamed louder. "I never let mine cry so loud," she snapped. Her eyes widened until, even in the dim light, the boy could see their whites.

"Please," he said, his hands clamped, prayer position in front of his chest. "Please, just wait."

The shrill sound from his baby grew and grew. Louder. Louder. Until it stopped. "Look," he said. "Its cheeks." His nearly baby on the floor, part knotted-wood, part frilly pink-white tissue, inhaled deeply through the gash on its top half. The two children watched on as the babe's cheeks puffed out.

"What is it doing?" she said. "Help it!" She wrapped her arms tight around her own collection of babes and kissed each one on where its fully formed head would grow.

"This. This happened yesterday. I couldn't take any more, couldn't hold it any longer. Its suction slit found my nipples. Look at them!" The boy lifted his shirt up and moved towards the lamp at his side. The girl gasped. "They're red raw. I bled, it bit on me so hard. And believe me, I wanted to let it carry on, because, for a moment, it seemed content, at peace, but it hurt. It hurt so much." He dropped his shirt, buckled forward in his seat, and cried.

"I don't know what to say. You just have to keep on loving it. Love it with all you have in your heart. You can do it. What do they say, the days are long but the years are short?" She paused and prized away one of her own babe's wooden spindles which had begun to search upwards for her breast. "Ouch. And they won't be babies forever." She reached forward and patted the boy on the knee, then brushed her hand against his face, wiping a tear from his cheek.

"I know. I'm trying. Believe me. It fills me with an unmatchable happiness when it eventually pulls its roots out from my flesh and unclamps its slit and dozes against my skin. But I'm so tired. I swear I'm delusional. That's why I came here. I need you to see this too."

"The breath-holding?" The girl tilted her head, looked down at the baby on the floor. "It must be some sort of protest. It's unhappy you've removed it and placed it on the floor, surely. Who can blame it?"

"Yes. That may well be the case. But that's not all, the breath-holding," he said. "Watch." He gestured with a limp wrist and pointed finger at his babe on the floor without looking up. "Please."

She crouched down by the side of his baby, drew her nose closer to the now tight slit at the top of the bundle of knots and softness, and observed.

"It's turning blue," she said, flustered. "I need to pick it up, please, let me touch your child. This is unbearable, watching it puff out its cheeks like this. I swear, the place where its face will form is swelling, growing. Its unhappiness is unsettling my babes. My youngest is arching." She pointed to the nearly baby draped over her left shoulder. "And this one here, on my hip, the first one I activated, it's writhing, pulsing almost, like it feels the pain of yours. You can't leave yours here on the ground. Please, before it attaches to the floorboards—pick it up. Look—it's putting out roots, see?"

"Please, be patient. Place your fingers in your ears, coo. Just wait and watch."

But she couldn't resist helping it. Mother's instinct. With a gentle hand, she caressed the side of part of its top. The roots the babe had laid down flash-recoiled, and the girl yanked her hand away in shock and fell back. The nearly babe on the floor opened up its slit and sucked in a large volume of air through its pre-mouth gash. The babe swelled up more, inflated. Its barky flesh stretched and widened, and it became globular in shape. The whole babe, now more a bark ball with flailing limbs, had tripled in size.

"Please, pick it up," she said. "It won't let me touch it." Her finger stung where she had tried to soothe the boy's babe.

"Just watch," the boy said. He was not watching. His face was firmly planted in the palms of his hands.

His babe slowly lifted off the ground, until eventually no part of it touched the rug or the floorboards. "It's floating," she screamed. Her babies matched her volume. She ran out into the hallway.

The boy looked up. *It wasn't a delusion*, he thought. *They float.* The baby's cheek pads puffed out further and further and it rose up like a light balloon until it hovered midway between the floor and the ceiling. "Look at its skin. It's gone blue," he said. "When you ignore them, leave them to cry, they hold their breath until they float. I just needed someone else to witness it, to know I'm not going mad."

"Just take it back into your arms, where it's supposed to be," she yelled. "Please. Take it back or get out."

"Yes. Of course. You're right. I need to hold it again. That feeling when they sleep on your chest. Nothing beats it." The boy sprung up, but just stood, statuesque, as if tethered to the spot. "But… I'm so tired of holding it. Alone in that dark house, with no food, with what might as well be the ghost of my mother banging on her bedroom wall, giving all her love to another bundle. Who holds *me*? Who soothes *me*?"

"Your nearly-baby gives you all the love you'll ever need," the girl said. "The slit, take it and angle the slit on your nipple again, please. Breathe through the discomfort. Endless giving, it's what a parent should do for their baby, in return for unconditional love."

"But it's not my baby," he whispered, quietly enough for her not to hear. "It's not even a baby." He looked at his feet then walked slowly towards the door.

"You can't leave it with me! I have four of my own. They give me all I need. I've nothing left to give another. Besides, yours won't even let me touch it." The girl marched towards the boy and pushed in front of him, her weak body working as a shield in front of the door, blocking him from leaving.

"And I need light. I can't bear to live in darkness any longer. You have so much light here and I have nothing." The boy seized the opportunity and grabbed a lantern from the cabinet by the girl's front door and lit it with a tea-light candle.

"If you're not going to love it, at least take it with you. Please don't leave it here, it takes up so much space. And what if it stops holding its breath and starts to cry again? Please, take it away with you." The girl lurched forwards, away from the door, and grabbed the floating nearly-babe by one of its unfurled limbs and yanked it towards the boy. "Please take it away." The boy took his chance and pushed past her, opened the girl's front door and stepped outside. The girl, again, pushed his bobbing baby after him, but he refused to hold onto it.

The two young parents watched on as the boy's baby opened up its slit and took in a large gasp of air, and grew larger. "Take it!" The girl yelled. The skin that held the boy's nearly-babe together had become stretched out so thin, it was translucent in patches. A muffled blue hue shone from it, illuminating it from within.

"That's new," the boy said. He pointed at his baby, which floated there, in the hallway between them. "That light." A pang of fresh love struck his heart and he reached out, shoulder height, and stroked his baby. "Perhaps I can tolerate it a little longer. Maybe it will get easier to care for as it grows." But as he placed his lantern on the floor and tried to reach again for his baby, the baby rose higher. The blue light within the baby flickered off and on and off and on. The boy grappled after his baby, jumped and tried to reach for it back, but the ball of nearly-baby just continued to rise. It became unreachable and its arm fronds wavered and brushed against the ceiling.

Too high. With another inhalation through its slit, the boy's nearly-babe flickered in blue, on and then off, and then drifted out of the door. The pair watched on, helplessly, as it rose up and away from the girl's house. As the limbed-ball baby came into contact with the cool external air, the strobing blue light within it shut off completely, much like the sun had all those months ago. But the boy and the girl could still see the baby, despite the darkness, as its taut skin reflected the light of the lantern. The boy lifted the lantern and stood and watched as the babe-orb inhaled and inhaled, increased in diameter, and rose further up.

"What now?" The girl yelled. "How do we get it back?"

Its flailing oaky limbs kicked and bent as the nearly-baby grew wider and swam up higher, into the dark sky.

With their necks flexed back, the children stared upwards until the boy's baby became a dot up in what, despite its hellish, lightless nature, must've been the morning summer sky. They squinted. One of the girl's anchored babes yanked free a frond which it pointed to the sky and released a piercing screech. The girl screamed in pain and forced the loose limb back in place on her breastbone. The boy cried. A sadness greater than the dark sky that stretched above him yanked at his heart, pulled his soul into an even more bleak place than the Earth had become since the sun had appeared to have taken its final breath. A misery with more depth than the author sharing this tale with you may have felt, when perchance, once she herself had become embalmed with the despair of watching on, helpless, as her nearly-babe took one final breath in her arms.

The girl cried too as she clutched at her restless nearly-babes which clung on tightly to her body. "Angle the lantern in such a way so we can see your baby," she said through sobs. They could do nothing but watch on as up, up, the boy's nearly-baby drifted, further from the young girl's house. The girl gasped. "Look," she said, her voice louder.

The boy's baby, a small orb reflecting the light of the lantern in an otherwise black landscape, bumped into another small flailing-limbed ball. "Another inflated baby," the girl said. "I can make out your nearly-babe, there," she pointed, "and another baby there, see, at its side." And she was correct. Up in the dark sky, the boy's babe nudged into another baby, which Newton's Cradled a cluster of other inflated, wood-skinned balls.

The two children shrieked. A sharp beam of sunlight broke through the blackness and singed their retinas as the bunch of float-ing babies rippled to the side. The boy dropped the lantern on the ground and closed his eyes to find a staggered rainbow of the outline of his own darling inflated baby imprinted onto the inside of his eyelid.

"The sun," he said, his voice reedy, desperate, dry with exhaus-tion. He rubbed his eyes then opened them again. "Up there. In front of the sun! The darkness is nothing but a thick cloud of inflated babes, lifting upwards, together, towards the Heavens!"

In a split second, the sunshine burst disappeared, and the sun became clouded over again, and, as if on cue, the lantern on the ground between them supped up the last of its kerosene and dipped out. Side by side, the boy and the girl and everything else in existence became immersed once more in darkness, lost to the eternal heart-break of the midnight of summer.

On her breast, one of the girl's nearly-babies began to stir, de-latched, and opened up wide its feeding slit. Despite the girl's efforts to soothe it, it broke into a cry, a piercing howl. With the cup of her hand, the girl clasped the place where she worried the full head of her babe might soon form. On the spot, she rocked slightly, a little broken, the way new mothers do when immersed in what seems like the forevermore of soothing a precious one, the one they love yet fear.

"There, there," she said to her nearly-babe, knowing not what else to say. She reached across and fumbled in the darkness until she found the boy. He had fallen onto his knees. She patted the crown of his head. On the long, unseen grass outside the house in which the girl would spend the rest of her life, the boy knelt and wept, his face once more pressed into his palms. "There, there."

LOVE LETTERS

She couldn't resist it.

She couldn't resist its pull, its magnificence. Such royal splendour. It had been this way for her since childhood.

Five foot two of red cylindrical sexiness, it stood outside of the village store, silently shouting out for her attention. You see, her Love was anchored to the concrete, so she had to put in all the work, and she did, although it never responded to her declarations of love. But she was happy, ecstatic even, when she was near it, even though, despite her frequent invitations, it never followed her home. Perhaps it's shy, she told herself.

Monday to Friday at eight forty-five and then again at five fifteen, she'd visit the object of her infatuation on her journey to and from work. She took the same route each day, the long route, just so she could brush past it. Often, she'd linger a little longer on a Friday afternoon by joining the queue for the store counter. Fridays were special. Fridays were collection day.

She'd line up with *Crochet Zone* magazine and her packet of humbugs in one hand, clasping the letter she had scribed to anyone who could read in the other, and she'd crank her neck while standing there in the queue, to see it outside of the shop.

She'd happily wait, caught up in erotica, until Mr Haddon the shopkeeper was free to serve. The longer he took with the customers in front of her, the better, in her opinion, so she'd let others queue-barge until she was the last in line, until Mr Haddon needed to flip the sign to closed, until she was asked to leave. Peeking back outside at its erect presence, at the tall, pillar silhouette popping, throbbing against the light from the low-slung afternoon sun, she longed. She'd pay for her goods and leave slowly, stalling a little, knocking something from a shelf on her way out, hoping that she'd timed her visit correctly so she'd get to witness it being unlocked and opened up and emptied of its contents. This was what she loved to see the most. It made her wet with expectation.

She felt the curvature and swing of its central door call out to her as the postman turned his key. The throbbing in her chest and elsewhere rose to an apex as she watched him shuffle the envelopes from the depths of the post box's guts out and into a hessian bag, and she wished she could sneak in and take the place of the letters and curl up inside her Love.

Once it had been emptied, if no-one was looking, she'd ditch the magazine and sweets and leave the counter queue early to drift home—to witness such a sight was almost too much for one day. On departure, she'd brush her palms against the ring of bumpy, heavily painted protrusions cresting its neck just below its slit of an opening before grinding the warmth of her thigh against its lower half, as long as no-one from the shop was watching. There are, afterall, societal expectations, rules, of a sort, aren't there? On how one should behave around international distribution services.

The lady was in love with the letterbox. Throughout her best years, she watched and touched it, caressed and felt it when she could, and filled it with letters to anyone and everyone and no-one. But alas, it remained stuck to the pavement, despite the fact that she'd whispered her home address to it many times. She eventually came to a place of acceptance. She wasn't mad. She realised it was never to be.

Broken-hearted, as nothing hurts more than unrequited love, and somewhat withering on the vine, she settled instead for a man named Stephen. 'Stephen with a ph' he'd first introduced himself as, in the queue at the post office, a copy of *Government Infrastructure Weekly* tucked tightly underneath his left arm. They'd struck up conversation about the handsome letter box outside the shop and he'd asked her out for dinner. Over dinner, the lady learnt fast that Stephen with a 'ph' adored phone boxes. He *really* adored phone boxes. He'd spend as long as he could get away inside of every concealed booth he came across, caressing the handset and the little metal buttons, you know, the way a man in love does.

The couple, in their early days, spent their weekends cycling around the cityscape, seeing how many pieces of government infrastructure they could spot together and they'd record their finds in a leather-bound book. For a while, Stephen with a ph just about ticked her box. He'll do, she thought—at least we have similar hobbies. They got married and she moved in with him, a good few miles away from her first true love and the village store.

Several years passed, and she grew tired of the fakery, sham marriage that it was, and she got bored of hearing him bang on and on about phone boxes. The stiff costume he requested she wore in the bedroom to help him reach climax was most uncomfortable and she didn't like what he kept asking her to do with the two foot of curly cord.

All was far from well.

One average afternoon, a row broke out between the two of them for not the very first time. That day, however, the heated debate continued, dragged on like a postal strike. While dusting the mantelpiece, he'd knocked off her favourite collectable plate, the Wedgewood one with the golden Royal Mail crown on its face. "Stupid butterfingers," she'd yelled. She hadn't appreciated her darling plate, the one she took to bed with her most nights, being broken. Not at all. This triggered her, you could say. It really pushed her buttons.

So she stormed off into the night. Up, and out she ran, without even switching her indoor footwear for outdoor shoes. She was clearly keen to put distance between them both. And down the streets, she moved as fast as the promise of a signed-and-tracked first class delivery. In her house dress and the ghastly slippers Stephen with a 'ph' had bought her for their wedding anniversary, she pounded, running all afternoon, until all that shone was the moon. She made it as far as her old village, the one with the corner shop, you know, the corner shop next to the Royal Mail post box? There she stopped. Wheezing and panting and sweaty, she felt she'd run far enough.

"You'd never break my plates, you really love me, don't you?" she whispered in the post box's circular ear, which she knew was located about half-way around its red-ribbed lid, as she caressed its rotund waist. It replied in agreement, with the voice that a letterbox has. It purred. It mewed back at her, only to her, like a merry cat on a lap. And like a ghost, she saw through its inanimate disguise, knew the letter box had to be of sentience, and knew, after all this time, that it surely loved her back. *What wasted years!*

The corner shop was closed and had been for several hours. There were no people. There was no Mr Haddon complaining about her ditching magazines without paying after she'd read them in the queue. Alone. They were alone at last—it was to be now or never, she decided on the spot.

She wrapped her arms around it and thrust herself against its cold, painted body, finding herself quite uninhibited thanks to the black canvas of the night. She wanted to kiss her lover. She needed more than a kiss. She pressed her lips up against its red neck and then licked its girth with her tongue. It tasted of vanilla and spice and the back of postage stamps and everything her husband hadn't. She couldn't hold back. Forty-nine years of repression. Forty-nine years of longing and lust. She slipped her fingers inside its slit and then slowly, entered her whole hand. Before her rational thoughts could stop her, her entire left arm had slid inside and down the letterbox's throat. Ripples of pleasure rose up her body from her toes to the top of her head. A swirling, a merry-go-round of passion spun in her solar plexus. As she tipped her head back and exclaimed her joy to the world, "Fuck Parcelforce and FedEx and UPS," her eyes rolled back in ecstasy.

And then the post box closed its own lips—down and hard and tight on her elbow. It ratcheted her in like a ticker-tape timer. Its rectangular maw cut and sliced her arm all the way up to her shoulder, and then it started to draw her head and torso through too. Her blood dripped down its outer wall and also into its core. From somewhere guttural, the letter box burbled with delight. The lady let out a piercing scream but her shriek was caught only by the wind of the night as the letter box next took in her waist and legs and feet. It spat out the slippers though, not before stamping 'return to sender' on them in bold black ink. They plopped onto the concrete, and shortly after, her dress was regurgitated too. "Cheap nylon," the letter box growled, "should be on the 'restricted items' list." In under a minute, the lady was fully inside her lover.

In the belly of the red columnar beast, the lady's skin was blended and chopped and mashed and pressed and formed into little flesh-mâché envelopes; her bones and organs were peeled and folded into red-inked overdue payment final demand letters and postal parking fines which were slid inside of the meat envelopes. The postman came at five fifteen the next day and scooped out the guts, and the lady who loved the letterbox was dispatched all over the world.

THE HAZE-ON LADY

"Do you ever feel like there simply aren't enough hours in the day, Miss, Mrs—"

"Fox. Mrs Fox… Tabitha, please," I said. It was hard not to be taken aback by the shocking orange lipstick and lilac eyeshadow that the saleswoman who was standing at my front door was wearing. I smiled politely as she pushed her Marc Jacob's tote a little more snuggly onto her shoulder-padded shoulder and then smoothed out the resulting single crease this action had caused in her tailored suit jacket.

"Tabitha, hello. I'm Dawn. I bet you'd *kill* for a few minutes more to yourself each day, wouldn't you? I can see you're a busy lady." She waved the touchscreen tablet in her hand at the pile of balance bikes, collected sticks, and muddy wellington boots scattered under my porch. "How many of the little—what should we call them?— '*blessings*' have you got?"

"Three." I pointed to the bags under my eyes. "All under five. All up, wide awake, full of beans every single bloody day, *before* five."

"I've four of the darlings. They're all a little older than yours, but I understand how overwhelming it can be." She showed me a digital photo of her children, all sat tidily, ducks in a row, on a pristine sofa in an immaculate living room. Behind me, I heard my stew bubbling over and my children screaming blue murder.

"Lovely shot, gorgeous smiles," I said, a forced smile hitched on my lips. Her children all looked so bloody perfect. It was hard not to notice Dawn's perfectly manicured neon-pink nails and perfectly fashioned chignon bun, not a hair out of place, as I hid my kitchen-dirty hands behind my back in shame.

"I was also finding motherhood exhausting until someone knocked on my front door and shared with me what I'm about to share with you." Her eyes sparkled as she spoke, like angler fish bait.

One of my children called out from the kitchen and interrupted her pitch.

"Mummy… Becky squished my dough giraffe. Now she's rubbing it down the gap by the side of the fridge."

I shuddered as I turned and caught sight of the kitchen clock. Five past six. Jack would be home shortly. A wave of adrenaline brought sickness to my stomach. When my youngest child had filled Jack's trainers with scrambled egg last week, he'd slipped them on, unaware, on his return from the office. He'd hit the roof, had thrown the trainers. The ding was still in the wall from the one that'd missed me. I'd covered it since with a painting.

Dawn smiled at the small, felt-tip-covered face of the three-year-old who'd poked around the side of my legs.

"Excuse me. One minute. I need to deal with this before it escalates," I said. Dawn gave an empathetic nod. Whilst I was dealing with the carnage in the kitchen, my husband returned from work.

After discarding his briefcase in the hallway, Jack asked Dawn who she was, why she was bothering us. "Don't you realise the working day has ended?" he said. "Coming here, interrupting families so late in the day. Despicable behaviour."

"I didn't mean to trouble you, sir."

With her shoulders back, Dawn nearly matched him in height. Jack glowered at Dawn, and stepped forward into what I would call her personal space. She did not budge an inch.

"And what is that hideous sickly smell?" He wafted his hand in front of his face and scrunched his nose in disgust. "Smells like baby vomit."

Dawn cleared her throat and stood a little taller in her patent yellow kitten heels. "That, dear man, is one of our best-sellers, *Eau d'Indépendance*. Praline, caramel, with top notes of bergamot. Would you like me to leave your wife a free sample?" She reached into her designer bag.

"Absolutely not. Smells like a brothel on a Saturday night. Don't you have a family to get home to, to cook dinner for?" Jack snarled at Dawn. She didn't so much as quiver.

Strangely strengthened by Dawn's presence, "Darling, that's rather presumptuous," I replied.

He cut me off with his all-too-familiar glare then stormed through to the kitchen, shouting at the children. I looked at my hands and finger-fumble-spun my wedding ring around.

"I'll pop back in the morning," Dawn whispered, then reached out and squeezed my hand before passing me a thin catalogue with a picture of three grinning, perfectly preened, champagne-sipping women my age on the cover. "Do take one of these in the meantime. I can't emphasise enough how life-changing our product is."

I thanked her. Perhaps a new concealer to cover the recurrent bruising on my chest and upper arms would mean I could wear something a little cooler in the summer months. I tucked the small catalogue discreetly in my jeans pocket.

"The house is a state. What on earth have you been doing all day—or *not* doing?" Jack's voice bellowed.

"Thank you so much for coming by," I said and began to gently close the door.

Through the narrowing gap, Dawn mouthed, "Word of warning, the make-up is terrible," and then pointed to her brashly coloured lips. "But look out for Mellow-Tek—towards the back of the catalogue. Our Haze-On smart tech is absolute fire. Shall we say ten, ten-thirty tomorrow?"

"Oh, um. Ten is fine." I said goodbye and made my way to the kitchen, a swirling apprehension in my guts. A conversation with another grown up, another mother… At least I had *something* to look forward to tomorrow I thought as I wrote the appointment down in my otherwise blank social diary.

∞

"Whatever ghastly make-up and feminist drivel she's pushing, we're not buying it," Jack said. As he cussed something I could not decipher, he lifted the lid of the stew. He drew the ladle to his lips, tasted it, and grimaced before spitting it out in the sink. "Disgusting. You've forgotten the meat again, haven't you, you scatty bitch. Your memory's rotten—IQ of a goldfish. I'll be getting a takeaway tonight. Scrap that, I'm going out for dinner. You and the ankle-biters can eat that filth."

I'll admit the stew wasn't perfect. I'd started leaving out the meat. Delirious with sleep deprivation, I'd done it accidentally the first time—relentless night feeds and nappy changes meddle with one's acumen—but when I realised it meant cooked meals would cost half as much, I'd started to omit meat deliberately. I'd always replace it with cheaper substitutes though, you know, tofu, beans, that sort of thing, so everyone got some protein, and in doing so, I'd stash away the difference.

"I'm off for some grub. And Bouncer will need walking after. You've clearly forgotten to take him out again, haven't you? I can tell by the way he's cowering in the corner. Useless imbeciles, the both of you." As he reached for Bouncer's collar to connect it to the lead, our poor dog whined. He'd already spent several hours at the park earlier that day with the children and I.

"Sorry," I said, "Must've slipped my mind." I'd learnt it wasn't worth contesting his opinion. He'd only justify his own view of how I'd spent my day after the kids were asleep with his fists.

By skirting around recipes and cutting corners on the weekly shop with the allowance Jack gave me, I'd managed to accumulate quite the nest egg. Nowhere near the sum I'd need to follow my dreams of studying Literature at university—something which Jack would never allow: *'Higher education is no place for women; you're far too ignorant and scatterbrained to unwrap and digest the literary greats—you struggle to even maintain a tidy household'*—but enough for a rainy day; a moment of frivolous freedom.

I did miss meat, its preparation, anyway: the piercing and slicing of raw, fresh slabs of beef brisket, the cleaving of joints of claret, bloodied lamb from its white sinew; the way animal flesh felt cold, dead in my hands, ready to be manipulated in any fashion I saw fit. The teasing out of cruor and blood clots from the vessels that would unfurl from odorous, packed offal had always given me some strange small pleasure.

Many an afternoon whilst the children played and I cut meat for Jack's supper, before I started to replace it with other things, I fantasised about what it might feel like to slice the blade into my husband's flesh, to watch the red squirt and spray from him, to hear him begging for me to stop. After all, he'd made me bleed countless times before.

Jack slammed the door on his way out, and the children and I enjoyed our stew. I bathed them, read them their stories, and sang lullabies before creeping back downstairs, alone, to study the catalogue that Dawn had left.

∞

Haze-On for Kids is our delicious vitamin and mineral-enriched supplement that can be sprinkled on breakfast cereals, added to smoothies, casseroles and soups, or taken as a single dose in capsule form.

Ditch those one-too-many sundown gins and sunrise hangovers. Haze-On powder is your modern-age mother's little helper.

Our smart technology will provide you more hours in the day at a fraction of the price of your local childcare provider. Brought to you by Mellow-Tek—Bring some 'Mellow' into your life.

'Sold to the unhappy lady with the frenetic life', I thought and finished my cocoa. 'But what is it? How does it work?' I traced my finger along the small print:

Just one dose allows your child's neuronal system to incorporate our new, safe, effective bio-tech. Haze-On powder is packed with hidden nano-particles which sequester in your child's forebrain, allowing easy and safe control with our compatible, easy-to-use Mellow-Tek patented hand-set. You want more hours in the day? We're giving them to you.

Speak with your local Haze-On representative—NOW!

I was intrigued. The image beneath the spiel showed two sleeping children curled up in their beds, each with a dreamy smile on its face.

∞

When Jack returned, I was in bed, scouring the internet on my phone for Mellow-Tek, to no avail. I couldn't find anything. As I heard him stomping up the stairs, tearing off his clothes and discarding them willy-nilly all over the floor for me to deal with in the morning, I deleted my browser history, then slid my phone and the catalogue under my side of the mattress. He rolled into bed next to me with a grunt. He stank of whisky and cheap perfume. I thought of Dawn, her fragrance, *Eau d'Indépendance*.

Then I thought a little more about Mellow-Tek and Dawn's perfect lifestyle, her perfect children, all the while feigning sleep.

൭൫ഌ

The next day, Dawn returned promptly at ten. I'd spent the morning breakfasting the children and attempting to tidy up the ever-replenishing trail of plastic detritus the three of them deposited in their wake. Dawn and I chatted briefly on the doorstep about the weather, the garden. She asked if I'd read the brochure, and I said yes. I told her I was very intrigued.

Should I have let her in, a stranger? *Jack would never need to know.*

She smiled as she pushed aside the offering of wooden cubes and pipe cleaners on the sofa, perched attentively on its cusp, and pulled a small bottle and an e-device from her mock-croc handbag.

"I tried to find out more from the net, but there's nothing out there," I said.

"We avoid the media. Prefer a more direct approach. It's an entirely female-led enterprise… you know… women helping women, empowering each other, our sisters? We're trying to remain off radar—grasping claws and vitriolic eyes of the patriarchy and all that."

"Ah, I see," I said, although I wasn't sure I did. I placed my hot tea down, drew my chair a little closer to the screen she was pointing my way, and watched the promotional video with intrigue and some awe.

"And you say it causes absolutely no harm… to their precious developing brains?" I asked once the video had concluded. She knew she'd reeled me in. The health benefits of the supplement alone would've made me part with a little of my savings, but the added bonus of being able to 'deep sleep' my darlings for the odd half hour was an absolute clincher.

"And *you* use it… the powder and the handset?" I asked. Dawn nodded. "And that's how you maintain such a smart family home? Why your children are happier… because they get more quality one-on-one time with you?" I shuffled forwards in my chair to take the portable screen that Dawn proffered in my own hands so I could swipe through the promotional imagery myself.

"Yes, in a nutshell." Dawn's grin widened.

"And now you manage to hold down a full-time job and parent full-time yourself, without any help?"

"Correct."

"I have to admit, I thought you were so smart when you knocked on my door yesterday—that photo of your immaculate family—I thought you were some kind of superhero!" I lifted my own grubby handbag onto my lap and reached into it for my purse.

"Yes. I've been a regular user for about three years now. As a single mum, it's been a godsend. Absolutely no regrets." As she smiled, I noticed a smear of lipstick on her teeth, a slight glitch in the otherwise perfect matrix which was Dawn.

She recommended the 'medium' pack, which she said contained all I would need; no additional purchases.

"So, I add a sprinkle to their food over the course of a few consecutive days, or I add the entire dose at once with a levelled scoop?"

"Correct."

"Then, an hour later, I press the button?"

"Yes."

"And you're sure it's completely safe?" I passed Dawn my debit card.

"Our studies actually show users develop stronger, enhanced neural networks, leading to intelligence gains and a significant increase in IQ."

"It makes the children brighter too?" It seemed too good to be true. I offered Dawn the last gingernut.

"Well, you'll find your children will be well rested when they're switched back on. We've noticed regular, transient pausing leads to improved behaviour, better outcomes at school, and increased happiness levels for all, but our main area of notable overall... improvement is actually recorded in the mother."

She handed me a bottle containing the capsules of powder and an electronic device no larger than a mobile phone. Would I be brave enough to use it? It had cost me over half of my savings. My heart revved as I considered the implications of spending this much, the length of time it had taken me to stow away the price of it all.

"You sync a dose with its recipient, give them a tag, set up an avatar. They'll love choosing their own characteristics for the display. This button here allows you to control each individual separately— great for giving dedicated one-on-one time whilst the others snooze. Much cheaper than childcare, I think you'll agree."

I thought of the additional cash I'd be able to save. This product would pay for itself in no time at all. Jack gave me thirty pounds to place the children with a minder every other Saturday afternoon whilst I gave myself up for what he called my 'wifely duties'. I could make a soft area in the garage, pause the children there, together, and tell him they were with Jane at the Teddy Bear Day Care Centre. I could put away this extra bit of money in my 'rainy day' pot.

"Thank you," I said. "Thank you, from the bottom of my heart."

"My absolute pleasure."

"I feel silly asking this, but I do have one more question…" I felt like her eyes were reading my mind. "Does it also work on animals?" I glanced at Bouncer, curled up in his dog bed under the stairs.

"There's no such thing as silly questions. We want you—the user—to feel reassured, to be able to reap the maximum potential from the device. Yes, it works on animals. Most people with pets actually try it on them first, though there really is no need. We've thoroughly researched the safety and efficacy of the tech. But if you do dabble—same size dose, same procedure." She paused. I watched her studying our family photographs on the mantelpiece. The five of us, sharing uncomfortable space, our bodies untouching, trapped within cheap metal frames, Jack grinning widely in each photo, his smile not stretching to his eyes. I don't look happy or 'well-rested' in a single one of them, and neither did my children. "I'll be in touch to see how things are… progressing. You'll probably have further questions in a few months."

"Thank you so much, Dawn. I can't wait to try it."

Dawn passed me a business card with her contact details and address on. "We do ask one thing of our customers, though. Please keep our technology to yourself. You know, proprietary patents, etc."

"Oh, of course," I replied. I didn't have anyone to talk to about it anyway.

⊗⊗

As soon as Dawn left, I gathered the children around the table and told them we were going to do some science experiments, with Bouncer as guinea pig.

"He'll love it," I said to three small, grinning, mucky faces. "My friend Dawn said it will make him super waggy." My children cheered and helped me mix the powder dose in with Bouncer's meal.

⚬⚬⚬

"Mummy, do it again!" All three children shouted in unison, buckling with laughter at the sight of our dog. I'd set up an avatar for him on the device and had linked it to the capsule we'd stirred into his meal an hour earlier. Oh how we giggled, together, as we took it in turns to pause and unpause the disoriented hound, showing him then hiding his toys between goes, as he scampered around the house in search. Bouncer, our very own befuddled, laggy, three-dimensional dog movie. Old lollop chops. What a delightfully bonding experience. Such glee! I took my turn and pressed the button and we laughed as his tail stopped, mid wag, leaving a creamy blur in his wake, so soft to the touch.

"Bouncer's happy," my youngest said.

"He loves it, Mummy. Do it again," said my eldest, who had folded over with a bad case of the giggles. Bouncer, in animated form, scuffled to the back door and scratched at it with a paw.

"He needs to relieve himself," my middle-child said. So we followed Bouncer out to the corner of the garden. The children fought over who would get to press the button next. My eldest child won. *Pause.* Our dog became stockstill, mid-wee, with a frozen arc of gold hanging in the air beneath him.

The only thing I found truly disconcerting? Bouncer's eyes. Where normally they were deep brown, loving, needy, always on the nudge for snacks, while on pause, both of his eyes became unreadable, hazy screens of black and white fuzz, like static on an old television screen; two eerie, bottomless pits, Bouncer's eyes seemed to call my own eyes in closer, yet violently repelled my very quiddity at the same time.

⚭

A little over a week later, the novelty having worn off for the kids in pausing the dog, I'd developed enough confidence in the technology. It was time to trial my purchase for real. I was ready to use it for what it was designed for. I crumbled up a dose in each of my children's desserts after their favourite spag bol, and monitored them carefully whilst they played in the garden for an hour or so.

I barely managed to hold them still for a minute that first go. What if they didn't reanimate? I'd never have forgiven myself.

Over the next few days, for only two minutes at a time, I stood and watched—as if I were frozen too—over their motionless bodies, strewn on the living room floor like beached carcasses spewed from shipwrecked vessels. It sickened me to see them this way, yet the new silence in my house gave me breathing space, filled my mind with a certain tranquillity, a numbness. Each time I put my children on pause, it did give me a little anxiety. What if they didn't come around? But the peace. The peace! Pausing my children was not a wholly unpleasant sensation.

I gradually drew out the time they spent under, upping and upping their downtime by a minute more each day. When dark thoughts kicked in, about what might happen if they were to stay permanently on hold, to make the time pass faster, I'd keep myself busy. I'd wander around, tapping their raised arms, adding or taking away layers of clothes to suit the temperature of the moment. I'd kiss their plump cheeks and wipe the residual food and bogeys from their faces that I'd never have had the chance to do while they were in their mobile phase. And they always seemed completely unaware once they came to me, once I hit play again, just as Dawn had promised.

In fact, they came out of each induced trance-like state much calmer and far easier to interact with.

A fortnight passed with nothing untoward occurring, so I decided to go large. I paused them for two hours on a Tuesday morning and indulged in a long-overdue deep clean of the bathroom followed by a thirty minute luxurious bubble bath. This extended pause became a daily occurrence.

I couldn't bear to look at their faces whilst they were switched off though, with their speckled eyes of monochrome vortex, so each time I paused them, I would carry my children to their beds. A little guilt bubbled in my stomach, but the benefits quelled this sensation quite fast. And Dawn had reassured me with her well-presented scientific evidence, hadn't she—the long term benefits of it all would rapidly outweigh my momentary anxiety.

Once I'd cleaned as much as I felt I could, rested, read a few chapters of my book, I'd spend half an hour preparing dinner: a vegetarian lasagne, a swede-and-potato casserole, or on Fridays, a delicious tofu and vegetable pie.

One bleak Wednesday afternoon, after a rather silent, still morning, with a brief period of hectic reanimation at lunch time, I decided to take a quick break from the chaos of the young ones again after our midday sandwiches. This time, I did no cooking or cleaning at all. I simply put my feet up and read two entire novels and then completed The Times crossword puzzle.

This pattern continued for weeks. Each day, I paused them for an hour or two in the morning to complete my duties, and then again for a second in the afternoon, the latter slot a more self-indulgent session. Still couldn't bear to see their eyes whilst they were under, though, no matter how hard I tried to adjust to the prickling void within their sclera. I attempted to gently close down their eyelids, but they just sprang back open like mouse traps, to reveal infinite pools of static. What were they staring at, I wondered. Did their minds, their frozen souls revisit the place they came from before they were birthed? Were they slowly walking towards a great light?

Pushing the unnerving sight and thoughts to the back of my mind, I reminded myself of how much more I managed to get done around the house thanks to this Haze-On technology. Things became tolerable. Things felt how I'd always expected motherhood to be: neat, clean, orderly, almost enjoyable when the children were 'awake'. Although Jack seemed to show total indifference to the tidying and improvements I accomplished with my extra time.

Three months after meeting Dawn, I finally felt on top of things. The house was neat, the freezer stocked with meals, and all three children had taught themselves to read before even starting school. For fun, when he was awake, little Billy had even taken up solving Diaphantine equations. I had accomplished so much around the home, I felt like Wonder Woman. With the kids all soon to return to school and nursery at the end of the long summer break, perhaps it was my time to shine. I wanted to go back and study; and to afford that, I needed a job.

I slipped Dawn's card out from underneath the mattress, and dialled her number. We spoke at length on the phone, each singing the praises of my new life.

After I'd hung up, I put the children on pause, and tucked them up in their beds, being sure to roll their faces away so I could avoid looking into their voided eyes, then I nipped into town to purchase a suit with some of my childcare savings; Dawn had offered me a sales role with Mellow-Tek.

"Sure, we'd be over the moon to take you on. All we ask of our saleswomen is that they target their customers carefully using the critique provided, that they don't discuss Mellow-Tek or Haze-On supplements with anyone unless guaranteed a direct sale, and that they have an additional spare room, basement or cellar at their property. Do you have a spare space somewhere at home, Tabitha?"

"I've a garage we never use. Full of old junk. No windows. Will that do?" I presumed the job would require some desk space for all the associated admin.

"Perfect," she said. "I'll pop round with all you need on Monday morning."

Monday could not have come soon enough. I slipped into my new suit and applied my make-up carefully: shrill orange lips, lilac blusher, perfect cat-like eyeliner flicks. A knock at the door came, ten am sharp. I ushered Dawn into my tidy home. "Looks fabulous in here," Dawn said before spreading out the training documents over my freshly polished dining table. "Let me show you the ropes. Welcome to the Sisterhood."

That same day, once I felt more confident in what I was going to be doing, knowing I could pop the kids on pause whilst I went out and found my customers, I couldn't wait to get started. It wouldn't take me long at all to save up enough to pay college fees on the commission rates Dawn had declared attainable. I'd decided I'd share my good fortune with Jack later that night, over our evening meal. How could he have been anything but pleased that his wife wanted to go back out to work, to better herself? Afterall, I was smashing it at home with consistently great meals, organised, stocked cupboards, neatly pressed laundry, and academic whizzkids for children.

That afternoon, the kids on freeze, I cooked a delicious dish just for my husband, made for the first time in a while with proper meat—organic steak. As I prepared it, I revelled in the snip and the snap of the fat from the lean as my knife slid through the fresh, the bloody flesh of the butcher's best cut. I laughed and sang as I sprinkled in my own delicate mix of herbs. I knew this meal would be essential if I wished to return to the world of work.

On his return from the office, Jack gobbled the whole steak pie down without comment as I sat next to him at the table with my bowl of slimmer's soup and the children sat quietly on the other side with their three-bean-stew.

Once I'd bathed and put the children to bed, I asked him if he'd like to at least give each one a kiss goodnight. He gruffly refused, telling me again, as I sadly knew he would, that bedtime was women's work, and slumped himself down in front of the television.

I waited until the children were asleep, then crept downstairs and told him the news of my gainful employment.

"You ridiculous woman," he snorted. "How on earth are you going to work *and* look after the family home? What about the children?"

"They can come out with me, walk with me, or sit in the buggy. It will do them good. Fresh air, seeing Mummy doing a little something for herself," I replied. Dawn had given me a script to follow.

"It's not happening. No woman of mine is touting cheap, slutty cosmetics for a pyramid scheme. What will people think? They'll think I'm not providing for you. It'll reflect terribly on me."

"Darling, it really won't. I've bought a suit too. Would you like to see it?"

"A suit?" He stood up. "Take it straight back to the shops or I'll cancel your allowance. You can't even hold the family home together, what makes you think you'll succeed at any sort of business venture?"

"But look around you, Jack. I've done so well in maintaining things. The silverware is polished, there are lavender bundles I made by hand in your underwear drawer… I even potted on the house plants yesterday! Surely you can see I'm doing so well and deserve a little something for me?"

"You'll become so tired and forgetful—you'll probably forget to collect my dry cleaning, or leave the gas on, blow the house up or something."

Jack's face grew red and his cheeks puffed out like a dragon as he became more worked up. His eyes became a malevolent shade of black, making them look almost more disturbing to witness than the static the Haze-On delivered. Was he about to exhale a fire of wrath in my face? He marched towards me, tossing angry words out at me, each one a painful swipe. His breath, sour and foul, blew hard on my cheeks. I backed away into the kitchen, feeling panic in my stomach as he followed. He moved closer towards where I stood, my back against the knife rack. My mouth grew dry; I knew he wanted to hurt me. He grabbed my shoulders and shook me hard with an uncontrollable rage; I almost dropped what I had clenched in the sweaty and shaking hand which I held behind my back. One of his mammoth hands moved like a vice around my throat and his other paw, in preparation for a mauling, lifted up into the air above my head.

I hit pause.

His looming arm froze.

Jack's body rested perfectly still, and his eyes became lost, razzle-dazzle portals to nowhere, vacant pitches devoid of soul. I wrenched myself from his grip and dropped into a pile, all shaking and teary. The encounter had been far too close for comfort. Thank God he'd eaten every scrap of the steak pie—the one I'd spiked with Haze-On. My heart was a churning mess of gunfire in my chest.

From my pocket, I pulled out Dawn's business card and placed it firmly in his grip, then made myself a cup of cocoa, allowing thirty minutes to pass. I paced the kitchen with my favourite chef's knife in my hand, fearful that he was going to somehow override the technology, switch on again, more furious, more enraged. Over and over, I tossed the plan in my mind, examining every avenue with a fine-toothed comb, ensuring there weren't any details I'd missed, loose ends I'd failed to tie.

"Have faith in the tech. Have faith in the Sisterhood." Dawn's last words from our conversation earlier resonated in my brain.

Once I'd reassured myself that all was fine, all would be fine and all was for the best, I turned my husband back on.

His brow furrowed as he lowered the hand containing the card, like a curious toddler pulling a caught handful of snowflakes to their eyes for the first time. With a muddled look on his face, he smiled as if momentarily unsure of his location and looked down at the card.

"Sorry, love. What was I saying? Was I thanking you for dinner? That pie was delicious. Much better than the usual crap you serve up."

"Thank you," I replied, trying to mask the sardonic grin I felt spreading across my face, as my sweating palms tried to conceal the knife I held in a tight grip behind my back.

"What's this you've given me?" His eyes ran across Dawn's telephone number and address on the card in his hand. I watched apprehensively as his eyes started to bulge with rage, as the cogs of his Neanderthal mind started to wind back up to speed. "This is her, isn't it? That pyramid-scheme-pushing whore with the shocking face of trampy make up?"

"Yes dear, I thought you'd be interested in—"

And like Dawn had guaranteed, before I'd had a chance to finish my sentence, he was slipping on his shoes and rummaging for his keys.

"I'm putting a stop to this right now. That home-wrecker needs dealing with. Meddling bitch has no right coming here, seeding ideas in my wife's delicate mind. Not enough room for any more information in that thick noggin of yours anyway. I thought we lived in a good neighbourhood. Can't believe such riff-raff lives around the corner. No-one's safe when there's trash like her about, are they? Where are my bloody car keys?"

"No idea," I said. I had an idea. His house keys, car keys and work keys were all hidden safely away.

"I'll have to bloody well walk over then. In the dark."

"Of course, dear. I understand. Do what you need to do. It was a foolish idea anyway. What was I thinking? Me and my feeble thoughts."

And off he stomped into the night, like a smoking chimney on legs.

ଓଃଡ଼

Rat-a-tat-tat

He knocked hard and firm on Dawn's secluded front door, and Dawn promptly answered.

"Ah, Mr Fox. Let's not have this conversation out here in the cold. Come in." Dawn told me later that he'd barged his way into her home and that she then had offered him tea.

"Water," he demanded with a venomous tone, huffing and puffing. A thick vein on his forehead was throbbing, and his irate fists squeezed and released tightly at his sides.

Dawn went to the kitchen, and texted me to let me know he'd arrived. I quickly swiped to his avatar and hit the pause button again. My husband stood there, frozen like a six-foot cardboard cutout, eyes like black holes, in Dawn's lounge.

It turns out that Dawn, like many women, was a lot stronger than she looked. The next day, over a glass of mid-morning champagne in a quiet corner of the local beauty spa, she told me how she'd hauled my stock-still husband into her spare room. There she stashed him, alongside all the other angry-faced monsters with their permanently open eyes, their eyes full of deathly domino static, before closing the door.

◈

Life as a single mum is so liberating. Things are much calmer at home now, too. I work whilst the children are at school. Don't feel the need to pause them anymore—which is lucky, as I've no idea where I put the controller. It's been lost for months. Can't seem to find it anywhere. I'm sure Jack would understand though, seeing as I have such a terrible memory. I'm frightful for forgetting the simple things, aren't I? IQ of a goldfish. Struggle to remember how to do up my own shoelaces some days.

Jack may have been right about the company being a pyramid scheme, but I do enjoy how working for Mellow-Tek allows me to make such a difference to women's lives. Dawn and I and the rest of the team have made such a big difference to so many troubled housewives. But I'm not going to be a door-to-door cosmetics seller forever though, I intend to follow my dreams. When I hit my target—I should have enough by the end of next month—I think I'll quit the sales job and enroll at university. You could say this is perfect timing, because my garage is nearly full.

GURGIE

"You're an ugly crier."

I swear, that's what it said. I hauled it up from the plug hole, and tried to scrape it and tap it and ease it off the straightened coat hanger hook, against the edge of the bath. My forefinger brushed against the tightly anchored slug of slime and hair, which made me dry-heave into the toilet. After dropping the gunk-coated hanger back into the bath, I rubbed my hands back and forth in disgust against a towel.

Had it really spoken, the plug dregs? How could it speak—it had no mouth. It had no anything. It was just a clotted tangle of dark hair woven together with ribbons of yellowed dental floss, some kind of plasm that'd been choking the shower up. I rubbed my cleaned hands against my ears in a protest of disbelief. Other than myself, the family bathroom was empty. The insult *must've* come from outside, through the air vent. Must've done.

"When you cry, your face looks like a dog's anus."

I spun around. Nothing. No-one. Just me. I looked down in the bathtub at the mass of runny crud I'd hoiked out from deep within the throat of the shower. The clump of drain treasure, repugnant, trembled like jelly as its words echoed around the bathroom. It had definitely spoken, and it was bloody rude.

"Pardon?" I replied.

"Truth hurts. Let it go—few people do look pretty when they bawl. And another thing—you shouldn't let your stepdad speak to you like that."

Whatever it was, wherever these words were coming from, they spoke with honesty. I *was* an ugly crier and I *had* had enough of Mark, with his awful 'vintage' record collection taking over our shelves—who even are Gary Glitter and Rolf Harris and Ike and Tina Turner, anyway? And his penchant for groping my derriere, and thrusting himself up against me whenever Mum wasn't around.

Mark was my mother's latest squeeze and the reason I, with a rusty, unfolded hanger, was unblocking the shower in tears. He'd said it was my fault the drain was blocked, and that I needed to sort it out or he'd 'sort me out'.

"What are you?" I asked the anonymous voice in my bathroom.

"Never you mind what I am. Your stepdad—you shouldn't let him tell you what to do. So what if the shower is clogged? He has hair as well. And he uses the shower, too, albeit probably not as much as he should—stinks like skidded knickers, that one. It isn't *all* your fault. I'm not made *entirely* of *your* hair, Ellie."

"You're right," I replied. "I know." I slumped down against the wall, hugged my knees to my chest, and let another wave of tears flow.

"Now, now." The voice sounded uneasy and largely disinterested, like it had no experience with—or true desire to quell—the emotions of a depressed fifteen-year-old girl. "You've got me all out now, anyway. The water is draining freely. Mission accomplished, so wipe away those tears. You've helped to release me… maybe I can return the favour?"

"And how on earth is a ball of slime, old hair, and a rusty clothes hanger going to help me?"

I sighed and thought about the biology practical I was meant to be doing that morning with Mr Turndike. I hadn't prepared for it all. I was probably in line for a bollocking from him too—and here I was, chatting to literal junk, when I should've been getting ready for college.

"If you could just pick me up, pop me in an empty Tupperware and slide me under your bed, I'll let you be on your way."

"I'm sorry, what? You want me to scoop you off the side of the bath and keep you? Under my bed?"

"Well, yes. Do you have a better idea?"

Stress does things to a person, doesn't it? It can make them delusional, see things. Hear things. I stood up and bent over the edge of the bath, and stared at the coat hanger coated in sludge. It didn't seem like it would hurt, not really, saving it, and maybe it could help me. It was certainly a good listener, attentive and truthful.

I ran downstairs, took the largest tub from the middle drawer—the tub Mum once kept fresh meringues or birthday cakes in, from an age ago when she used to bake, when she used to care—and ran back up to the bathroom. Using the cleanest part of the wire, I lifted the collection of repulsive mess and dumped it all down in the transparent plastic box, hanger and all. I swear I felt it exhale on me.

"And the lid, if you don't mind. I'll catch a chill without it. Don't worry. You'll still be able to hear me."

I clicked the lid on—I'd clearly already lost my mind. What difference would adding a lid make? Then I slid the thing under my bed.

☙❧

"Ellie, you haven't done the reading, have you?" All six-foot-six of near-skeletal Mr Turndike loomed over me. His hot coffee breath stank worse than the formaldehyde pong of the dead frog splayed out on the chopping board on my desk.

"I… I've had a lot going on at home," I replied and pulled the sleeves of my shirt down and over my wrists. I didn't want him seeing the bruises on my arms. He'd be more annoyed than I would at all the additional paperwork such a discovery would deliver.

"I see." He rolled his eyes at me, took a scalpel from the pot, and made a firm slit from the amphibian's neck to where I'd expect its genitals were. "Ox heart next week, Ellie. Make sure you're more pre-pared."

"I will be. Sorry, Mr Turndike."

"You need to jab the skin with assertion, confidence. Then gently peel away the visceral fascia like so." With the steel needle and forceps, he teased away a transparent tissue to reveal a set of purple-pink organs not that dissimilar, I imagined, from those you might find in a tiny human.

"Thank you," I said. I covered my mouth with the back of my gloved hand. The pain au chocolat I'd scoffed on the way into college repeated itself, and brought acid and bile up into my throat too, for the ride.

Turndike moved to the front of the class and started to issue instructions on what to do next. It was then that I heard the other voice.

"Take it," it said.

I said nothing, petrified that someone else may've heard it. What if one of my peers thought the deep, mildly threatening voice had come from me? It spoke again, louder, more firmly. I felt terrified this second time, not because of what it said, but because I realised that no-one else, not a soul in the entire class of twenty-eight, had also heard the booming words which had sprung from nowhere. I *was* losing the plot.

"Take the tract—the digestive tract and the kidneys. Put them in your pocket. Bring them home to me."

I froze. I wanted the voice to stop.

"TAKE THE KIDNEYS. They're yours for the picking. Just like your stepdad helps himself to your mum, to the food in your cupboards, to you." To hear these sorrowful truths voiced aloud triggered a sadness within me, but I couldn't cry, I wouldn't. How would I wipe tears from my face? My fingers were covered in bloody frog guts.

Its instructions were deafening and resonant, yet around me, my classmates plodded on as normal. David and Gemma, my desk neighbours, were carefully slicing away tissue, pinning back membranes like guy ropes on a tent, deftly exposing and fondling frog innards. I decided against asking them if they'd heard the bossy voice too. The whole college already thought I was odd; this would undoubtedly have added fuel to the fire.

I hacked the parts out crudely with the scalpel, picked them up in my latex-gloved hand, turned the glove inside out—trapping the organs within it—and pegged it out of the lab.

"Ellie… Ellie Harper… come back now." Turndike's words hung in the hallway, but I was already through the college gates, on my bike pedalling, halfway home.

On arrival, I threw my bike down against the hedge. Panting and red, I puked on the pansies in our front garden that Mum had been so proud of. Fiddling and twiddling with the key in the front door lock, I finally got it to turn. *Click*. In.

Mum and Mark were out. I crept up the stairs, a little fearful of what I might find.

"Come, take off my lid."

I slid the cake box out from under my bed and did as I was told. I felt sick again as I looked down at what was inside. It was as if Egon Spengler had tipped out the contents of his proton pack and garnished it with furballs.

"Drop in the intestines, the stomach, the kidneys. Yes… all of the digestive organs. We all need to feed, don't we, Ellie?"

Delving into my pocket, I pulled out the gloved contents and inverted the demanded parts onto the congealed shower-slime. My heart thudded hard, my stomach turned over, yet I watched on in awe. Within the container, the slime seemed to absorb the organs into its erratic, tangled net of gunk; strands of hair octopus-armed each of the gifted organs around. It squeezed and channelled intestine and kidney and stomach as if searching for a good fit, a home for each gobbet of amphibious meat. The lump of stinking jelly started to pulsate as slime of its own soma was drawn in through the top of the stomach bag and pumped in and through and out of the length of frog gut and anus. A rhythm of intake, propulsion, and expulsion became established—most revolting but also, oddly intriguing.

"Good," it said. Its voice had quietened, somewhat satisfied, satiated. "Lid on."

I clipped back on the lid, slid it back under my bed, and, gladdened that it was content and silenced, tried to think nothing more of it.

⊗⊛⊙

The following week at school, Turndike slapped down the promised ox heart onto a wooden slab in front of me. "You'd better not be thinking of bunking off early again, Miss. Ellie. I'm watching you." My hand trembled as I lifted and moved the organ meat into position on my surgical steel tray.

"Of course not, Sir. I've read up on it, too. I know what I'm doing today."

I didn't want to be in trouble at school as well as at home. I'd stayed up until midnight the night before, until exhaustion tugged down my eyelids. I'd crammed up on the cardiac system, partly because I wanted to impress Turndike (I like biology), but largely because I'd had to listen to Mark screaming and Mum crying downstairs.

I followed the instructions and sliced the heart in half. My sensory system tried to ignore the stench of formaldehyde and stale meat, and the sounds of my classmates mock-retching. Worming my gloved fingers through each of the major vessels, my hands enjoyed playing God. I picked out a rancid blood clot the size of a grape from the ox's aorta, flicked it onto the chopping board on which my steel tray was mounted, and then continued to explore the cold, grey flesh. The white webbing—the tendons holding the bi and tricuspid valves in place—was easy to snip away, and doing so allowed me to splay the ventricular and atrial chambers apart to identify each quadrant correctly. Turndike was most impressed.

"Well done, Ellie. Well done. You may pack up now. Enjoy your lunch."

I started to peel off the latex gloves. But then the voice returned.

"Take it. Tip your sandwiches out, pop it in your lunch box, bring it to me."

Shitting fucksticks! I thought I'd heard the last of it. I'd planned on disposing of the mess under my bed, before the smell from the rotten, furring frog innards permeated out from my room. Again, I panicked. My own heart, still hooked up within me, shuddered and squeezed double-time. I scooped up the dead ox organ from the table and bundled it into my bag.

"BRING IT."

I left the laboratory and jumped on my bike. I pedalled, hard and fast. Doing what it ordered seemed to be the only way to get the voice to stop. After I'd silenced it this time, I'd chuck it in the waste disposal or, if it had dried up, I'd set it alight in the fire pit in the back garden. *Kill it with fire!*

⚜

Mark was in the living room, listening to terrible rock music and playing with one of his creepy reborn baby dolls and drinking Special Brew in the middle of the day. He gave me a wink. Repulsive. Mum wasn't home. I felt unsafe. I ran up the stairs, lunch-bag slung over my arm. I needed to silence the voice and then I needed to get out of the house before that creep came up.

I yanked the tub from under my bed and placed the ox heart in the centre of the sludgy, throbbing intestinal ribbon.

"Come on now, don't be shy. Give me a stir," it ordered. I shook the deathly soup while trying not to gag.

"Yes. *Yes!* Thank you," it said with a tone not dissimilar to Brian Blessed.

Thank God, I thought, *now the nagging voice in my head will stop.* But it didn't. The box of bits wanted more from me.

"Now cut your fingernails. Dust me with your keratinous tips."

"I'm sorry, what?"

"Your nails, girl. Chop chop." A moment later, with the sharpest scissors in the house in my hand, I set to work. The smelly, lumpy gloop slurped up each black polish-coated nail clipping I sprinkled on its top. Once done, my nails trimmed as short as they could go, I took the scissors back to the bathroom to put them away in the medicine cabinet. On returning, I gasped.

A multitude of undulating tentacles had unfurled over the sides of the tub, each tipped with a three-inch razor-sharp black talon of nail. Within the centre of the tub, amongst the mass of slime and dark hair, the ox heart had started to beat. The stomach of it rumbled and a peristaltic mass of twisted, pretzeled intestines the size I imagined a dog's or a cat's might be squirmed.

"Eyes and teeth. Need eyes and teeth, girl."

I staggered back and fell against my bookcase. A stack of papers and trinkets tumbled to the floor around me. What on earth was this thing I'd dredged from the bathroom sewer pipe? What thing from Hell had I released?

"EYES AND TEETH."

Its words punched my eardrums, its demands echoed again and again. I needed it to stop. I didn't have any eyes and teeth to spare. I thought of my milk teeth, which Mum kept in a pot in her underwear drawer. Would that collection of rice-grain sized teeth satisfy this organ-hungry monster?

In a pile on the floor in the corner of my bedroom, I started to cry. I heard Mark's heavy footfall thumping up the stairs. And there I was, trapped in my room, between two awful, hungry monsters. What choice did I have but to stay there in the corner and just contend with the demanding voice which I was no longer sure was really just coming from my head. Mark would've killed me if he'd caught me rummaging through Mum's drawers.

The door swung open. The thing in the tub leapt out and slid over all greasy-ghost towards Mark. Streaming, gelatinous tentacles pushed the organ mass across the floor, and it left a trail of hair and slime in its wake. The heart I'd given it thrummed through transparent tissues. Inches of vile frog's intestines pulsated and writhed like maggots. It doubled, trebled, quadrupled in size as it moved, until it became a tower of madness and primal urges. Riding the large wave of gloop bareback, the metal hook of the coat hanger bobbed along up top where I could only imagine some sort of head should be. The meatmarket apparition travelled toward the door frame where Mark was standing.

Mark, terror stamped into his features, screamed at the sight of the hair-clot beast as it hastily approached him. Too late. Too late for Mark now, I thought, frozen in my place. With the metal hook needle of its hanger head, it gouged out Mark's left eye first and then his right. Mark released a guttural scream which shook dust from my bookcase. As I shuffled further away, I knocked Noodles, my favourite Beanie baby, from my collection off my desk. I grabbed Noodles and held him up to my chest in fear.

Two blue-irised eyeballs, each dribbling blood and black vitreous humour, were skewered on the steel tip of the hanger sludge beast's crown. Mark's eyes. Although I didn't think they belonged to Mark anymore—sitting above Mark's still-attached nose and mouth were two spurting red-and-black sinkholes. Mark's arms flailed about as he swung at the beast I expect he could no longer see. Screaming again, Mark's mouth fell agape, and that was when the shower-gunk beast really seized its chance.

"TEETH!" it screamed.

A giant tentacle of goo shot out from the wobbling tower of depravity, and the tentacle latched onto, and moulded around Mark's open jaws like a gigantic limpet. I covered Noodle's eyes as black talons swiped and shredded and rent Mark's meaty torso into human puree.

I stood, still with my back against the wall and a shaking palm over Noodle's fluffy visage and watched the horrific scene I had absolutely no control over at all play out. This creature's work was nowhere near as neat as Turndike had demonstrated a proper dissection should be.

Blood dribbled and spurted from Mark's core. As his intestines unspooled, he somehow managed to catch them briefly, only for them to waterfall onto the floor between us. The clot sucked and slurped on Mark's mouth, in some kind of satanic fellatio. Noodles and I heard the snap, crunch, and pop of each tooth as it was yanked from its socket. Fountains of blood sprayed over the beige deep-pile bedroom carpet.

Mark's frame swaggered backwards, listing from side-to-side, a captainless ship adrift in a sea of pain, until he reached the top of the staircase. The drain monstrosity, now with a full set of dirty gnashers suspended amongst plasm and tangled black hair goo, snapped at Mark, and took off and swallowed his nose, which was pulled down through the beast's guts, only to re-emerge seconds later in the centre of the beast's own vulgar, shifting face.

It punched him with a translucent tentacle and Mark tumbled down the stairs. I swear, I've never seen anything tumble so oddly. The thing, I still have no idea what it was, then became arrow-like, fronted by the sharp, unfurled hook of the hanger and a pointed cluster of talons. In a trice, it lifted itself up from the floor and through the air, and shot after Mark.

As quickly as a plague of locusts, it devoured the sad remnants of my stepdad. Then it shot back up the stairs, slid into the bathroom and flung itself straight back down the plug hole.

"Mum," I yelled from the top of the stairs, "where do you keep the carpet cleaner?" I needed to clean my room. A tidy house is a tidy mind, afterall, and Mark's departure had created a terrible mess.

Surely no one could've studied in such a state of disarray? And I had to get back to the books, straight back to the books—and I know it's been a journey, a wild ride, and Mum's had to go back on the tablets, but I swear I've told you everything and after all I've learnt, I'm certain I can get an A in Biology.

And this is the story I stand by, Officer.

LIKE SARDINES

Without sedation, Marie knows the amount of money she will receive for her egg donation will be a little higher and it is this thought, at least, which helps to keep her calm as the procedure begins.

Skilfully and rapidly, the doctor inserts the rusted oocyte retrieval needle through her vagina until its tip meets the germinal epithelium which lines her left ovary. Sensing the change in tension, for the sake of precision, the doctor pauses to examine the ultrasound screen at his side. "Little scratch coming up," he says. He pierces through. Cold. Sharp. Inside of Marie, the tip of the needle encounters its sought treasure: a ripened follicle.

Marie balls the single-use tissue-sheet beneath her in tight fists, crimps her eyes closed, and internalises her pain, just as she had done in labouring all three of her children.

The doctor draws back on the plunger. Suction. A pop. "All over," he says and withdraws the device from her body. "You may feel some discomfort over the next forty-eight hours, but I'm afraid the service you elected does not include post-extraction analgesia, nor anti-infective medication."

"I know," Marie replies. She wonders how many others this needle—which the doctor passes to his sombre colleague—has ventured into, in the hope of drawing out something useful for the wealthy and infertile.

"And I'm afraid this will be the last egg donation we'll be able to receive from you." The doctor discards his gloves in the clinical waste bin. "Due to your age."

"I understand." Marie slowly swings her legs around, ignoring the smarting pain in her womb, and sits with bony buttocks on the hard steel table. She drags her old trousers back on, then barefoot, makes her way through to reception. Her children are waiting for her there, each of their stomachs rumbling; a torturous sound audible only to Marie, perhaps.

Too tired to argue the unfairness of how most of her male lodgers can make unlimited sperm donations in exchange for hard cash, she lifts her youngest from his seat and requests her other children get ready to leave. "The payment will be in my account before the end of the week?" she asks the sallow chap on the front desk. He nods without lifting his eyes from his screen. A familiar twinge springs in her groin. Marie hurries home, although home does not feel like home anymore.

☙

For the next few hours, due to her discomfort, she has no choice but to lie down while her children wait outside in the rain. Her bed, in which each night herself and her young ones squish up against each other in an attempt to rest, is pushed up against the window in the smallest room of her house. From the bed, with one hand, she massages her stomach, and with her other hand, she scrunches the draped newspaper tacked up over her window to the side to look down at the street below.

A chalk-rich rock her youngest had pocketed on the long walk home has provided her offspring with entertainment: the faint outline of a hopscotch grid can be seen on the pavement outside. Marie grapples at her waist, her ovaries, apologises to her body. *Needs must,* she thinks and smiles softly at the sight of her kids fighting over the rock—she's proud of how her kids are so thrifty, how they always make the best of what they've got—although inside, her heart cries, singing an all-too-familiar song of poverty. Eventually, she dozes off.

☙

Her children argue over who owns the sheet of half-popped bubble wrap which has drifted down the street. This noise wakes her. *How long have I been out for?* she thinks. She massages her midriff. *Long enough for the discomfort to have settled, thank God.*

She peeps out of the window and sees the sun low in the sky, but does so discreetly, so as not to let her children notice she is awake. With Barry and Lydia and Mohammed asleep in the hallway, there is not enough space for her children to come back inside yet.

She descends the stairs, stepping over the items her lodgers have not yet been able to flog, which are stored on the bannister side of each step, and attempts to enter her kitchen.

Excuse me's and *pardon me's* and *if you wouldn't mind's* fill the already minimal air space there. She will allow her children back inside soon, once Barry and Lydia have set off for their respective night shifts. Once Mohammed has shifted position, moved in, away from the thoroughfare. She will not keep her children out at night—the dark is no place for young ones. Nowadays, everything has a price.

With sadness and disgust in her chest, she squeezes past James and Roderick and Martha and Clive, and peels down the veil of sticky fly-tape which drapes above the pile of excrement—bait—kept in the place where the pawned fridge-freezer once sat. From the insect trap, she scrapes off with the back of a butter knife plentiful wings, legs, and antennae onto a chipped plate.

With a little frying oil, a sprinkling of vitamin powder stolen from her first lodger's—Lucy's—drawer, and enough salt, at least her children will eat this evening. She sighs, thinks on her feet, *How can I make this more of a meal*, necessity being the mother of invention. The scraped arthropod protein stretches out the final can of 'Whiskas' tuna she'd salvaged last week from a skip. "Like sardines," she says to her children as she serves it up, "but with more crunch."

≈

Despite the rent she collects from the nineteen other people Marie sublets her small house to, she still accrues massive debt each month, still exists terminally in the red. *The boiler must go*, she thinks, *it takes up too much space.* She has not dared turn on the heating for over three years. *Perhaps the metal casing in which the old pipes sit may be worth something in scrap?*

≈

The next day, she asks Bill, who lives in the upstairs bathroom along with Jody and Pete and Olivia H, to disconnect the unused gas supply. He agrees to this begrudgingly, although his opinion is that the house is cramped enough without taking on an additional lodger in the small cupboard in which the disused boiler sits. But he does as

Marie asks—after all, his rent with her is cheap. He cannot, despite working three jobs, afford to move elsewhere. He certainly does not wish to join those who have lost the luxury of a roof over their heads: the people who exist under the bridge and haunt the abandoned parking lots.

The new 'spare room' is filled before the end of the day. Angela, a recently divorced sales rep, moves into the airing cupboard, and uses the small aliquot of space where the microwave used to be to store her worldly possessions.

Cheek-by-jowl, the inhabitants of Marie's dwelling move around the living room, the hallway, the kitchen. Like crabs, each of them sidle from one cramped spot to another. The queue for the downstairs bathroom is verbal and constant and the stench from the blocked drains, relentless.

ͼ₰ͽ

Over the school holidays, Marie's children complain. There is no room for them to play inside, and none of them rest well at night now Harold sleeps on the slim strip of floor between the end of the bed and the bedroom door. Harold had his hours cut, had to downsize, and Harold's wife, Barbara, must slumber in a straight line, for she has no room to curl up at the foot of the matchbox-like cot, which Marie and her children share. Harold, who sleeps on his back despite Marie's complaints, releases throaty snores which wake them all at some point each night.

Marie realises, as her youngest bursts into tears for the third time in one day—because Adrian's breath stinks and Barbara is such a fidget and Richard's voice is a notch too loud—that this is not living, just existing. Marie knows, feels her children's pain. She is also strongly aware that it is her duty to solve this crisis. With every inch of space within the property rented out, she must do something else to try to make ends meet.

⚭

The holidays draw to a close and Marie drops her children off at school, each dressed in dirty trousers exposing more than an inch of bare ankle. She waves them goodbye, blows air kisses, and tries not to cry as each is dragged into its respective classroom for a day of hard manual labour. *It is for the best,* she tells herself. *At least they have a little more room to move, to breathe at school, up and down the factory-floor line.*

She does not have time to fluster over their tears, or to dilly-dally a moment longer; an appointment has been made. Marie has ten minutes to walk to the surgery. Despite the fact that she is up to her limit with blood and egg donations, and no woman can feel entirely well with less than one whole kidney, Marie is confident; she believes, with this upcoming procedure, she is making a wise choice. After all, what option does a single mother have but to provide for her family, the days of benefits and government subsidies long dead?

She had begged the doctor to take a cornea, figuring she could manage just fine with only one working eye, yet the doctor had declined. He had, instead, suggested something else.

⚭

Marie sets off down the road, the school gates shrinking in her wake. Her stomach groans. She reminds herself she does not have the privilege to feel hungry or nervous, and the cash she is about to receive will provide ongoing sustenance for her and her precious young family.

She arrives at the clinic, where she exchanges small talk with Robin, a surgery porter who has just finished his shift. Robin is a man of minimum stature and also on a minimum wage. She learns he used to collect stamps before times got hard, and now he likes to take long walks at the weekend but enjoys less so napping under trees. *Seems like a pleasant enough chap,* Marie thinks, as she tilts her head while he spouts off his pitch. Robin follows her through to the procedures room where he signs and dates the contract which, afterwards, the doctor asks Marie to sign in a similar way. She reads the details carefully, does as she is asked, then Marie is instructed, once again, to strip from the waist and lie supine on the steel table.

"Knees apart, ankles together," the doctor says. He slips on latex gloves. Marie obeys, and watches without blinking, feeling fear yet also a sense of relief. This payment may afford her and her smalls something decent for dinner at least—although she has been warned the procedure may somewhat increase her appetite. The doctor lubricates the tip of the speculum in his hands. "This will be no more uncomfortable than a smear test. Are you old enough to recall those? Before the NHS fell apart?"

Marie shakes her head.

"You may experience some post-procedure settling pain," the doctor says, and then instructs Robin, the off-duty porter, who stands at the end of the hospital gurney, to wrap up the rest of the thin sandwich he holds in his hand and take off his shoes.

Once the widening device is inserted, the doctor cranks open Marie's cervix. Marie cusses as her opening is stretched several centimetres more than it had been in childbirth. "Okay, we're good to go," the doctor says, his nose close to where his speculum rests. He waves Robin on as the plastic device tugs Marie's spread labia. "Seems small but cosy inside."

The porter, on hands and knees, climbs in. "Could you pass forward my shoes and sandwich," he whispers, before assuring Marie his direct debit payment is set up to cover the next six months in advance. *One more tenant can't hurt,* Marie thinks, as she balls her fists tight and thinks again of sardines.

BONUS KIOSK

"Maybe it's a typo?" Sam called out from the fridge.

"A typo? An entire additional, fictional bloody month? You're off your rocker. It's knocked all the other dates out of sync. Rest of the year is a write-off." Ralph tossed the spiral-bound calendar onto the sofa, on top of the plastic wrapping from which he'd just unsheathed it. "My birthday is meant to be on a Saturday this year, not a Tuesday."

"Help me give the shelves a wipe before I load in the meat, will you?" Sam was kneeling on the tatty laminate flooring of the Air BnB kitchenette, reaching into the corners of the old refrigerator with a threadbare J-cloth he'd found under the sink. "This place isn't as clean as I'd hoped. There are… sticky black feathers… everywhere. Gross stringy gloop all over the salad tray. God, this stuff stinks of stale death." Sam stood, mock-wretched, and wrung the dirty cloth in the sink.

"This calendar is a piece of shit. What a waste of money," said Ralph.

"We'll go back tomorrow and get our money back, after a good night's sleep. It's just a calendar."

"S'pose so."

"You've got one on your phone anyway. I don't understand why you wanted that one so much—" Sam's words petered off, as with one glance at his well-built husband, he detected a trace of 'the red mist' descending over Ralph's face: the narrowed eyes, the tight lips, the volcanic brow.

Ralph growled before he spoke. "I thought it'd be nice to tack up on the wall while we're here, and then back home. In that space on the wall above the airfryer. A souvenir. It's got nice photos of beach sunsets in it."

"Sorry darling, I know how much you love your sunsets—"

"The shopkeeper said there were pictures of fossils in it too, from the digs along the bay. I thought that might interest you. I guess the old bag was a sharp saleswoman."

Ralph picked back up his faulty souvenir and thumbed through its pages again, searching for the additional month. He flipped over July. There it was, the month of 'Beachtember', with its thirty-one additional days, slotted in right after July and right before August, accompanied by a large photograph of a semi-excavated Apatosaurus fossil and an artistic impression of what the prehistoric beast might look like in real life by its side.

Ralph studied the image again then rubbed his eyes. Had the sketch of the old thunder lizard just furled its upper lip, revealed its dagger sharp teeth, winked at him with a blood-red eye?

"I mean, seriously, 'Beachtember'? If they're going to mess with paying customers and prank tourists like this, they could at least come up with a better name," Ralph muttered. He slumped back into the dusty faux-leather recliner. "Can't believe that old crone conned us out of 150 pesos. Imagine if it *hadn't* been half price…"

"Love, let it go. I'm guessing it was half price as we're already halfway through the year. Who buys calendars in July anyway? Speaking of which, summer's whizzing by, isn't it? I can't believe it'll be August tomorrow."

"Not according to this calendar, it won't be. It'll be ruddy 'Beachtember'. Wonder if I can find that bastard 'Bonus Kiosk' on Trip Advisor. Might leave a bad review." Ralph dug into his pocket for his phone. "Bet it's not on the net—it's all a tad backwards round here."

"Language, Ralph."

"Oh, come on, I don't mean an actual bet—it's a figure of speech, Christ. Idiot."

"Ralph, darling. Please." Sam spoke gently, in the hope soothing words might calm his husband down. "Put your phone away. The doctor said to minimise stress. 'Digital detox'—work on reconnecting with your higher self. It's the only way you'll silence your demons."

"No bars anyway." Ralph hurled his phone on top of the calendar. "Booking accommodation without Wi-Fi was not your best idea."

"There's plenty to do here without the internet. We can laze in the sun, walk, swim, search for nearby digs… How about we hire a *fotingo* and head into the city to find some rumba?"

Ralph let out a long sigh. Sam closed the fridge door and came and crouched at his partner's side, and softly squeezed Ralph's thigh.

"What we're not going to do though, mister, is keep on grumbling. We're not going to spend every evening online, ignoring each other. And we're not going to think about gambling."

☙❧

In the morning, after coffee, Ralph picked up the faulty calendar, wrapped it in his beach towel, and slid it into his rucksack.

"It's roasting. You could've picked an apartment with air con. My sun block's sliding off."

"Ralph. Please. Can we do today with positivity, even if you have to fake it? I-it's not all about you—this is my holiday too."

"Don't I bloody know it… I'd have chosen somewhere a little less focused on digging up old bits of crap from the ground and a little more lively, for sure. This place is a graveyard. There isn't even a bar here."

Sam's smile dropped. "You don't have to get involved with the digs."

"Surely there's *something* left of the inheritance. A few pesos to put us up somewhere more… refined… air-conditioned?"

Sam unscrewed his water, glugged half of it back then rammed the bottle hard into his bag before dabbing away pearls of sweat from his brow. He snapped, "Funnily enough, after paying off your sizable gambling debts, there wasn't enough left for butler service and five-star accommodation." Then he retreated to the kitchen end of the open plan living space, for fear he may've overstepped the mark.

Old Aunt Ely, whom Sam hadn't seen since he'd been small, had left him a couple of thousand in her will—just a squeeze more than they'd needed to clear some rather threatening illicit arrears Ralph had acquired. There'd been enough left over to get them both out of the city for summer, so Sam had taken the opportunity to book a trip to the place he'd so often lectured his palaeontology students about but had never visited, and figured the break might also help Ralph with his addiction, might help the couple with the 'marital issues' they'd been having for months.

"Why don't you flog that revolting ring she left you too. Free up more capital. Treat us to an upgrade, some cooler air?" said Ralph. Sam hid his hands behind his back. This was not the first time Ralph had attacked the piece of jewellery Sam's aunt had also left him. Yes, it was of a certain taste, but it was all Sam had left as a keepsake of the aunt who he had recalled being very kind to him when he had been a young child.

"You know I can't sell the ring. Her will specifically said to keep it—for good luck."

Made from blackened metal, the ring bore a miniature bird skull with two red rubies for eyes, and it fitted Sam's pinky perfectly.

"It's disgusting, Sam. You and I both know that."

Sam busied himself with tidying away the coffee mugs. "I've packed sandwiches for breakfast. Egg and tomato, extra salt—just how you like it," he said. A change of subject was often the only way to avoid conflict.

"Thanks," Ralph grunted.

"Come on, let's check out the beach."

⳥

As they made their way down the long, winding trampled path which broke between a jungle of six-foot tropical grasses, rubble eventually merged into hot, white sand that stretched either side as far as the eye could see. The sun beat down on their fair skin from a ceiling of perfect azure sky.

"Think I'm going to keep these on," Sam said, waving his flip flops, hopping as his feet screamed with the heat of the sand.

"I need some new ones," said Ralph. "Any chance of some cash?"

Sam looked directly at his partner. "If I give you cash—"

"You don't need to say that," Ralph interrupted. "I don't need a lot anyway—sandals, water, and crisps. It'll save you coming shopping with me."

"Are you sure?" Sam's eyes widened, seeded with doubt.

"Sam, come on. There's nowhere here to gamble anyway. The place is dead."

He spoke the truth. White sand made up most of their view and not a dinghy or a soul was out on the flat ocean. All they could see was the beach: desolate, apart from the small shop a good walk away—the Bonus Kiosk—where they'd brought groceries and a useless calendar yesterday.

Sam reached for his wallet.

Ralph took the bundle of notes proffered and stuffed them into the front of his rucksack.

"Isn't it gorgeous here?" said Sam, reaching out to his husband, searching for affection. "You know, it's our wedding anniversary next month? Fourteen years. Ivory, I think."

"Really? Ralph replied, missing the prompt to wrap his arms around Sam, kiss him on the lips, tell him he loved him. Instead, he stood stone-faced as tears collected in the corner of his partner's eyes, before reaching into his bag to retrieve a warm sandwich.

"Speaking of months, I'm going to take that calendar back. Now. Said she was open twenty-four seven, three sixty-five. Three ninety-six more like. Joker. A thirteen-month calendar? What a rip-off merchant."

Off Ralph stomped through the blistering heat and Sam sloped against a palm tree, one of a cluster of five which provided the only shelter from the sun in the area. There Sam sat and stared out to sea for a moment, and twiddled his thumbs, but then he stood up, flustered on becoming aware that he'd misplaced his aunt's precious ring.

ೞ

"Yes?"

The same old woman who'd served them yesterday stood behind the counter, hawk-eyeing like a dumpy vulture over Ralph from the moment he entered. Yesterday, Sam had said he'd found the shopkeeper familiar. Ralph had said that was ridiculous, as they were seven thousand kilometres from home and on a deserted beach. Ralph had found her glare vexing.

The door of the Bonus Kiosk swung shut behind him as he trudged up to the counter, trapping him inside with the stifling air. It seemed less well stocked than it had yesterday. The area where the groceries had been stacked was now bare, all save a few two-litre bottles of water, and the exposed wall behind where the produce had been was now messily plastered with pages of text, several hundred loose sheets, ripped from books and pasted willy-nilly as wallpaper.

He looked at where they'd collected eggs, tomatoes and bread from the day before, and tried to make sense of the strange scripts covering the wall.

"Hi. I came in yesterday," he said, slapping the calendar down on the counter. "You sold me this. From there." Ralph pressed his angry finger down hard on the disappointing calendar and then thrust the same stiff finger at the rotating display in the centre of the floor.

"Ah yes, half price. Bargain," the shopkeeper said, peering at him through beetle-black eyes over her half-moon glasses.

"I want my money back."

"Sorry. No refunds." She thwacked a long length of bamboo cane against a section of pasted text stuck on the wall to their side, where the fruit and veg had been. "Says so here, in the rules."

"Don't be absurd. It's clearly faulty."

"Rules are rules. And here's another," she said, the tip of her stick leading his eyes to another sentence strewn amongst the wall of text: *"Proprietor is always right."*

Ralph leaned in, rubbing the sting of sweat and sunblock from his eyes and took a closer look, only to confirm the lady's words.

"This is ludicrous. If an object's faulty, I'm entitled to a refund—it's the law."

"Where you're from, maybe—but you're not home now, are you?" She winked and laughed, hee-haw cawing like a randy magpie.

As she pushed the calendar back towards him, his eyes were drawn to her hands. Despite the heat, both hands were gloved in elbow-high black velvet and each gloved finger was decorated with a ring—all except for the fourth finger on her left hand. Each of the rings bore mounted upon it a miniature black bone. As he stared at her peculiar attire, Ralph felt a shot of ice run down his spine which was anything but refreshing despite the shop being hotter than an oven. As he backed away from the counter, he knocked into the carousel which still held hundreds of sealed, reduced, identical wall calendars. Managing to grab it just in time, he saved it from tipping over.

His heart picked up. How dare this crone speak to him this way, with her stick and her ugly jewellery and her rip-off products and her stupid wall of rules—he wanted his pesos back.

"But it's got an extra month in it. Thirty-one days that don't exist. And after that, the days are all out of whack. It's useless."

"You mean Beachtember."

"Yes, I mean 'Beachtember'. Of course I mean Beachtember." Ralph's cheeks fired red. He snatched the calendar up, riffled through its pages and shook the made-up month in the shopkeeper's face.

"Pinch punch first of the month," she said.

"What?"

"First of Beachtember. Today," she said. As she spoke, her thin lips pricked up a little higher at the sides. "Pinch punch."

"You're crazy." Ralph pulled out his mobile phone—still with no bars—and tapped on the calendar app to try and prove her wrong. To his shock, as he opened up the digital calendar widget and displayed it on the screen, it too presented the entire month of Beachtember. "What the—"

"You like the beach? Beautiful, isn't it. Hot white sands, deep blue seas. So peaceful—and all yours. Yours alone for the entire month."

Ralph switched his phone off and on again, hoping to fix the glitch, but Beachtember flicked back up on the screen.

"I just want my money back," he said, giving up on the phone and sliding it back into the pocket of his trunks.

"No refunds." The old woman tapped her stick against the wall rules, then swung her stick towards the carousel. "Happy to exchange for a different calendar."

"What? Do they all have Beachtember in them? I bet they're all the same."

The shop worker paused and stroked her chin as her eyes narrowed. "Do you want to make a bet?"

"No. No. I don't. No bets. And no, I don't want another one. Look." Ralph took his towel out from his bag and used it to pat the sweat from his face, "What's this all about? Where are the cameras? Joke's over. I get it. I'm being pranked."

"Not at all—no cameras here. No electricity," she said, and he realised she spoke the truth. There were no plug sockets in any of the walls. No till. No ceiling lights.

He laughed. Had his sanity started to melt in the heat?

"Tell me about this Beachtember, then." Ralph exhaled slowly and leaned over the counter, bringing his face up close to the old woman's.

"Simple. You get to stay on the beach for an entire month. Thirty-one days. Holiday time."

"Sounds great." He shrugged and shook his head. It was hot and he realised he had no option but to go along with the woman's game. "Keep your bloody calendar. I'll just take this water. Do you have any crisps?" He pulled a note out from his stash.

"No, we don't sell food. Only food is Bonus Ice Cream. Van comes every Tuesday. Range of flavours. Bound to find one you like. Why not try them all?"

"You were stacked with food yesterday. We brought a bag of groceries!" He gestured at the wall to his left, where boxes of delicious fruit and vegetables had been displayed the day before, the same wall now bare other than the pages of text covering it. Sand started to pour in through a narrow slit where the wall met the ceiling. A trickle at first, and then, a waterfall of grains, faster and faster. A continuous gush cascaded down over the glued book pages, forming a pile on the floor where the broccoli and mangetout had once sat.

"No. We've never sold food here. It's in the rules, look." She pointed her bamboo cane at a tiny sentence amongst a page stuck down amongst the wall of other pages. "*No food is sold in this shop.*"

"You're completely mad," he said. "Keep the change." After picking up his water, he marched towards the door and slammed it behind him on his way out of the shop.

"What about your free seventeen percent?" she said softly to his back, waving a smaller bottle of water she'd lifted up from behind the counter. But it was too late. Ralph had not heard. "Always something extra with every purchase in the Bonus Kiosk."

ରେଃର

The sun was strong. Ralph made his way back over to the cluster of trees to find Sam gone. He looked up and down the beach. His husband was nowhere to be seen. Nothing except for blank white sheets of sand in either direction, a dense thicket behind him, the kiosk, and the ocean were in his sight.

"Christ's sake." Ralph muttered under his breath and started to walk back along the beach.

His feet slapped on hot sand. Thwump, thwump, thwump. He searched for the clearing where the path began that would take him back to their rental property. Where was Sam? Where was the clearing? He searched and searched and walked and walked, but couldn't find either.

On and on along the scorching sand he walked, accompanied only by the continuous wall of thick jungle on one side and flat blue sea on the other, but Sam was nowhere to be found. And where was that damned clearing that led to the rubble path? He tried to phone Sam, the battery draining of juice fast, but there was no signal no matter how much he thrust it up into the air, and the screen still told him it was Beachtember the first. After walking for what felt like at least an hour, his mouth was dry and every part of his body ached, so he stopped and finished his water and the rest of his salty sandwich.

Ralph turned around to examine the route he'd taken. He could no longer see the kiosk behind him, or the cluster of trees under which he'd left Sam. Where was his partner? Where was *he*? Still on the beach, that was evident, but seemingly no closer to where he wanted to be. He contemplated turning around and retracing his steps, but, with his innate bull-headed arrogance, he knew he could not have missed the break in the dense shrubbery. And so onwards, he continued.

His skin hot to touch and turning a shade of lobster, he noted the sun had taken a full arc of the sky and was touching base on top of the ocean. Night would come soon. Mosquitoes chipped at the back of Ralph's neck and legs as his feet slapped down and down again, onwards.

He had to stop again, had to take a moment to rest. Had to. A man should not walk all day in such heat, especially not when on holiday. He placed his sore, burnt hands in the dips of his lower back and stretched out his spine and yelled at the ocean, then he looked back at the trail of his own footprints in the sand.

"Christ alive," he whispered, his throat as dry as the sand beneath his feet. Squinting to dull the white light of the sun, there, just behind him where it should have been miles away stood the cluster of palm trees under which he'd left Sam, and just behind that, he could make out the shape of the red and white storefront and sign of the Bonus Kiosk.

In any better state, it would have taken an army of stallions to drag him back into the shop, but as the sun appeared to be about to set, and as he was out of food and water, he swallowed his pride. He had no other choice but to step back inside to ask for directions.

☙❧

"Yes."

"Hi," he said. The floor of the shop was now as sandy as the beach outside. As the door shut behind him, a small avalanche of more sand tipped in hard and fast from the hole in the wall. "Look, I—"

"Came back for your bonus water?"

The lady plonked down a small bottle of water on the countertop.

"No, but… well, yes. Thank you," he said. He swiped the bottle and unscrewed it with haste. Gulp gulp gulp. "I'd like to buy another. Please. Two." After wiping a dribble from his chin with the back of his hand, he placed a bank note on the counter. "About earlier… sorry. Too much of this bloody sun."

"We all have our mad moments," she said.

"Could you just direct me back to the path, the one that leads back to my rental property, please?"

"Path? No paths in Beachtember. Just sand, sea, sun. And ice cream every Tuesday."

"Pardon?"

"No paths. You're on the beach. I told you. Pinch punch. It's Beachtember. Thirty-one days."

"You're saying I'm trapped on the beach?"

"Well, yes. You are. Just you, on the beach. Sun, sea, and icecream on —"

"I don't give a shit about ice cream right now! You're telling me I'm stuck here? On the beach and I can't leave. For a month?"

"Yes. It's beautiful, isn't it?" The old lady folded her arms and smiled.

"What about Sam? I left him under the palm trees. Where is he? What have you done with my husband?"

"It's a lovely beach. Beautiful sunsets. Postcard picture perfect. Would you like to buy a postcard?" She gestured at a range of cards, each one a variation on a theme, each small card an image of the hot ball of fire in the sky touching down on the top of the ocean. As he stared at the selection of postcards the lady placed on the countertop, each close up of the setting sun appeared to radiate more unwanted heat in Ralph's direction. He stepped back, his right hand held up with its palm to her face.

"No." His voice came out loud. The lady's brows rose, furrowing her already deeply wrinkled brow even more. Ralph paused, considered his manners—this was the only shop for miles. And this woman, antagonistically odd as she was, was possibly the only other human for miles. He needed to be polite. "No thank you. No. I don't need any more souvenirs. I just need water, and some food."

"Ice cream," she winked. "Bonus Kiosk does ice cream. Every Tuesday."

"It's Monday."

"Yes. Monday the first of Beachtember. Ice cream tomorrow. Ice cream on Tuesday. So many flavours."

Ralph, volume adjusted, stammers in response. "I-i-it's getting dark outside. What am I supposed to do? Where do I sleep?" His legs ached like he'd run a marathon, and his feet were sore. Really sore. His t-shirt clung to him with sweat stung as he tried to flap air onto his chest through the neckline. Had he ripped off a layer of skin in this attempt to cool himself down? The sun, it appeared, had burned not only his exposed skin, but the skin that had been hidden under his clothes.

"We sell hammocks. Each hammock comes with a free bottle of mosquito spray. Bonus spray." The shopkeeper bent to retrieve something from below the counter top and dragged it along the floor to where the kiwis and watermelons had been sat the day before. "Bonus Kiosk—always a bonus with every purchase." She pointed at the brown cardboard box then pushed it up towards Ralph with her foot.

"I guess I'll take a hammock and some spray then." Ralph reached into the box and pulled out a heavy sack and a small pink, dusty bottle. He placed the goods on the countertop and then reached into his pocket to retrieve another couple of notes. Over half the money Sam had given him he'd spent in this woman's kiosk already. But he needed somewhere to sleep, somewhere off the sand. What value did paper notes have in such a harsh environment? His brain needed rest and his body needed some sort of miracle.

He left the shop and set his hammock up under the trees just before the sun sank completely. And there, he lay in the make-shift bed, in the dark, with only the light of the moon for company, as the mesh of the nylon weave fabric sliced into the red raw flesh of his back and buttocks. Ralph, his skin hot to touch, yet his bones shivering and his skin peppered with mosquito bites, struggled to distinguish the stars in the sky from imagined stars that flickered in and out of what remained of his peripheral vision. Moments of pained, restless, fretful sleep ensued.

∞

Waking up at the crack of dawn from his fitful sleep, Ralph found himself scratching—the mosquito spray hadn't worked. Ralph glugged down a few mouthfuls of water, but each mouthful felt like deep-throating a cactus. The night had not been good.

His phone told him it was five o'clock in the morning, the second of Beachtember. He was still there, imprisoned on the beach, and his skin was blistered, red, nibbled, and sore. He rubbed the sleep from his eyes and fantasised about coffee and eggs and paracetamol as he took another sip from the bottle. He'd have to drink more slowly if he was going to be here for the month, he thought. As he itched his forearms and shins, strips of skin like fried bacon sheared off under his nails.

Rocking himself with care out of his hammock, he slid his flip flops on, snapping the thong on one as he did.

"Shit. Shit shit shit shit shit," he said, lobbing the broken foot-wear into the thicket behind him. He couldn't do another night on this beach, let alone another twenty-nine days. The sun was already churning out its fire. He looked to the horizon, blurred by the haze of morning and his sun-singed retina, and placed his bare foot down on the sand in the shade.

Tolerable. Just.

If he was going to walk the other direction in order to escape, he knew he needed to do it now, before the sun rose any higher and turned the sand into lava, into burning coals. He packed his stuff up and set off in the other direction.

He'd been walking for several hours with nothing but undrinkable water and bramble to his right and to his left, and white-hot sand underfoot, when he saw a red shape on the shore in the distance. Mustering his inner strength, he ran towards the something, which turned out to be a tent.

"Digs," he shouted into the void around him. Never before in his life had the thought of something so dull as dusting off dirt from very old things dug up from beneath the ground made him so happy. There must be people there who could direct him. Help him. He thought briefly of Sam. Maybe he'd be there, inside, exploring whatever old fossils had been excavated. *Bloody ammonites*, he cussed aloud.

He lifted up the canvas curtain of the tent, dipped his head and entered. Muggier inside than out, at least the canvas roof offered protection from the deadly rays. The tent was more than empty. Where the sand should have been was a pit, propped open with wooden struts, and its edge was scattered with abandoned spades and brushes. Ralph edged closer and saw at the bottom of the pit what looked like a row of black elephant tusks poking up and out of the sand, like a linear bunch of sharp-nailed fingers. It didn't look like fossils, more like bones. If bones were black and serrated.

The bones seemed to beckon him closer, offering whispers of refreshment and direction.

Climbing down the sandy walls of the pit, he neared the bottom. Reaching out, enticed by a beseeching murmur that seemed to speak to his heart that came from within the pit, he placed his hand on a black bony finger poking up through the sands of the beach. It brought an instant coldness to his fingertips, causing him to lose balance and topple over. A sheet of sand slid down, burying the black finger tips. Or had they sunken of their own accord? Rubbing his eyes with sandy hands, he jumped up and back, unsure of what he'd just seen.

The walls of the tent suddenly felt a little closer, as if closing in. And Ralph wanted out.

He climbed up out of the pit and floundered out of the tent, and on exiting, he looked ahead to the journey he had no choice but to continue on. But where before, there had been nothing but more white sand, now he could see the kiosk again. He'd come full circle.

Exhaustion and frustration shook hands with pain and despair as the sun beat down on his red, raw face.

The fire of the sand burned his bare foot, ricocheting pain up his leg. The acrid stench of his own flesh cooking slapped him in the nose. Hopping, he hurried to the edge of the sea. In it he dipped his feet, howling with pain as the salt of the water bit like lemon sharks. He held and looked at his foot, which had been cauterised by the griddle of the sand. Cooler in the water, he saw he'd lost some of his toes. *Argh, the pain!* Panic and tears followed. What was he going to do with hardly any money left and no shelter and now, not nearly as many toes as he had had in July? And where was Sam?

His heart thrummed like a bag of bees. There was no way left or right to escape: the beach was an infinite loop. He'd need a machete to get through the greenery at the top of the shore and would most likely only be returned to the spot from which he had begun. Madness. *Have I lost my mind?* he thought, and this thought reiterated on a loop akin to the insane beach loop in which he appeared to be trapped. His only option was to swim. *Away from this bastard place.*

Bundling his belongings up into his bag which he balanced on top of his head, he waded out into the water, salt stinging every inch of his flesh, infiltrating open wounds with toxic marine bacteria.

The sea floor fell away gradually, and got so deep that he had no choice but to swim, and swim he did, as far as he could. Tendrils of seaweed and unknown creatures tangled and snagged against his legs in the dark waters beneath. He coughed and sputtered as he swallowed down screams with fetid water.

Ralph grew tired. His arms felt exhausted, and his body was sick, close to collapsing, dropping like a rock to the ocean floor, and his mind skirted dangerously close to cracking. Pain pinballed through every part of him.

Just as he thought he could swim no more, game over, his foot hit the seabed. Then both feet. Placing his raw soles flat on the rough terrain below, which he still could not see clearly, he began to walk again. Sharp shells, rocks, needles, teeth of glass for all he knew, lay along the ocean carpet. Razor clams or razor blades took off more flesh from his feet and legs. His shins and thighs, rended by things of the deep, puffed red-smoke swirls out into the water behind him.

The sun hung directly above and his shoulders, exposed again as the water became shallow, bubbled with pearly blisters. In front of him, a wide strip of white grew taller, until it became the sands of a beach like the shoreline he had swum from.

And it *was* the shoreline he had swum away from. There in front where it should have been behind stood the cluster of trees and that *bastard* Bonus Kiosk.

☙❧

Ralph, out of the water, shipwrecked himself under the collection of palms. Sand stuck in his countless wounds, decorating his body like salted tiger stripes. He looked like he'd been peeled. Badly. And here, he passed out.

❦

Hours or days later, Ralph was woken by music. The minor key of 'Greensleeves' caromed through the thick air into his ears. He fumbled in his bag for a bottle and drained it of its last few drops of water. His eyes, fried like egg albumen, made out the silhouette of a truck in the distance. Tuesday. *Must be Tuesday,* he thought, remembering the shopkeeper's words. Ice cream Tuesday. He watched the truck progress toward him until it pulled up at his pitch.

Pulling out a note from his bag, he stumbled over toward it, the sand a little cooler, more tolerable in the evening light.

"Yes?" said the lady, the same shopkeeper from the kiosk, as she picked up a scooper.

"Ice cream," he murmured, his words barely forming.

"Flavour?" she asked and reached around and pointed with her cane at the options displayed on the side of her truck.

"Can't read. My eyes," he said, indicating each black pupil, hidden behind white fog.

"Ah, solar cataracts."

"Don't care what flavour. Anything. Need to eat."

"Okay. Well, today, we have special flavours for our special customer to celebrate the first of Beachtember. We have: 'Can't Believe It's Not Chicken', 'Tallow 'n' Shavings' or 'Miscellaneous'."

He felt a dry retch of vomit burning up his throat. Still the first? Surely not. And this wasn't ice cream. But it wasn't July, and this wasn't a holiday.

"Miscellaneous. Please," he croaked, desperate.

"Here you go. Complimentary flake," she said, snapping off her un-ringed finger, sucking out the marrow from within it and shoving it on the top of the cream ball in its cone. She dressed the cold treat with a squeeze of strawberry sauce from her stump. Ralph, largely sunblind, was oblivious to it all. "Bonus ice cream."

Ralph bit into the cold dollop with fervour, the initial shock of ice on his teeth a pleasurable experience, only to spit it back onto the floor of the beach.

"That's fucking disgusting," he said, dropping the cone, buckled by waves of dry-heaving.

Standing back up, he wiped his face with his hand, and lumps of minced, frozen cartilaginous gunk sloughed off from his cheeks onto the sand. Ralph, unsure if the textured slush was ice cream or parts of his face, hurled again as he caught the scent of his fingertips, which stank of the dankest rot.

"Maybe. But it's all you're getting." The lady slammed the shutter down and drove off. The trail of a melody: 'You Are My Sunshine,' rippled out in the van's wake and hung in air so heavy you could cut it with a knife.

"And you didn't give me my change," he shouted. Ralph, in agony, limped across the beach, a ribbon of bodily detritus behind him. *Where am I? And where is my lover? All I want is for Sam to hold me in his arms and tell me everything will be okay. And then I want to pummel the life out of him. How could he bring us here? This is all his fault.* Tears rolled down his red raw cheeks.

Back at the shady patch under the trees, he curled his aching body up in the hammock. A soft whoop from above stilled his sobs. Through his damaged eyes, he could just make out the shape of large wings circling. And then more—could it be a wake of vultures bothering the sky? A black beast of feathers cut through the air, dive-bombing down towards him. In one deep swoop, the bird of prey clean tore off the hand that still stank of vomit and meat cone and flew off with it in its talons.

Ralph screamed. Blood squirted from the end of his arm, making a ruddy mess of the sand. With his other hand, he pulled his towel from his bag, wrapping it around and around his wrist stump, then folded over in pain in the hammock, screaming and crying. *This must be a mistake—a nightmare!* he thought. *I'll die if I don't do something, if I don't leave this bay.*

His only option was to go back into the kiosk.

With his last modicum of strength, he dragged himself up and out of the hammock, placed one painful foot in front of the other and made his way. He'd had enough. He was going to demand she helped him, bargain and barter with whatever he had left to offer. *Or God help her*, he thought.

Forcing the door open, he stepped again into the shop, left hand raw, right hand gone, bandaged in a crimson towel. As he staggered up to the counter, every step through the rising sands of the shop floor hurt. Sand was flooding in through the gap in the wall, faster and thicker than on his last visit.

"Yes?" Same greeting, same beady eyes, same fists full of black rings.

Without words, he pulled out the last remaining notes from his bag. Then with the only word his dehydrated lips could muster: "Help."

Pushing the last of his money over the counter, with his left hand, he gathered two bottles of water from the shelf.

"Bonus water," she said, swiftly shoving the notes amongst her cleavage, and placing two additional, miniature bottles on the counter.

She placed a coin of change on the counter and pushed it toward him. After downing half a bottle, he managed to regain a reedy voice. "Thanks," he rasped.

"Your change," she said.

He looked at the coin. It wasn't enough for more water. "Keep it," he said. "S'not worth anything to me. S'not enough for water. Still no food in?"

She lifted her stick and pointed it towards the wall of writing. "We don't sell—"

"Yeah. I get it. Rules. Don't sell food."

"Correct—but if you want something in exchange for your coin, I could offer you some entertainment…" Her voice trailed as she shuffled out from the counter, past the calendar carousel, and over to a shelf.

"What do I want with bloody entertainment? Look at the state of me. I need urgent medical attention. I'm burnt—no toes, no hand. I've a fever too. An infection. I'll die if you don't help me." Odorous pus seeped from wet wounds from countless sites on his body. "Look at my legs. A butcher's bin."

"Looks like lumpy ice cream." The old woman licked her lips.

"And my eyes. I can't see further than the ends of my hands. Hand! Something took my right hand, for Christ's sake. Help me, you witch!"

"We've entertainment," she said. "It's only the first of Beachtember. Entertainment might help time pass faster."

He let out a crazed laugh. "Pass time faster? Without water, food, antibiotics, a bloody good surgeon… I'm going to die!"

Reaching down, she picked up a small packet from the shelf and carried it to the counter. "Cards," she said. Ralph recognised the rectangular packet, the black and white lattice pattern of the box immediately. "You can afford these."

Ralph sighed. He brought his spread hand up to his forehead and shook his head into it in despair, his eyes winced with pain as his hand made contact with the raw, cracked, oozing, infected skin of his brow.

"Play me and win," the crone said, through black eyes narrowing, "and I'll help you home."

He dropped his hand and looked up. "For real? All I've got to do is beat you at cards and you'll get me out of this shithole? This… zero-star holiday trash can?"

"Yes. Name your game."

"Now you're talking," he said, dragging across a small step ladder through the rising sand of the shop floor on which to perch on, with little strength left for standing. "What have I got to lose?"

"Exactly," the lady said, with a sparkle of ruby to her eye.

"Poker," Ralph said, his eyes also brightening, despite his weathered body burning and shedding and flaking layers of purulent skin with every movement he made, unwrapping with every heartbeat.

"Let's play a few games for fun first, to warm up," she said, brushing black feathers from the counter and placing down the cards.

"Sure," he said. He took a swig on his water. "I used to be pretty good at this though, I'll warn you early doors."

০৪৪৪

Time unlike no other passed as his exhaustion and fever grew, his pain ebbed and ebbed. His hand throbbed and dripped onto the rising sands, but, addict he was, he got a buzz from the cards. The buzz spurred him onward. Each win seemed to energise him, to power him on. Bursts of adrenaline and dopamine got him through each round.

The lady played poorly, her face as old and still as the fossils the beach held, and Ralph started to feel a minutia of hope. As addiction demons roared inside his gnarled, empty guts, with each win, he felt a little closer to home.

"Let's do it. One final hand. I'm ready. I need you to take me to Sam, to hospital." A pool of blood had collected around him, darkening the sand that had risen up to his knees, and a circle of flies hovered over his stump.

"Final game then," the lady said, palming out fresh cards. "This is it."

He lifted his hand, drew his pair close to his face to check what he thought he could just about see. Through his near-opaque eyes, Ralph saw the one-eyed suicide king winking at him, axe in hand, and the Jack, the laughing boy—a diamond too. On the countertop lay an old queen, diamond, and the ten, too, amongst the row of shared cards. The game played on, his hopes of rescue elevated. The shopkeeper twisted over the final card on the countertop, ace of diamonds, and Ralph yelled out from his seat, "Fuck, yeah. I'm going home!"

Royal flush. An unbeatable hand. *Unbelievable,* he thought and yelled again.

He slammed his fist down on the counter so hard the postcard display fell over. "Yes! All in. Get the fuck in! Yes yes yes yes yes. Thank the fucking Lord. You won't beat this. You can't beat this," he said.

Spreading his cards out wide so the old lady could see his luck, his heart banged as he waited with bated breath for her to reveal hers. Sand poured in, waist height. "Hurry up, you old hag. Get me out of here."

She tilted her head to one side and looked at the state of a man in front of her.

"I've won, haven't I? That's it. I can go home," he shouted, white spittle frothing like lace at the corners of his mouth.

"I'm sorry." She stepped back from the counter and tossed her hand down for him to see. He looked down at her cards and up at the lady and down at the cards again.

"What is this? What is this one here? This card? With the bowl on it. Here," He tapped the odd card with his finger, his red face whitening. Where a Jack or Queen or King would normally be found, on this picture card, an image of a bowl or a cauldron with a handle sparkled.

"I'm afraid you have lost." She picked up the card, and tipped it forwards towards the countertop. "As I have the Bucket of Skulls."

Hundreds of small, avian and humanoid skulls, ebony black, spilled out from the bucket on the card like rice from a bag. All over the counter, out and onto the floor, skulls tumbled, spreading out as they came thick and fast with and into the swamp of sand that was ever rising in the shop.

Ralph, a face full of panic, looked at the woman and brushed the flood of skulls away from where he was getting stuck. "No, this can't be. There's no such card."

She lifted her stick and tapped it up high on the wall of words behind him where the fruit and vegetables used to be. *"Bucket of Skulls wins outright,"* she said with a squawk in her voice.

Ralph scrabbled together all of the cards, including the rogue one from the Bucket suit, which was still hurling out small skulls, and counted them. Fifty-three. He recounted, questioning his own ability to think straight, to count straight. There were still fifty-three cards.

"There's an extra card, you can't do that, you can't bring in new suits," he wailed.

"Bonus card," she said, and then tapped the rules on the wall again. "Bucket of Skulls *always* wins. Beachtember always wins."

Her neck elongated, coming up out of the white ruff of her black dress. She tugged at her head with her ringed fingers until her hair fell out in clumps. In its place, black feathers spurted through the puckered skin of her head. Pop. Pop. Two nubs bursted from her clavicle and branched wide and sideways, each pronged with more feathers. Longer feathers. Darker feathers. Feathers sharpened at their tips like blades. Her mouth, pinching forwards, grew forwards and reddened: a beak!

Ralph's heart skipped a beat. Ralph was scared. But he was also angry—angry at the lady, angry at his own eyes for failing him in such an evil way. "This can't be happening. This is madness! I have gone mad… I'm going to kill you, you crazy old bitch."

After wriggling and dragging himself out of the sand like a moth from a cocoon, despite his stump, his missing toes, he lunged towards the counter. "I'll get you, you witch," he yelled as he tried to grab the woman by her shoulders. He wanted to shake her hard. He needed to beat sense into the vitriolic old crone, like he had beaten his husband so many times before, but his arms—instead of meeting the now-aquiline hag to crush her, came crashing in together. Shockwaves of pain sped through his burned and bitten torso as his hand and stump collided. Ralph fell forwards in agony.

The woman was gone. Ralph was alone in the shop, now up to his chest in sand. Only her caw of a voice remained. A final sentence Ralph wasn't sure was in his head or vibrating in the hot air of the shop echoed all around: "Bonus life for me. You can't kill the undead." The words pecked at his eardrums, as if driving glass shards into his brain. He needed to get out of the kiosk, away from her hellish nest of sand and cards and faulty calendars.

Scooping his way out as fast as the sand would allow, he managed to get through the door and out of the kiosk, and back to the heat of the beach.

He staggered until he was as far away from the Bonus Kiosk as he could possibly manage, each slap of foot on sand burning like murder, sending lightning bolts of agony jolting through his body.

Screaming and burning, exposed to the heat of the sun and the sand again, he could go no further. He dropped to his knees and the red tent appeared again before him.

Crawling through canvas wings, he found himself back in the pit where the black finger-bones had lain.

Sand gave way beneath his weak wrist and feet and he rolled down into the pit, the sides of which caved in after him. The excavation site had been dug deeper, revealing not black fingers, nor tusks poking up from the beach floor, but a giant humanoid rib cage, black and bone. And the giant ribcage belonged to a huge, black skeleton. Propelled by gravity, he tumbled towards the dried corpse. His face slammed into the tip of a sharp bone. The sting of it! It pierced him like a whittle-sharp elephant tusk, and in the momentum of the collision, his torso met with the bones in many other places too with great force. Finger-like projections skewered his core, leaving his broken, bleeding body split, anchored there like a sandy kebab. Ralph hung from the bones of the giant black ribcage. In unison, a long final groan came from Ralph and one from the bones on the beach. Ralph closed his eyes for the last time and his soul sank down into a sandy, flaming-hot vortex.

The roof of the red tent flew off, carried up into the air and away by a ruby-eyed vulture, leaving Ralph's body to further barbecue in the sun.

⁜

The following morning, August the first, Sam woke up in tears; his husband had still not returned. He ran down to the beach. In the light of the day, he could see the sands and the ocean that appeared to stretch out for eternity in all directions. At the furthest point he could resolve in the brightness of the day, out far on the white-hot sands, Sam saw something black, like the prongs of a fork, like black fingers, or the bones of a rib cage poking up from the beach. And from the distant scene, something small and red glinted like a winking eye in the sun.

Sam ran towards what he thought could only be a mirage. But as he got closer, his heart up in his throat, he realised it was not. He fell to his knees and covered his mouth with his hands. In front of him lay the body of his husband, his precious Ralph. There Ralph lay, splayed in the sand, pecked at, torn like teased ham, his sunburnt black ribs like witches' fingers projecting from his shredded and cleaved chest.

Oh dear God, no. My darling Ralph— A pulse. I must check for a pulse. Perhaps there's some chance he's still alive? he thought as he knelt by Ralph's side, although he knew this was most unlikely, but the clouding nature of love can sometimes make things appear far, far better, far more hopeful, than how true things ever really are.

The burn of the sand on his knees felt irrelevant to the pain in his heart at the sight of his injured husband. Sam reached for the left hand of his lover and took it in his own. In doing so he yelped at the sight of the end of his lover's right arm and averted his gaze from the blood-and-sinew stump which was all that remained of where Ralph's right hand should have been. With his fingers pressed gently, shaking, on the inside of Ralph's wrist, he probed for a throb, a sign of life. No beat. He found no pulse there, and in all honesty, no flesh either, but as he inspected Ralph's limp arm, where Ralph's own simple gold wedding band should have been, the bold ruby ring Sam's aunt had bequeathed him squeezed the dead flesh and bone of Ralph's ring finger tightly. He dropped his lover's arm and vomited hard onto the sand.

⚇

And a few hundred yards along the shore, in the Bonus Kiosk which looked out over the beach, a newcomer was selecting groceries from the well-stocked shelves and browsing for souvenirs to send to his family back home. The holiday-maker asked the shopkeeper, whom he thought resembled a fat vulture, if she had anything cheap—"You know, really, really cheap"—that he could purchase as a gift for the relentless chore that were his children. "I only see the little rats at weekends, which is more than quite enough, but oh, how the ex-wife will moan at me if I return from three weeks in the sun with my new girlfriend without so much as a trinket for the little cash parasites." The shopkeeper tilted her head in the manner of an inquisitive crow and doddered out from behind the counter.

"We have nothing really in here for children, Sir, I'm afraid… but… perhaps I could interest you in a small gift for yourself? How about a little something to decorate your holiday let with—something to bring a little sunshine to the walls?" She shuffled to the central carousel. "Perhaps you'd be interested in one of our half-price calendars?"

EMILY'S JOURNEY

"…God did not spare the angels when they sinned, but cast them into Tartarus and committed them to pits of deepest darkness to be kept until the judgment…"
— 2 Peter 2:4

The wrought-iron shackles come as quite the nasty surprise, but they are not as much of a shock as her second dawning realisation: the heavy chains around her ankles are connected to other bodies.

It is not the first time she has been incarcerated, nor bound to something, but she struggles to withhold a gasp as she observes how, in front of her and behind, a continuous line of bodies, all connected by the weighty chains, form a seemingly eternal spiral.

She has lost track of time, hasn't a clue at all if she is still part of 1913, and there is no way of even knowing what season it is, if here, seasons still exist. Here, in this furnace-hot space in which she appears to be trapped. All that lies within her field of vision is an encompassing wall of blazing flames, the never-ending circular staircase on which she treads, and infinite chain-shackled semi-sentient cadavers.

How can such a place exist, Emily worries, *with a peripheral as bright and as hot as the sun, but with a central core as black as my darkest nightmare?* She looks down and then up the centre of the coiling staircase along which she trudges. Darkness, ringed by fire, projects in both directions.

Her body aches as if she has been in some sort of hideous accident. Each inhalation of scorching air burns her throat, her lungs, and as her ribs move up and down, she is certain some of them are broken.

Over her right shoulder, her 'Votes for Women' sash is slung, coming to rest on her waist. The sash's coarse fabric catches on a sore spot on her back. She reaches round to re-adjust the sash and there, sliding her wrist inside of her collar, she probes beneath her clothing. Her fingers find one sure source of her pain: two wet stumps. On inspecting her fingertips, she finds they're speckled red. The body in front bears, she notices, a similar injury at the top of its spine, betwixt its jutting scapula. Two crimson-soaked, weeping feathered protrusions—a place where wings had once, perchance, sprung from.

Emily looks ahead, past the grey body in front of her: a relentless string of bodies, all shuffling along, trancelike, not dissimilar to an unending concertina of slow-marching paper dolls. Each animated mannequin moves in sync with the one ahead, with the slow lift and drop of limbs. Are they ascending or descending with each step? Emily cannot tell, but somehow, she knows she and they must carry on walking in time with the one-one-two-beat chant which echoes thick, source unknown, through the blazing air:

Tar-Tar-Us

Tar-Tar-Us

Tar-Tar-Us

She feels she has no choice but to take each step in time with the others—who stretch as far as she can see—along to the rhythm of the ethereal chorus, stopping briefly, feet together, on the third syllable for a count of two, before proceeding to move forwards again.

Where am I going? she thinks. *Where are we travelling to?* There is no horizon, no sky or ground for comparison. Just heat. And plenty of pain.

Beneath the twinge of bruised ribs, there is a small feeling of joy in her heart—or in the place where a heart may have once been; she cannot feel it beat. Despite her current predicament, she has an awareness that she lived a most worthy life and died doing something she was proud of.

She walks and walks and walks, trying to make sense of her situation. Occasionally, a body tumbles down the centre of the infinite circuit around which Emily marches. Every now and then—although she has no concept of time and has given up trying to keep track of her duration in this plane by counting the constant metronome of footsteps—flailing limbs spiral past, spinning like tumbleweeds. Some of the fallers scream. Others, it appears, cannot scream or, perhaps, have given up attempting to make sound. There is never a thud.

She trips on her ankle-length Edwardian dress, and in lifting her arms to ascertain balance, her elbow brushes too close to the wall of flames which stretches up and down around the staircase on which she plods. She draws her arms back readily, bites her lip as a stinging kicks in. The cream silk fabric of her sleeve singed, the skin of her arm beneath burnt, Emily, defiant, stoic soul that she is, does not let out a shriek.

She stops momentarily, takes check of her body. Her legs ache. Her chest smarts. Sweat trickles down her décolletage. Her cream tussore slip is most impractical for this never-ending hike, so she hoicks it up. Her switch in cadence causes a problem. In pausing, the grim body behind her can't progress. Emily feels the strike of the body behind her as it slams into her back.

"Sorry," she says, and continues on her insane voyage, concerned if she stops for too long, she may be pushed over the edge of the step.

A small cherub floats to her side and, with chubby hands, rolls out a scroll. "Mrs Davison. Your first sin, for which you must repent—"

Emily, although taken aback by the blackhole mouth of the otherwise faceless creature which flutters by her shoulder, interjects. "Ms, if you pardon. I was not foolish enough to marry." She wipes a dribble of sweat from her brow. Perspiration trickles from every part of her body, yet she does not feel thirst, nor hunger, and cannot quite remember the quenching sensation of cool water in her mouth.

"Ms Davison. Intercepting King George V's finest horse in a successful attempt to commit suicide," the cherub says.

Emily closes her eyes. A flash of hooves beating down on her. Her face in a puddle. Both legs, myriad ribs cracked apart in several places. A final true breath of water and mud and blood.

"I wasn't trying to martyr myself," she seethes. Clearer memories flood through. She is angered that her protest had ended the way it had, as full recollection of her last moment in the Land of the Living returns. "If you had taken the time to investigate properly, you would have seen the suffragette flags in my hand. I had hoped to pin them on the King's horse's reins to raise awareness of the insidious sexism in the British voting system."

"You could've hurt the horse."

"Anmer went on to finish the race, did he not? And the jockey went unharmed?"

The cherub crimps its void of a mouth then speaks again. "A second attempt at suicide was made. You barricaded yourself inside of your prison cell on a hunger strike."

"What I choose to put into my own body is my choice, and always should be," Emily replies, "and I do not see how that is a sin. A few days without food did not end me, did it? Everything I did was in aid of the greater cause."

The cherub *tsks*.

"The state responded to my abstinence by force-feeding me. Under restraint, a tube was forced down my oesophagus by a man who had the nerve to call himself a doctor. If anything, I was physically violated. How can such a situation be deemed a sin of mine?"

The cherub's pit mouth shrinks and it flutters away. Emily walks on, unsure still if she is descending into more fire, or moving away from the source of the heat.

Will this go on forever? she wonders. *There is no sign of an end.* Despite fear in her belly, and blistered feet, fiercely and with audacity, she taps the shoulder of the body which marches in front of her, with thoughts of asking its opinion. It turns. No face. Just grey sweat-drenched skin. No hair. No expression. The body shrugs and turns its head back around. Emily shudders but continues on her journey.

The cherub returns and again, rolls out its scroll.

"Your second sin, for which you must repent—His Lordship is quite adamant that you should take penance for these unholy misdemeanours."

"Go on." Emily sighs.

"Obstruction and assault of a policeman, and assaulting a second man you mistook for the Chancellor of the Exchequer." The cherub's mouth hole slips up into a smug grin. "His Holiness is exceptionally perturbed by such earthly behaviours and wishes you to consider how best to repent or you will face His ineffable might."

"Both men touched me first," Emily replies, rolling her eyes, "in most inappropriate ways. And I'd do it again. Self-defence. So perhaps you can let His Majesty know that." Emily sways in the heat, careful to correct herself for fear of searing her side on the flaming wall. She shakes her head at the awful cherubic guardian of the steps. "Don't you understand what we were campaigning for?"

The winged guardian unfurls the scroll further. "Third sin. Mass vandalism, which includes setting fire to a pillar box, breaking windows in the House of Commons, and throwing stones."

Emily finds it impossible not to laugh as she takes step after step while recalling each protest event. As she laughs, she inhales sharply through her nose. The ever-pressing heat singes the hairs of her nasal passage.

"And how, pray tell me, are each of those incidents worthy of being classed as sins? Was a single individual hurt? A drop of blood shed? No. How can damage to material property be classed as a sin worthy of this… Hell you have me shackled up in?"

"Oh, Ms Davison. This is not Hell." The snarling cherub curls up its scroll, tucks it under its arm. Butterfly-sized wings beat heavy on its back, struggling to counter its voluptuous form. "The heat here is nothing compared to the flaming agony of the eternal pit far, far below. You are in the Place of Indecision, the Steps of Tartarus— God's waiting room for fallen angels. He has not decided where to place you yet. And until he does, until you repent, you will keep marching in time with the others, sweating out your potential sins, for as long as the judicial process takes."

Emily buttons tight her lips, says nothing in response. The guardian of the steps flaps off, either up or down, Emily is unsure, and rolls out its scroll at another poor body.

I shall not repent, ever, Emily thinks, and continues to lift one tired foot after the other as the unsettling consideration of eternal purgatory spins in her mind.

Minutes or years pass, Emily has no idea which, and the guardian cherub returns to her side. This time it does not roll out a papyrus, but instead, pulls out a small brass horn. It places the metallic mouthpiece to the black hole in its face and blows a jubilant tune. Emily places her fingers in her ears. The cherub places away its horn in a special pouch draped around its neck, crosses its chubby arms, and flaps closer to Ms Davison.

With a hint of resentment, the being addresses Emily again. "God has decided you may ascend to Heaven. He is content that many of the actions you have taken in your life are not, perhaps, as sinful as He had first imagined. His Greatness would like you to join Him for a welcome supper. So, if you wouldn't mind following me—"

The cherub flutters down to Emily's ankle chain and draws out a large key from a space between its wings. Emily's brow furrows. She kicks at the guardian, as one might do in the event of a dog attack, and knocks the key from the cherub's hands. The key is lost, falls downwards, or upwards—who is to tell in a place of such nondescript direction—and the cherub tumbles back in the air and into the maddening curtain of fire.

The stench of singed marshmallow and eiderdown floods the eternal staircase. Emily pegs her nose. The cherub flaps back out of the fire wall, its wings slightly a-smoke. "What in Heaven's name did you do that for? Are you not aware of the overarching power of His Almighty? His magnificent omnipotence?" The cherub's angered black hole of a mouth twitches as it speaks.

Emily coughs, clearing her throat of sooty air. "You can leave me locked up, thank you very much. I am quite content to walk here forever, on this endless, agonising oven of a treadmill. You see, I have no intentions of ascending to Heaven. The last place I want to spend eternity is under the close authority of a man."

EMPTY NEST

Folded neatly, that's how she left a pile of freshly laundered and pressed towels in each room. Every nook and cranny, and each bare shelf and untouched toy in the children's rooms, she dusted every day, despite the cribs now resting, unused. The made-up beds lay as cold and quiet as the expectant, refrigerated body lockers down at the dead house. One day, they would return. She was certain that one day, they'd need her again.

A fortnight ago, she'd lost her eldest son, Freddie. He hadn't so much as looked back, merely cornered his head for a final goodbye as she'd waved him off in the death trap he'd toiled all summer to buy. Music had blasted out from his car—a most unwanted farewell gift to her ears—and he'd fled the nest for university some hundred and fifty miles south.

Jennifer, the daughter with the red hair, had departed five months earlier, with her first love, a factory worker of some kind, to the coast. Never called her mother.

Her husband, rest his soul, had been gone six years to the day now, too. Before leaving, the children, which they were until ever so recently, had encouraged her to try and pack away his belongings. She had of course ignored them, her opinion on the matter being the only one of any value. His books on chess, billiards, and all the other sports that had so absorbed him screamed at her from the shelf. Yet, untouched they rested, gathering dust like a grey settling of snow, like the frosting that had appeared at her temples. The children had taken no interest in the games, but she couldn't take them down—she couldn't remove them because even though he was long dead, deep in the ground, a luncheon for snaking worms, his belongings dotted around the house made her feel like someone other than her own sagging figure was still present; these lifeless items of paper, wood, metal, and glass made her feel a little less alone.

In defiance of her spiralling solitude, she had brought in his fishing rods and clutter and other ghosts from the garage, and had displayed them on the sideboard in the living room, perhaps hopeful his possessions would encourage him up and back from the plot at the boneyard. She'd grown bored of sitting on her behind and watching re-runs of *Great British Bake-Off* and *Is It Cake?* alone in her deserted house. She'd settle for anyone's company in her prison-cage life, even a resurrection of the husband with whom words had run dry decades ago.

She hadn't loved him. Not really. But her husband had been a support for the family home. He'd paid the bills, had eaten her food with gratitude. He'd loved her deeply despite knowing his love was travelling aboard a one-way ticket. He'd propped them all up, especially her, when she'd had low moments, when nothing would quell the heat from the angry furnace that burnt inside her or plug up the tears that would rain from her eyes each month, each cycle. She had liked the man in her own way though, although love was a word of higher value, a one-off payment that he had known she'd already spent elsewhere.

No-one had been there to mop up her tears since he had departed; her children were heartless at best. The Change that followed the loss had triggered a cacophony of emotions that even half quart of gin could not suffocate of an evening. No amount of fanning or air conditioning could counter her flushes either. She'd taken to stripping off naked in the night, around two or three, feeling lost, shipwrecked on the surface of the sun, dripping with cling-wrapped limbs coated in her own perspiration as she'd glided about the house, sticky, searching for something to cool her down and something more than gin to bring her sleep.

Whilst cleaning, a hobby in which she partook on her better days to fill her hours, a hobby that played out quite synergistically alongside the hoarding of Robert's old belongings, she found an old photograph album. It poured out faded, dull memories—images of another time—from well before she'd met her husband. She leafed through the black and white photographs mounted on fragile sheets, each picture triggering little within. Perhaps time and the loss of the hormones that'd once made her shine dulled her senses, numbed her essence. Her well of emotion had perhaps run dry like every other part of her papery, parched shell—until she reached the end of the album.

And there it was, popping out at her, jumping out and off the page, striking her heart—a cue ball potting a red on a break—bringing a flurry of warmth to her core. The woman felt a hot rush in her joints more so than any of the moments the Change had delivered so far. There it was, exhumed from wherever her subconscious had chosen to bury it, smothered by the tiredness of early motherhood and the demands of running the family home and sustaining a mundane marriage… there it was: the photo of her happiest memory.

Michael Baker had been her high school sweetheart, her one true love. He had been the steak knife to her fork and they had been together at one point in time, although only for a turn of a season. With him, she'd felt invincible. Never since had she felt a passion so strong or the obsessive need to be touched, felt, and held so badly. Not even the joy she'd been informed each of her children would bring to her life had matched the sensation. In the snapshot in the old album, there, Michael Baker and her stood, embraced like knotted vines, her eyes only on him and his eyes only on her. Her palm travelled to her chest and rested against her heart, guarding it, uncertain whether the chest-plummet she was feeling could be caught as ecstasy or pain. He had sold her the world—Michael Baker. He had given her the moon on a stick, but of course, as her parents had hinted, it had all been puppy love.

Over the summer before they'd parted to go to college, to carve their own paths through life, she'd caught him kissing another in the spot where they too had taken their first kiss. The sight of his lips, his hands, on another had cracked her heart in two that day; her heart had split like a dropped melon on a stone floor. She'd slowly tried to patch the pieces back together after discovering him with the other woman. But it'd been too hard to make some kind of mosaic from the thousand shards scattered by his dastardly deed. Everything had felt surreal since: distorted, fractured and untrue.

She peeled out the single photograph, held it tightly to her heart, and carried it, her face now full of tears, into her bedroom. Here, she propped up the cherished photo in front of the long-ignored bedside filigree frame, back-seating a snap from her wedding day of her and her late husband jointly holding a knife in preparation to cut their three-tiered cake.

Bitter tears rolled hellward down her cheeks as she threw herself back onto her bed at three in the afternoon, and there she remained half-spun, until three in the morning, falling down a shaft of misery and nostalgia, drowning in tears merged with the sweat the night brought her, with no soul there to pull her out.

She'd not even bothered to draw her bedroom curtains. It was pitch black when she woke. From her bed, she saw all the stars were asleep. Even the crescent-sliver of moon must have been taking a timely blink from its eternal stretch of velvet sky. Darkness. She flicked on her bedside light and grappled around in the sheets for the photo which had featured heavily in all of her bad dreams. But she couldn't see it. The cherished photo of her and her high school lover must've slipped down, been dragged down too, most likely, into her well of misery. Lost at sea, somewhere in the bed amongst the drenching waves of worn cotton, *it* must *be here somewhere,* she thought, as she rummaged for her treasured photo. But she could not find it. Her framed wedding photo stood proud, erect, glaring at her victoriously from its pompous frame. If you were to look closely enough at her face in the wedding snap, on her Special Day, you'd see she was indeed smiling though, despite the matrimony being, at least on her part, rather a pretence. You'd see the bright red slash of lips across her pale, smooth face—quite a vision before time reaped her beauty—and the corners of her lips were pinned up, nailed almost to her apple cheeks. But her eyes were flat, dead, as if she wasn't fully there. And her heart had always been with Michael.

She fumbled in the bed again, in search of the other photo, the one of her and Michael Baker that she'd bawled at and stared at until she'd eventually capsized and dropped off into a hurricane of hori-zontal insensibility, but it was to no avail: after much searching, she finally gave in. Emptiness smacked her and lifted her like a hand, depositing her back into sweet waking Hell. At least she could still see her young lover's face when she closed her eyes. Her heart bled out, pain flooded her arteries, and she cried until her eyes ran dry, until no tears were left to shed.

Eventually, under the devilish slice of a honeydew crescent moon, now open and staring again, she slumped out of bed, crouched on the floor amongst many an old thing, and pulled out the suitcase in which her wedding dress was stored. She flipped open the metal clasps of the trunk and carefully drew out the over-engineered garment. Thirty years, and the fabric had not perished even slightly. The gown was still as cream as the day she'd worn it all those years ago, as milky-white as the parts of her body untouched by the sun. But also, due to cramped storage, as crumpled and folded as her own badly-aged skin-suit. She tossed the dress aside, onto the floor. It was not the dress she was after.

In the case, several more photographs rested in between her matrimonial silk garter and a wooden spoon a great aunt had gifted her for one superstitious reason or another. But these nostalgic items were not of any interest. She was searching for something else.

In a zipped compartment at the bottom of the case, her finger-tips finally found what she was probing for, almost recoiling in delight as they struck gold. There it lay, the item, shrouded in tatty yellowed newspaper from the sixties. Huzzah! *This* was what she was after.

A smile slit across her face, cracking the dried rivulets where tears had fallen before sleep had come. She unwrapped the baroque-handled knife from its old home and held it in her even older hands. The knife: the sharp tool she'd used to cut up her wedding cake into fifty or so small slices. It had cut through the first piece of iced sponge as sharply and keenly as the last, all those years ago. Large and long and still as sharp as a throat-razor, oh how she loved the feel of its weight in her hands. She held it up in the air. Drunk on tiredness, drunk on the Change, inquisitive as to what she might see, searching perhaps for a vision, a prophetic mirage—she noted how the blade was lightly tarnished as she peered into it, but it was still shiny enough to catch the light. How disappointed she was to only discover her own somewhat haggard reflection on display. Who was this careworn witch looking back? Was this why Michael Baker, her first love, her only true love, the one she had loved perhaps more than life itself, had left her for another?

He'd married her friend—her enemy. They were still together as far as she knew; back down in the backwaters, the boondocks of Claretville. Although gossip was quite thin on the ground as most of her old school acquaintances had moved away by Ford or by hearse, she most likely would have heard if they'd split up.

Her sadness swung to rage, a weathercock on a windy day, as she tried to block out the face of the friend who had stolen her Love all those years ago. But even with her eyes closed, she still saw the woman's face as if it were imprinted on the insides of her eyelids. She pulled on clothes and shoes with no thought of her appearance and, wrapping the blade back up in its newspaper casing, she placed the bundle into her handbag. With her keys in her hand, she strode out to her car, while something strong whipped up inside her body.

Out in the car, hands on wheel ten-to-two, trapped in a dark dawn cold enough to see her own breath in, she tried to block out more thoughts of that woman. She tried to replace them instead with sweet memories of Michael. She could still remember the scent of his breath: coffee and caramel. Saccharine. Distinctive. She remembered how she loved to kiss him in the evening, or after he'd come off the rugby pitch, when the tang of his lips would taste like a more concentrated version of himself. She reached for the glove box and pulled out an old red lipstick, *Ruby Kiss*, that, like herself, hadn't been handled for years. She smeared it over her dry lips without so much as a glance in the rear-view mirror, circling her mouth with it thrice to be sure; her lips, now akin to a bleeding womb, became primed with pure determination. She had never enjoyed kissing her husband and was thankful once the children came along, as it qualified exhaustion as an excuse to avoid intimacy. They'd rarely touched, let alone snogged, after the birth of their youngest. And after a while, her husband had simply stopped trying.

But Michael, oh—

She returned her hands to the wheel and closed her eyes.

He will be mine again.

She needed to fight for her man—the man she wanted. She needed to claim the prize she deserved for all the suffering she'd endured. All those nights in her family home with two children who ignored her and a husband she had grown only, through slow time, to like.

How dare that Carmine bitch steal her lover! That is not what friends do.

She hadn't spoken to the thief, Carmine Bridewell, since the day she'd caught her kissing Michael, although she had screamed the trollop's name into the wind on many a full moon. And now, just thinking that wretched name, Carmine, Carmine, Carmine, just mouthing that godforsaken word in angry silence to the space inside of the car, felt abrasive to her crimsoned mouth and tongue.

She drove off into the dark dawn, one hand on the wheel and the other in and out of her bag, as her restless fingers fulfilled an urgency to check that the blade was still there. All the while the tired stars continued to turn in the sky, in search of respite, and the fading crescent moon continued with what was left of its strength to judge down.

She flicked off her headlights and pulled up outside the house of her former lover, where he lived with Carmine, the piece of work Michael'd left her for. The sun broke the horizon, shouting out suggestions of soundless amber and rust. She drew out her knife from its newspaper wrappings and watched on from the warmth of her car as curtains were drawn open in the house of her ex-lover.

Carmine Bridewell, now Baker, appeared at each window, moving from room to room with haste, spreading open each set of floral drapes, wiping away condensation with a cloth, frowning at the break of day.

From her car, the vengeful woman contemplated where she'd strike that whore Carmine first. Where would the silvery blade—last used to cleave slices of sponge from a stupidly oversized cake—enter this stupid, life-robbing slut's body? She bit her lip thinking about the blood that would leak, no, spurt out from Carmine's chest and thighs and stomach as she'd jab jab jab and twist in the knife. *Is it cake?* No! Of course it would not be cake. It would be flesh. Rubbery, tough, oozing, flesh. And once her vendetta against Carmine had reached its peak, she'd scarper, lay low for weeks, a month maybe, tops, time enough for a funeral, a wake to come and go, before claiming back the man she loved. She *would* get her happy-ever-after.

She closed her car door behind her gently, so as not to awaken neighbours, then crept closer to the house: up the path marked out by well-pruned rose bushes, thorn-sharp, to the front door of her ex-lover's cottage. Her blade lay hard down her blouse, held there by the wire of her bra, warming against the heat of her chest and concealed by a flap of cardigan, as she knocked three times on the door.

Through the door she heard a man's voice, it was his voice for sure—her Love—but it boomed and yelled and did not bring joy to her ears like the sweet whispers of nothing she remembered from all those years ago. This voice made her quiver and her heart beat at double pace.

"Car, who the fucking heck is that, knocking on our door at six o'clock in the morning?" He paused only for breath, to add more venom to his spit. "Answer it then, you fucking lazy cow. Then fetch me my breakfast. And if you burn my bacon again, you'll speak to my fists."

A thump followed, audible enough to shake birds from the tree-top. Then a scream, then silence. Then footsteps.

The lady ran with a capricious change of heart, back down the path, back around the bush that shielded her car, and climbed back into her driving seat. And there she sat as a thousand bats crashed into her rib cage as her heart pumped them out from the abandoned belltower she had become. In a cold state of dread, hunched low with one eye squinted open and the other firmly closed, she sat as still as rigor mortis, afraid of seeing the state of the beast of a man her Love sounded like he had become. Despite her sharp tool, she felt a little fearful for her own safety.

The front door opened to reveal the same Carmine from school, the very same friend who had stolen her man, but this Carmine had not travelled well with time. Her hair, mostly grey, was swept up into a tangled bun and her eyes were both bruised black. On the top of her bare, sagged arms were more bruises, yellowing but large, the shape of a man's thumb print, and once-open wounds too, from where a ring or belt or both may have struck. A scar ran down her left cheek that looked like it had received stitches, a strip of train track from eye to jaw, and as Carmine looked around, searching for who-ever had knocked, the lady in the car could see that murdering her would be pointless. Carmine's eyes were already dead.

Carmine didn't see the lady in the car, so she shut the door, and scuttled off to fetch her husband breakfast, like the dutiful wife she was. The lady in the car waited, unsure of her next move, until screams and shouts permeated from the house.

In the car, she wept, hoping for Carmine's sake that the violent row would peter out. There she sat, crying and rewrapping the knife which had been concealed in her blouse in the newspaper. Then she scribbled something on the newspaper in red lipstick. When she could no longer hear shouting or thumping or dishes being smashed, she took her chance and ran back up the garden path. She left a gift wrapped in newsprint packaging by a flowerpot, with 'For Carmine' scrawled in *Ruby Kiss* on its top, then rushed back to her car and drove away, top speed, like she had someplace else she needed to be.

And she did.

And she didn't.

She drove home.

And on her return, her home felt like a place of freedom, a place of no responsibility. It may have been an empty nest, but it was her nest and it was a nest from which she could now leave at any time she wished, either as a dropped egg or a winged bird.

After a lengthy bath to wipe the smudged rouge from her lips, to cleanse her skin of panic, she went out and had herself a blue steak for breakfast, followed by a slice of delicious Victoria sponge. And why not? Who could tell her otherwise?

Middle-age was, after all, perhaps a dish best served alone.

EVERYONE, MONSTERS

There's a horrendous smell in the chicken shop this evening. The pungent odour—not unlike bin tuna on a hot day—overpowers the MSG stench of deep-fried poultry and the greasy fug of soiled oil filters, and it comes from behind the freezer units in the back room. There, in a dark, hidden space, sits the bucket in which Jayden's alien swims.

Jayden is at the shop counter. He shakes a tray of battered fillets out into the brightly lit, heated unit and spreads the pieces with tongs so the wire rack beneath is barely visible.

Once the arrangement of deep-fried food meets his satisfaction, with steel forceps, he picks out the smallest chicken piece, carries it into the back room, pegging his nose with his other hand in preparation, and drops the chicken chunk into the red bucket tucked behind the freezers.

Thrashing appendages make light work of the deep-fried meat, and the alien belches, satiated. *Good,* Jayden thinks, *it's full.* It's after a good feeding, Jayden has learnt, that his hostage will probably want to chat.

Mellowed and heavy with a full belly—if the largest of its glistening sacs is indeed its belly—the alien rotates in its putrid liquid, and opens its solitary iridescent eye. It releases an incomprehensible noise, screams blue murder; this is no easy prisoner. The smell Jayden's alien creates before it is fed is repulsive and if he allows it to build up, it makes his eyes sting. Luckily, Jayden has found that once the alien has been fed, and has consequentially unloaded in screams and nonsense whatever junk it needs to dispatch from what Jayden presumes is its mouth, the smell disappears. For a while. And if Jayden is careful, he can capture what it is *he* needs from his alien companion in exchange for meaty titbits, with the aid of the inner card tube from a cheap commercial toilet roll.

A flurry of hungry customers will soon pour out from the pub over the road and come to Jayden's shop for fast food or a little illicit street-treat from under the counter, and Jayden likes to be prepared. He has also learnt, quite incidentally of course, that his 'exchange' with the alien facilitates this, makes the transactions of the evening all so much easier.

But he never gets high on his own supply, knows careful analysis of customer needs and attention to profit margin details are key to achieving financial freedom within the next five to seven years. Jayden is so glad he does not take dirty street drugs, only sells them. His opinion, which he keeps to himself, is that illegal substances are for losers.

CRLESS

Thwang. Jingle-ting. Big Gary bursts in.

"A'wight, Jayden, top dog, you about?" Big Gary's cockney twang disturbs Jayden from his alien-bucket dabbling.

"Coming." Jayden tosses the cardboard tube he'd been using to the corner and stands, staggering slightly, to return to the shop front to handle his Friday night regular.

Big Gary, born just Gary, is big, in all directions. Built like a brick shit house. Six pints down, like clockwork most evenings, Gary will stride across the red, tiled floor of Jayden's gaff towards the counter. Jayden wants him in and out as quickly as he can manage. Gary, you see, is a blight on society. But an easy source of income for Jayden.

"Two of they then, and a bag of wings," says Big Gary, metabolised beer emanating from his facial pores and armpits.

Jayden nods. He puts five wings in a card box and passes it to Big Gary. With nicotine-stained fingers, Big Gary lifts each piece from the box, devours the meat, belches, then tosses the container in the bin.

"Good night?" Jayden asks.

"Yeah, blinder. Some chick at the bar's coming on to me strong. Gonna fold her up like a pretzel and fuck the shit out of her later." *She isn't at all interested in me, why would she be? With my tiny cock and three chins. But if I can get her high enough, maybe she'll tug me off in the car park. Then I'll ditch her before the rave so I can get mashed up with the boys.*

The edges of Jayden's mouth twitch. He restrains his desire to laugh at Big Gary's truth, which elucidates in flickering neon text, visible only to Jayden, above Big Gary's head, as the large man fumbles for his wallet in the pockets of his stained jeans. Jayden's truth vision helps him pitch the right drug to the right customer, gives him the power of the all-seeing eye.

Jayden reaches under the counter and taps his Beretta 9000 pistol to the side to retrieve his stash. Without taking his eyes from the demanding gigantic idiot, Jayden's fingers find two discreet wraps of

Bolivian marching powder which he slides across the countertop to Big Gary; a stack of notes slides back to Jayden in exchange.

"Nice one," Big Gary says, and winks at Jayden. *Better not be under, like it was last time, you thieving shit. I'll fucking do you.* "Can I use the bathroom, mate? Need a slash." *I'm gonna sniff half of this gak now, then go find that dollybird.*

"Sure, help yourself." Jayden thumbs Big Gary towards the toilet, although he knows Big Gary knows where it is.

Jayden spreads out the chicken pieces to cover the gap his sale has made and stares out of his shop window at the drunken crowd outside the pub.

"What the fuck's that stink?" Big Gary is out of the toilet, making his way back to the front of the shop where Jayden is still ogling the drunken crowd outside while scrubbing and spray-disinfecting the countertop. Jayden puts down his scouring brush and cleaning bottle and narrows his eyes at Big Gary.

"You what, mate? Don't come in here and take a shit in my gaff and chat at me like that. There's a fucking toilet brush and air freshener in there for a reason."

"Nah, mate, it's not me. I'd own it if I did a shit that bad. The fuck you got cooking back there? Health and Safety need a visit." *Might have been me, actually. That coke went straight to my guts.*

"Fuck off, bud. With respect." No witnessable mark of respect is evident in Jayden's expression.

Big Gary laughs a disgusting laugh and snorts back up the reddish-clear stream of fluid which had been slugging its way out of his left nostril.

"A'wight mate. See you down the rave later? I'll ping you the party line." *I expect you've got the party line already. I just want you to know I also have the party line. I might be balding at the temples and pushing fifty, but*

I'm still a badman junglist. Still got connections. Bet you get all the girls, with your pretty-boy face, baggy Carhartts, and your stash. I hate you.

"Sure mate, safe. Might head down after I close." Despite clearly being able to read Big Gary's truth, Jayden plays along with the game. He knows full well you catch more bees with honey. And the bees pay for the hire purchase on his '07 plate BMW 3 Series M Sport.

"Put a couple of grams back for me, if you come," *I'll need more cocaine by midnight to try and fill the void in my soul because tomorrow marks the five-year anniversary of my father's death and that bastard used to beat me black and blue. I'm not an addict, though. I'm not addicted. Definitely not. Could give up any time. It's still all shits and giggles.*

"Man, you know I don't carry when I'm out." Jayden folds his arms. "But I've got E here though, good Mandy, if you want to have fun tonight, peak by three am, and maybe get some sleep tomorrow?" Jayden tries to help people while lining his own pockets—sometimes he'll encourage them towards MDMA, and all of the other 'heart chakra' drugs, a sidestep from brown sugar resins soaked with Taliban ghosts or freebase powders tainted with the blood of ruined Columbian farmhands, plus, this week, Jayden has got an excess of E to shift for one reason or another. But most people don't want to hear what Jayden has to say, they only care about what it is they specifically want which they know he'll have under the counter. Most people are controlled by their specific addictions. And Jayden knows this. *Stupid losers,* he thinks, *stupid, money-squandering losers.* All the drugs Jayden sells are bad in one way or another, he knows this too, but he sees addicts for what they are: lost souls with a little cash, there for his exploitation.

"Nah mate, pills are for hippy wankers and girls."

Jayden surveys the space above Big Gary's head and waits for his subtext to appear, but nothing does. Jayden sighs, shrugs. Nothing lasts forever. He's tired of chatting shit with users, feels tightness in his neck at the stress of it all, and now, he just wants this skittish oaf out of his chicken shop so he can go behind the freezer unit to feed his alien again. To try and clear the stench. He must get rid of that blasted stench. "Laters then, bro," says Jayden and widens his stance, taps his nose and clears his throat. "Nose, Gazza."

Big Gary wipes away the thick crust of white powder haloing his left nostril with the back of his football shirt sleeve. Then he yanks the door open and stomps out of the shop.

⚬⚬⚬

The smell. It really is becoming quite unbearable, enough to make his skin crawl, so Jayden shoves a handful of warm meaty bites from his display into a card box and dashes to the back of his chicken shop. He crouches then tips nine cheap nuggets into the bucket. With silky suckered limbs, the alien whips the feast into a cyclone of sinew and breadcrumbs and gulps it all down. Armed with his toilet roll tube, Jayden just manages to capture the *'vraggleshclok ptshptsh schwirtszimmersimmer tiktik'* which follows and then he slumps against the wall as the pungent stink begins to clear. Jayden's shoulder tension dissipates like a released spring.

Jingle. The door chime catches. A gaggle of girls all loose on alcohol stumble in. "Alright ladies, coming now," Jayden shouts from behind the freezer unit as he pulls himself up from the floor.

He stands and strolls through the beaded fly curtain which separates the shop front from the preparation room with the confidence of a man who can read the minds of beautiful women and manipulate the direction of their conversation. Leading the group in is Bella, Jayden's current squeeze.

"Bella, babe. How you doing?" Jayden hops over the counter and slaps Bella on the bum.

"Alright, Jay." Bella, aloof, slinks away from him. "This is Amy, Sienna, and you've met Tasha before." Tasha nods, then sucks on her pink vape and puffs out a plume as Bella gesticulates, laissez-faire, at the three life-size Bratz dolls she's brought over to score. Nothing scrolls above Bella's head. Jayden furrows his brow and scratches his goatee. He'd been able to read her like a book last night, learned all about the terrible relationship she had with her mum, and had managed to get in her knickers. But this evening, nothing.

"Safe," he says and nods at the girls, then hugs each in turn. As Amy leans in for an awkward greeting, she stumbles on her three-inch Buffalo sneakers. Sienna lunges to catch her and cackles, exposing a gold implant which matches her oversized hoop earrings. Amy snorts and hoots.

"Any chance you could sort us out with a few of they? We're catching a lift with Dray from UnDo Crew in a bit. His mates have already taken a rig down for tonight," Bella says.

"Yeah, sure. Dready Dray? He's a tosser, Bells." Jayden hops back over the counter and fumbles through his stash, eager to please his girl. "Surely there's a better ride? How many beans d'you want?"

"I'm good, thanks, but Tasha wants a gram of Mandy." Jayden looks to the space above Bella's head. Still nothing.

"You sure, babe? The gurners are on me."

"No, I'm okay," she says and adjusts her leopard print Nike crop top so it only exposes three inches of cleavage.

"If you can wait half hour, I'll lock up, join you at the pub. If there's space?"

Bella picks a half moon of grime out from under her thumbnail and flicks it onto the floor. "Sure."

Tasha's stomach rumbles. Jayden grins. "A gram of Mandy, Tasha? Sure you don't want a side of chicken with that?"

Tasha laughs, sucks on her vape, exhales. Caked-on make-up cracks around her eyes. "No thanks, I ate earlier. Just a gram of MDMA, thanks. Nice one." Jayden pauses in his rummaging and takes in the stream of neon information which flashes above Tasha's head: *I hate my body. Haven't eaten a decent meal all week. If I lose ten more pounds, maybe I can win my ex back. Until then, I'm just going to get so high I forget about how sad I am about the breakup and how uncomfortable my boss makes me feel at work and how very lonely just existing makes me feel.*

"I've got something that can take the edge off the hunger—all the supermodels are on it." Jayden gestures at Tasha's stomach, noticing its already concave nature, and with a smirk like the driest wine on his face he winks at her.

"Sure, okay. I'll take some posh," Tasha replies. *Looks like I'm phoning in sick on Monday.* She pulls out a wedge from her pink-sequinned fanny pack and passes the notes to Jayden in exchange for a small baggy of lilac-tinted crystals and another of white.

"So what y'saying then, Bells. Wait for me?" Jayden asks.

"Ok, sure." She wafts her hand in front of her nose. "What's the foul stink in here?"

Jayden shrugs. "Drains, I guess."

"Laters." Bella says. She blows a kiss roughly in Jayden's direction as she opens the front door and the girls leave as loudly as they entered, leaving a cloud of strawberry-scented e-smoke in the shop front. Once they're out of view, lost to the crowd of revellers the other side of the road, Jayden nabs a half-chicken from the display and hurries back to the alien behind the freezer unit.

⋘⋙

An hour later, Jayden shuts up his chicken shop and heads over the road. It doesn't take long to spot Bella. She's with her girlfriends, joking around with other drunken imbeciles —Dray and a bunch of the Retox lads—on the pavement outside of the King's Arms. Jayden notices Dray is standing dangerously close to Bella. Jayden doesn't like the way she's laughing, seemingly fixated on Dray's jokes, hanging on his every word.

"Alright, babe," Jayden says as he strides over to Bella. He hugs her and plants a kiss on her forehead but Bella shrinks away from Jayden's draped arm.

She takes a step closer to Dray, trading her proximity to Jayden for a tight-lipped smile instead. "Yeah, all good. Too hot for hugs." The whites of her eyes are tinged pink and her jaw juts as she speaks.

"How many pills have you dropped, Bells?" Jayden asks.

"None."

He narrows his eyes and offers her a swig of his water. "Go steady."

Jayden sidles up to Dray and places his bulky record bags and Eastpak rucksack on the pavement between his feet before proffering a too-heavily-greeted fist bump. "Space for me in your van?" Jayden grimaces and squeezes his buttocks as he tries to channel the sting in his knuckles into his gut.

"Yes, mate. Bella said you'd be coming. Brought out every record you own again, have you? All of them still shit though, I expect." *Your girl is fucking fit, bro. And she's high as heck. I'm going to snake her up this evening, just you watch. My limbic system will alpha male the fuck out of you tonight, you piece of shit.*

Jayden swallows his anger. "If I'm on *your* rig, then yes, mate. Your speakers are older than your old man's jokes. Time you upgraded. The Neverlution lads just shelled out 10k on new Funktion-Ones. Bit pricey for a roofer who still lives with his parents though, I guess." Jayden thwumps Dray on the back and passes Bella a stack of notes. "Here you go, Bells. Treat yourself and your mates to some Special Brew from Sonni's on the way."

"Thanks babe," Bella replies and smiles and takes the cash, but her eyes look wrong to Jayden, and there's still nothing scrolling above her head. Jayden wonders if she might be ill.

"Come on then, you riffraff, let's get going," says Drey to the crowd of girls. He slaps Jayden on the back and points down the street to where his van is parked before whispering something in his ear. "Fuck you, dude, seriously, fuck you. I'm only letting you come with us in the van because Bella asked if I'd give you a lift." *I'm making Bella mine tonight, mate. But you're more than welcome to watch it happen.*

Jayden and the Bratz girls pile in the back of Dray's beaten-up old panel van and Bella hops up into the front seat next to Dray. She dials the party line and sets her mobile to loudspeaker.

"Nah, Bella. I know where it is, put your phone away," says Dray. He pushes her phone and tickles her thigh. She blushes. Jayden sees it all. He hugs his rucksack on his lap and seethes in the back seat, jealousy roiling up his spine.

⚘

They drive out of the city for an hour towards the secret rave location. From his backseat spot, Jayden hears the party before he sees it, even over the loud music which blasts out of the van's speakers. The rickety vehicle careens down the last rocky valley, with everyone onboard swinging from side to side. The party is in an abandoned farm in the countryside somewhere on the edge of the Blackdown Hills, on the edge of the moors. A vast, gloomy landscape of mist stretches out all around them, bar the other odd party wagon searching for the venue. The last time Jayden had been to a rave in the area, his mate had fallen into an old mine-shaft sinkhole which had been riddled with piles of unexplained sheep skulls. Jayden hadn't discovered him there until sunrise. Two broken legs. First thing he'd asked Jayden was if he'd had any more gear on him for sale.

Tasha is the first to spot the rib of red light which stretches from the dishevelled barn into the black sky, making a red eye of the full moon. This projected beam is the visible beacon which calls the ravers closer.

As they tumble out of the van, Jayden tries to take Bella's hand, but she declines and chooses to ribbon off ahead with her mates, towards the barn. Jayden follows, picking up the rear. The straps of his bags cut into his shoulders.

Diesel powered generators. Two stacks of speakers, each ten-foot tall and five-foot wide, stand either side of the make-shift DJ booth. 150bpm techno bursts out from the rig, shaking the mammoth wooden outhouse. Razzle-dazzle fabric and psychedelic banners hang on the walls and UV inflatable tentacles dangle from the ceiling. At least a thousand other wasters, dressed in desert camo army surplus and leopard print lycra, dance to the beat, pie-eyed, like they've sold their souls to the Devil. Sweat and dissociated ket-heads drip from the rafters.

Bella and her mates slip away from Jayden and into the crowd before he has a chance to ask her if she wants a drink, so he heads over to the DJ booth to try to lose himself in the music. *Maybe they'll let me spin some records if there's anyone sound up there I know,* he thinks as he battles his way through a sea of idiots.

⚮

"Want any 2ci, 2cb, bath salts, WD40 mate?" *I wish my parents hadn't sent me to boarding school at age five. My housemaster was a cruel and perverse man.* Jayden laughs at the string of neon words which flash above the head of some posh kid who's trying to sell *him* drugs.

"Nah, mate. I'm all good," Jayden replies. Then he tries to lose the trust fund kid who is dressed, for reasons unbeknownst to Jayden, as The Joker, but the kid proceeds to follow Jayden around the VIP space behind the DJ booth, pushing his crazy new-age drugs. Jayden grows impatient and stops and turns and holds his palm up to the youth's painted face. He shouts at him to be heard above the music.

"Look mate, I don't do drugs. Just here to play some tunes."

"You sure? I've good shit. Hallucinogens, man. Research chemicals." *I'm so unhappy with my existence I want to reach a state of nihilism, be as I was before birth.*

Beads of sweat curdle the white greasepaint on the kid's brow and neck as the bones of his jaw fidget. *It's as if the twat isn't listening,* Jayden thinks. "No, dude. Not my bag. Have you seen Sparky or Wrong Dan?"

"Who? Nah. Sorry." The kid shrugs.

Jayden bats the kid out of the way and continues his search for a more familiar face, someone who'll let him play a set.

ༀ

Despite offering him free chicken later in the week, the wasted DJ won't let Jayden spin any records, so Jayden steps down from the raised platform and decides to search for Bella instead. He asks people he vaguely recognises, all in various states of temporary mental decay, as he barges his way through the dance floor of the barn.

Some stumbling girl with ketamine stalactites hanging from each nostril, a customer from his chicken shop, waves him on, points to a crowd standing around a girl spinning fire poi by the entrance. "Nice one," Jayden says and heads in that direction. There, Jayden finds

Bella, sat against the wall, huddled around something with Dray. Jayden hoists up his baggy trousers and crouches to meet Bella at eye level. Here, he squints to try to make sense of whatever it is the pair of them are so enthralled by.

On the ground, between them, sits a large glass jar with smoke trapped inside. Strobe lighting catches the jar's contents, highlighting the dancing white wisps within it. Dray grunts at Jayden. Jayden grunts back.

"Alright, Jay?" Bella slurs, then opens the jar, plucks something free from the gas cloud inside it, and slides what she has withdrawn—a featherlike flake of shifting white plasma—in between her lower eyelid and eyeball. Jayden cocks his head closer to Bella's face. She giggles, shoots Jayden a wide-eyed stare, flicks her hair back, and then sticks her tongue out at him.

"What the fuck you two doing?" Jayden asks.

"Hedgehog, mate," Dray replies. "And there isn't enough for you."

Irritation tightens Jayden's face as he waits for the bubble of neon information to spool above Dray's mass of matted hair. "The fuck is hedgehog?" Jayden asks and stares at the shit they're fiddling with then looks up again to the space above Dray's head. Nothing. "And, fucksake, man. You *know* I don't do drugs."

"Spines of ghost hedgehog. In your eye." Bella is barely coherent as she speaks. Her sore eyes roll from side to side, her tongue lolls from the side of her mouth; it's as if her very essence has been excavated. She reclines and sprawls out on the barn-floor and slowly snow-angels in the dirt.

"Gives you total freedom," Dray says, "like nothing else out there, man. Stops people from knowing your business, stops you caring what other people think. When you're on hog, you don't want or need anything else. Liberating as fuck."

Bella sits bolt upright, suddenly alert and back within her own body. She lifts the lid of the jar. "Yeah. Total freedom." She echoes Dray's words. "I need another hit. Dray, babe, can I take another spike? That rush of freedom is quite moreish."

"Sure, hun." Dray winks at Jayden, grins a sardonic grin. Jayden's fists ball up. He wants to punch Dray in the face. "It's twenty a pop. You can pay me later, Bella babe, one way or another." As Dray speaks to Bella, he doesn't break eye contact with Jayden.

Bella plucks another wisp of smoke from what Jayden can now make out to be the rotting corpse of some kind of wildlife riddled with white fungal spores. He grimaces as she slides it into her eye socket.

"Bells, come on. Leave this alone. This shit is dark," Jayden says and tries to take Bella by the hand, to lead her away from this madness, but she refuses his advances.

"There will always be other drugs, better drugs, than what you have to offer, Jayden," she says. She blinks. Her bloodshot pupils begin to flit again, from side to side. Jayden can't read her, can't read Dray, can't make out if the pair of them are pulling his leg, although he's pretty certain that this is not all some sick joke. Bella's eyes are red but void, empty, as if everything has been poured out of her.

Bella pushes Jayden on the arm. "And why the fuck does your bag smell so bad? Fuck off, Jayden." As she speaks, Jayden knows all is not right. The girl's vowels are drawn out too long. Jayden watches, speechless, as Bella strokes some sort of imaginary air kitten. She is present, yet not. "Just… fuck… off," she slurs. Despite the hollowness which rings in her voice, every blow lands. Jayden realises she does not want or need him anymore.

⊗

Jayden storms off to the fire pit several hundred yards from the barn to try to clear his head. He has an urge for something, a strong longing in his heart, but does not think it is for Bella. *I'll walk this feeling off,* he thinks, *I'll go chill by the fire,* and he places one foot in front of the other in an attempt to put some distance between himself and the girl he thought he knew. As he walks, an image is imprinted in his mind, of her, Bella, high on the spirit of some poor dead woodland creature. It turns his gut.

He uses the narrow beam of light from his phone to avoid turning his ankle as he walks; the long, wild, purple moor-grass is dashed with dense bushes of gorse. Focusing on the uneven ground, his ears drenched by the hellish pelt of double-time wobble-tek shitting out from the rave in his wake, he does not see or hear Big Gary come up behind him.

Gary grabs Jayden and gags him with a sweaty hand and drags him several metres over the moorland before coming to an abrupt stop. Gary slams Jayden's spine against the bark of a pedunculate oak, a monolith of nature midway between the barn and the fire pit. The barn is far, far behind them and the firepit is nothing but a candle of light some distance away.

Pinned there by his neck, Jayden blanches. The angry cokehead breathes hard in Jayden's face, his nose an inch from Jayden's. The tip of Big Gary's knife finds the flesh of Jayden's waist. Lit by the wedge of light from his phone, which he has managed to remain holding onto, Jayden can see Big Gary has lost it. When something circles in the air for long enough, it's got to run out of fuel and crash at some point. Big Gary's pupils are blown, as large and dark as black holes. Too. Much. Cocaine. Gary's sneer reveals stained teeth, yellow and brown like rotten corn kernels.

Over the moorland, electronic music thrums with a distorted baseline but all Jayden hears is the blood rushing through his own cranium, and then, Big Gary's low cockney tone. "You've got two choices: give me the drugs, or give me the fucking drugs." *I've run out, my heart's clacking double time, and I'm full of the rage of the farmer who was forced at gunpoint to grow this heinous coca in place of his sugar cane crops while corrupt soldiers pillaged and raped his family. My brain's as desperate as Peruvian children, working for a handful of Soles, dancing barefoot in troughs of gasoline and acid-soaked Erythroxylum leaves, their feet blistered and bleeding. My mind's as lost as the ghost of the pregnant woman coerced into smuggling condoms full of this shit inside of her who died as one exploded,* in utero, *on the boat over to our country. I will cut you if you don't put out.*

"Jesus, mate, I don't carry when I'm out. You know this. Come on, let me go," Jayden says, his heart valves flapping as fast as he's sure Big Gary's are. *Fucking junkies,* he thinks. The tip of the knife at his waist nicks in. Jayden gasps. Big Gary pulls back, grabs Jayden's rucksack from his shoulder, rips open the zipper and tips the contents on the ground.

"Fucking Christ, what have you got in there? Fucking stinks. It's enough to make a grown man vomit." *Fucking Christ, what have—* As Big Gary speaks, Jayden notices Gary's fog of subtext cuts out midsentence.

Gary staggers back, drops Jayden's rucksack on the wild heath, then buckles forward, and retches into the darkness. Jayden seizes this opportunity to lunge for the knife that Big Gary, overwhelmed by the obnoxious bouquet, grips limply in his hand. Jayden tussles, wins the blade, and with all his might, plunges it into Gary's neck.

"You fucking stupid addict," Jayden says as the serrated knife opens up something very red inside of Big Gary.

Jayden panics and drops the knife and watches Gary grappling at his opened throat, trying to catch at the blood which jettisons out, failing hard. Gary collapses into the overgrown grass in the dark, in the middle of nowhere, as Jayden wipes the mud from his Nike Air

Max 90s all over the handle of the blade on the ground, then collects up his scattered belongings and hoists up his bag. The backpack contains, after all, his most precious possession.

The lid of the Tupperware—in which Jayden 'travel-modes' his prisoner—has come loose within his bag. Vile waters are spilling from the tub and leaking through the bottom of the bag and onto the grass. Jayden lifts the tub out and attempts to reseal it but fails. He needs to get away from Big Gary's body, fast, so he lifts his backpack over his shoulder, and with the tub now in his hands, he holds his breath and runs back to the barn, trying to reseal the lid as he moves.

The stench. Jayden must get rid of the smell. He must! For the wellbeing of his alien. The smell is all he can think about while he runs, the smell, and making it stop. It's causing his nostrils to itch… and it can't be good for the alien, can it? To be swimming around in such a bloody awful odour?

Back in the barn, Jayden hurries to a dark corner, away from the crowd. Here, he peels off the lid of his alien's tub, yanks out an A5 nightclub flyer from his rucksack and a near-flattened multipack of chicken-flavoured crisps. Ripping open the crisp packets, one after the other, he tips them all out hastily, into the opened tub. The alien swirls and scoffs and churns out a string of babble, which is lost to the ears of all the munters in the barn in the middle of nowhere, but Jayden hears his alien's noise clearly. His alien is calling to him. His alien needs his help. It's thanking him, perhaps? And it's Jayden's responsibility, isn't it? To feed the alien, to clear the stench, and to suck up and tidy away all of its nonsense? He must do it every time the smell comes, which is happening, he realises, more and more regularly. He must always feed his alien, and he must feed his alien more often, before the smell has a chance to build and make the itching in Jayden's nostrils spread to all the other parts of his body. He must help his alien clear its stench and then he must inhale the conse-quential babble. It's a duty of sorts. A responsibility.

Fingers all buttery with haste, Jayden rushes to roll up the flyer. With one end of the make-shift paper pipe resting on his lips, he angles and probes the other end of it into what he presumes to be his alien's mouth. He sucks up into his own throat and lungs the mish-mash of elongated, distorted vowels and high-pitched screechy gibberish the alien twaddles out. He's making everything better. He's taking one for the team.

Afterwards, Jayden exhales slowly. The air around him sparkles with a glittering transience as he releases all the unnecessary commas, semi-colons, and em-dashes. The babble he retains spreads quickly in his bloodstream and his nostrils immediately stop itching. The inhalation begins to turn the aching, stiff cogs once more in his skull. Non-descript sensations unravel within Jayden's nervous system, causing his limbs to shudder, his feet to jerk, and his mind to press at the edges of understanding everything around him and all that occurs within the universe. His internal eye of providence opens slowly. It is a familiar feeling, one he has become accustomed to, but one that has grown weaker with time. His all-seeing eye has never opened as fast or as wide as it had on his first dose, many moons ago. He scrabbles around on the ground, retrieves the crisp packets he had hurriedly emptied, and frantically empties the last few crumbs into the tub. The alien feeds on the morsels and releases more gut-tural wails. Jayden lifts the curled tube up to his lips again and jabs it into the alien's word hole, and sucks, sucks, sucks up, the stream of discharged alien nonsense, with all his diaphragmatic muscle and might.

The stiff cogs in Jayden's skull turn, but not as fast as they did the time before. His legs judder, but only with a mild wave, not enough, this time, to trigger his Achilles reflex again. He exhales a small shimmer of transient unwanted punctuation as a smidgen of balderdash circulates in his blood.

Jayden stares down at the floating translucent glob, and one wide eye stares right back up at him. "Talk, you fucker," he shouts at the tub. "Talk." The alien continues to bleat out more verbal hieroglyphics, which Jayden desperately wafts into his lungs with his hand. Above the alien's bulbous body—which is also, Jayden presumes, probably its head—a string of font bubbles tap out.

Jayden has never considered his alien's truth before, never understood a word the jellied ball has had to say. But it appears this evening is a first time for several new experiences. Jayden's real eyes widen as his all-seeing eye translates the alien's mumblings:

Feed me more fucking chicken. What's a chap go to do around here to score some fucking fried chicken. I just want some more—

The alien's subtext cuts out mid-sentence. *That dose of gabble barely lasted ten seconds,* Jayden thinks. Jayden craves for the turning of cogs, the shuddering of limbs, to be able to inhale more poppycock and tripe, but he has nothing left to feed his prisoner.

He covers and shoves the stinking beast back into his bag and sets off to find a lift back to anywhere near his chicken shop. 'Wings and Things' opens in a few hours. His alien needs feeding. His alien is bloody starving. And Jayden will have no choice but to clear up its stink.

HE HAS NOT SEEN A BIRD

One tree, a metal climbing frame, an empty sandbox: this is all that stands in the middle of the brick-walled play space which sits in the centre of the housing development. At night, lit by one flood light, the other lights broken and not repaired, the climbing frame casts a monstrous arachnid shadow over the wall of Caledonian Heights - Block B.

Around the small park, a circle of apartment towers stretch up, flat upon flat upon flat, all the way to the sky. Ms Theroux tells delivery companies she lives on the seventh floor of the 'concrete wedding cake'. Up there, on the seventh floor of Caledonian Heights - Block E, young Blake lives with his mother, Ms Theroux.

☙❧

Blake looks out of the reinforced window of his bedroom. The window does not open, has never opened, for fear of someone falling out or something climbing in. With a chubby index finger, he points at the tree. Today, a tattered bird perches on a skeletal, brown branch and fills the air with a sorrowful tune. Blake smiles; he is elated. He has not seen a bird before other than on the e-screens which line his play-pen.

"Birdie," he says to himself, sounding out the consonants with his tongue. It is the first time the tree has made the boy happy. The tree is the reason Blake, sometimes, cannot sleep. Blake often cries out for his mother in the night, complains through wet eyes that he senses the tree is watching him.

Blake presses his cheek and eye against the window in an attempt to look closer. "Mumma, tree falling," Blake says, and again, louder, as the creak of a heavy branch is audible through the triple glazing. Blake's mother runs from the kitchen to Blake at his window and drags her son away. The boy and the woman fall together onto the toddler-sized mattress as the branch looms towards the building.

"Dear God, no," the woman says, wide-eyed, as the bird, pre-empting what is about to occur, screeches, lifts up from the tree and launches in panic, smacking headfirst into the glass. A dark mark, like a ruddy snow angel, now dirties the pane. Neck broken, the bird's soulless vessel plummets to the ground sixty feet below.

The woman's hands cover her child's face, protecting his eyes and skull, as the branch, larger than the boy, splits away from the trunk of the old Caledonian pine, instructed by gravity and a rot that has come with age, and thwacks into the blood-stained glass. It all happens so fast. The glass splinters into a silver-white-red cobweb, but, thankfully, the window does not shatter inwards.

"Blake, darling, are you okay?"

She soothes her son, finds his favourite comforter, then carries her babe on her hip through to the living room, away from the damaged window. Here, she places him in his interactive playpen, a walled box from which he cannot climb out, and kisses him on the crown of his head. "Watch some cartoons in your holo-den. Mumma needs to make a phone call."

She finds herself drawn back to the boy's bedroom, to inspect, to bear witness to what has just happened, aware of the sheer nightmare that could have unfurled, and she cries. She has hated the tree ever since they moved in. Pulling the door to her son's bedroom closed, she returns to the kitchen to make her urgent call: something must be done about the dangerous pine in the park, before more blood is shed.

With two firm claps of her hands, the apartment operating system greets her with its duteous tone. *"Good evening, Ms Theroux. How may I be of service?"*

"Call the building manager," she says.

A dial tone pulses out through the speakers built into the ceiling. With deliberately slowed exhalations, she tries to breathe panic out from her chest and into the clinical void of her kitchen. She drums her fingertips on the stainless-steel kitchen work top and waits for the manager to connect.

◌◊◌

Harrison tosses his mobile back into his bag. He has had no reception for three hours, not since he'd first stepped out of the car and into the grey container unit hut, his office for the next few months. It hadn't mattered, the lack of connectivity, when he'd been with his team of surveyors and contractors. They'd snaked after each other through the labyrinthine maze of cramped Scots pines following a hired guide.

The guide had handed out to each of them a paper map of the area, warning them all reception would be lost as they ventured deeper into the noir of the woods, but most of the men had left the sheets behind in the hut, smugness and ego splattered on their middle-aged faces, Harrison's included. This was Harrison's project after all; he was self-appointed deputy lead of the board who'd purchased the vast area of woodland. The blueprints for a luxury housing development destined to provide homes for 10,000 new residents are pinned up on the wall in the hut. He'd studied the technical drawings for weeks prior to setting foot in the Scottish Highlands, knew the future layout of his city-to-be like the back of his hand. Soon all these bastard trees would be building timber. Harrison had stopped to take a leak, nipped off the track for a moment, and on returning to the spot in the forest he'd left his team, he's dismayed to find the group gone. He spins round, desperate to find his crew, only to see trees, shrubbery, a solitary deer which scarpers immediately at the sound of his heel turning in leaf litter, and more trees.

He walks in a straight line, hopeful his feet will lead him out of the forest. Some sort of grouse darts out of nowhere, jolts him, and this spurs him into walking faster. He fastens his jacket and pulls the flaps of his hat over his ears. Despite the shelter the trees provide, there's a chill in the air, a mist descending. The rare, small pockets of already bleak sky which break through the canopy grow dimmer as he walks. Night will fall soon. In his hurry, he trips on a tangle of cream-encrusted, rotting tree roots and hits his head.

"Fucking mushrooms," he says to no one and pulls himself up into a seated position.

"Tooth fungi." A voice. The crimp of white fungus he'd tripped over bleeds red, jam oozing from its myriad gaping pores. "You've damaged it."

Harrison looks around. No one. He looks to the fungus then up again. A woman with one good arm, her other arm ending as a stump above the elbow, looms over him. She takes his hand in hers, an intimate act Harrison is not prepared for, and helps him onto his feet.

"Th-thank you," he stutters. "Sorry about the fungus." Harrison rubs his eyes.

The woman smiles at him, softly, with no anger in her jaw.

Through the mist, he studies her. A member of his team? He squints. Through the impending darkness, a slice of light falls. In it, her eyes sparkle. Flecks of golden light shimmer from them and scatter around her face, like unfurling galaxies birthing new stars. *I have concussion*, Harrison thinks, *the thin strip of light must be reflecting motes of dust.*

"It will survive," she says. Her smile drops. "But as for the forest—" She lifts her palm, gestures at the trees around her and shakes her head.

Harrison's cheeks rouge. He can't tell the woman he is, in part, responsible for the logging on the forest periphery, for the new roads which connect this patch of nature to an adjacent city in preparation for the people who will spill into the apartments his company will erect over the months that follow. She may turn her back on him, and in this moment, he needs her help.

"Could you direct me to the edge of the forest?" he asks. "The grey hut."

Again, she takes his hand in hers, and as her cool skin brushes against his palm and her fingers knit with his, a longing pulses in his chest. He can't recall the last time a woman has touched him with such tenderness, without some sort of financial exchange.

Together, they walk, run, as she leads him over tumultuous ground, through branches and shrubs. Ribbons of her long autumn-red hair bounce as she strides over rocky pockets and mossy tumps. He does not know who she is, but he knows he does not want to let go of her hand when he sees his hut and his colleagues in the clearing upon reaching the edge of the forest.

She stands under the shade of a tall pine and says goodbye, says she will not travel with him any further. Harrison thanks her, wishing more than anything he could spend more time with this woman with firefly eyes. He plucks up the courage and asks, "May I take you out for something to eat this evening, to thank you for your kindness?"

"No," she says and steps back into the forest, hiding herself from the crowd of men who are just out of earshot, all drunk on cheap bourbon, playing cards around a makeshift table. "I cannot leave."

"Will I see you again?"

"Maybe." She beckons him back towards where she stands, and Harrison watches as she plucks out a six inch black feather from what appears to be a skirt, but may also be her flesh, the tip of its quill bright red with fresh blood. "For you, a piece of my forest, a keep-sake."

"What is it?" Harrison accepts the feather. It has an iridescent shine to the blade of its vanes.

"Tail feather, caipercaillie," she whispers. Her words of nature are a fresh balm to his ears after months of only hearing about spreadsheets and budgets.

Harrison slides the feather in the pocket of his cargo trousers and as he looks up again, she is gone.

❧

It is all Harrison can do over the days which follow, think about the red-headed woman with celestial eyes who had led him out of the thick tapestry of mist and trees, as the construction team start to slowly clear the land. He dreams of her, sees her face in the faces of strangers, hears her voice in the night. It is as if she is calling to him as he lies in his hotel bedroom in the nearby city, several miles outside of the forest.

A week later, he ventures back into the woods, with his paper map this time, on a quest to find her. It does not take him long, as if she wants to be found. He finds her leaning up against an alder tree. She is wearing what looks to Harrison like a black mourning veil over her face.

She tips her head to the tree as he approaches her and tells him, "alder," then plucks and shows him the heart-shaped, leathery leaves the tree wears in its broad green crown.

He identifies each alder proudly as she draws him deeper into the dark forest, the tree branches wavering slightly overhead, as if sentient.

"Correct," she replies each time, and teaches him "hazel," and "birch". As she names plants, she passes him small branches of each, instructs him to cherish them. He takes the gifts from the mysterious woman and places them in his bag.

Minutes become hours as they glide and weave through the woodland. Harrison wishes she'd hold his hand again, as they walk side by side, as the woman points out tracks left by red deer, a pile of leaves she insists is a hedgehog's nest, a cluster of white creeping lady's tresses in bloom. Eventually, he asks her if he may take her hand in his, and she allows this.

Barefoot, she leads him further, further into the forest, her skirt train of black feathers and twigs trailing behind her, her hair streaming out like unfurled, red ghosts. She stops to point out rowan berries. He asks her if he may kiss her; her lips have become his obsession, are as red as the berries she points out. "These are sour berries," she tells him instead of answering his question. "But waxwing adore them." She shows him waxwing birds, how to locate them up above by their distinct high-pitched trilled *bzeee* and their prominent tuft of head feathers. He smiles when he sights his first, unaided, and later, she lets him kiss her.

After their lips press, Harrison touches her eye veil. Up close, he realises the eye covering is stitched from a dark red thread, not black. "Sac spider webbing," she says as he lifts it from her face. He is shocked, gasps audibly. Her eyes do not sparkle like they did on their first encounter, instead, today, they weep slightly, red. "My tears have stained the webbing." Harrison is taken aback by the crimson which drips from her eye ducts, yet he is still overwhelmed by the enchantment of her beauty.

∞

He visits the woman in the forest again and again while, under his command, his team chip away at nature. Each time he learns more about the woods, and less about himself, and always departs with a gift from the lady: posies of lesser twayblade, intermediate wintergreen and twinflower, woven baskets of pine cones, dried leaves filled with juniper and crowberries, a pouch of tooth fungi she says can heal memory loss, anxiety, infected wounds. He takes each gift and thanks her, embarrassed, unsure as to what he might offer from his world of construction and machinery in exchange.

∞

Over the next few weeks, more loggers arrive. A metal army of heavy machinery pitches up on the outskirts of the wood. Harrison fears for his forest lover's habitation. He is too heavily invested financially to withdraw from the development, but has fallen in love with this woman with bleeding eyes. Her eyes see into his soul like no lover has before.

One afternoon, loosened by gin and after a long meeting with colleagues, Harrison finds himself again walking in the woods. He no longer needs a map. The forest has become smaller. He recognises each tree, each shrub, and uses them to guide himself to her. He finds her. With her one arm, she drapes herself around him, pressing her lips on his. Pushing her hair out of the way, he kisses her neck, works kisses down her arm, lifts up her skirt of feathers and presses his lips and tongue in other places. She wails with pleasure, guides his lips back to her mouth, and unbuttons his trousers. "Is this what you want?" he asks.

"More than anything, yes," she replies, "It is what I need," and she takes him and guides him inside of her body. Each thrust is exhilarating. Locked in desire, they stumble back until pressing against a sturdy pine. Lost in the moment, eyes closed, faces kiss close, he does not see, or feel the rivulets of vermillion which gush down her inner thighs as they make love.

I'd rather die than stop now, he thinks; the friction of his flesh on hers feels like this is all he was ever meant for. His worries and thoughts unravel and his thighs shudder as he comes.

They lie together in the leaf litter afterwards: him propped up against the tree, her curled with her head on his lap. Red tears follow the line of her nose and drip-drop between his legs, onto the forest floor. Harrison strokes her hair and realises he does not even know her name.

"It's Nàdair," she says, although he is certain he had not asked.

"Harrison," he replies.

"I know."

Harrison gasps. His cargo trousers are stained dark red, too dark a stain to be due to her bleeding eyes. "Your arm, where you had an arm, I mean— The stump of it…it's bleeding."

Nàdair shrugs, reaches for a handful of leaves, and wipes her weeping elbow. Blood continues to trickle out. She is unphased. "It appears I am becoming undone."

Harrison clears his throat, swallowing back the impulse to vomit that'd risen in it. "How did you lose it?"

Nàdair drops eye contact. "Once, I tried to leave the forest," she says. "I do not wish to talk about it." She pulls away from him.

Harrison stands, lifts her up only so he can again pull her in close, then kisses her. Her body feels light, too light, weak in his arms, and her kiss tastes of copper.

Harrison asks if there is anything he can do to help her feel better as his heart floods with guilt. He feels, in some way, responsible for her illness, her constant loss of blood.

"I love you," he says.

"It is time for you to go home," she replies.

On their walk back to the edge of the forest, it is dark, so he does not see the additional trail of red which leaks from the soles of her naked feet.

They reach the boundary. *She is pale*, he thinks, *perhaps exhausted from the intimacy.*

From the shelter and shadow of the forest canopy, she tells him, "I will go no further," then presents him with a fallen antler. With sixteen tines and covered in ragged velvet, it is a majestic thing of beauty. Harrison thanks her for the gift, kisses her passionately fare-well, and wipes away her red tears.

He carries the antler home in his hands, the beautiful souvenir too large to fit in his bag.

CRSO

Harrison struggles to sleep that night, his nightmares haunted by lost limbs, visions of rutting, eyeless monarch stags, and forests drowning in red. As the sun rises, he realises he must try to halt the final stage of the forest clearance, preserve what is left, but he fears it may be too late to stop the project—deep foundations have already been dug over nine tenths of the purchased land.

❦

At work, from the window of his grey hut, he sees giant, robotic cranes lifting girders, long-wheelbase trucks zooming in to deliver bricks by the tonne every hour, machines with steel teeth: angled, poised, ready to bite. The metal and concrete jungle he had stared at in blueprint for so long now nears completion. The project has snow-balled out of his control.

❦

He decides he must visit her immediately, the woman of the forest, to tell her to leave the ecosystem she calls home, before auto-mated machinery bullies its way in. He will guide her out, bring her to safety, then teach her there is nothing to fear in the modern world in which he has grown up. He wants to look after her, marry her if she wishes, but today, she must relocate. A convoy is on route to tear down the last cluster of trees. The loggers have refused to delay this, despite his reasoning and offers of cash. But talk of his descent to madness echoes between the workers.

Harrison marches into the forest, which is now no more than a grove, a copse. Light passes through from one edge of it to the other. It is no longer swamped by the thick canopy-cloak of gloom he has grown to love. A few strides in and he reaches the sentinel pine, against which he has so often found his lover leaning. But today, she is not sat at the bottom. He follows the trunk of the tree up and searches for a glimpse of black and red amongst the branches. He steps back, his face contorted.

Nailed to the tree bark, pulsing, pumping in time with his own, a little larger than the size of his balled fist, he sees a heart. Blood dripping from its pierced core, the heart still thrums. It beats faster as he moves closer, as does his in response. He vomits, narrowly missing his shoes. A noise, from above: the sound of a woman crying. He hears her sob over the angry roar of engines revving and other motorised cutting machinery chomping at the bit. She is there, twenty feet up in the tree, her legs hunched up, her face in her hands.

"Please Nàdair, come down. I tried to get them to stop, to leave you time to say goodbye, pack—"

Through a gap in the forest, the first automated tree feller machine bursts. Its sharp blades churn and spin. Harrison screams at it to stop, but it is unstaffed, controlled by a man in the hut a mile or so away. Harrison scrambles up the tree and pulls Nàdair over his shoulder. She weighs but a feather. *It is as if her bones are hollow*, he thinks, but as he lifts her, he sees her belly is swollen.

"I can't leave," she says, her voice reedy, weak.

He drags her down from the tree. "You have to."

"It's yours," she says as he places her on the ground. Her single hand wraps around her belly protectively. "I cannot leave my tree. It is my heart and I, its." She pushes his head hard, his ear turned in, onto her chest. There is no beat, no repeating push of blood coming from behind where her ribs must sit.

"I'm the father?" he asks. She does not have time to tell him again.

The blade of the chopping vehicle rams through the wood of the heart-tree's trunk, slicing it, pushing it over. "Quick," Harrison says. He lifts his love and runs with her in his arms to an exposed clearing, a spot already logged, where a scattering of thin forest soil and leaf detritus dusts the ground, and there, he places her gently down.

Nàdair screams, crouches. Her face crumples in agony as she lifts her feathered skirt, reaches up, between her legs, inside of herself, and pulls hard, extracting a large brown seed. She places the seed, covered in blood, into Harrison's shaking palm, folds his fingers around it.

"Our child. Nurture her. Keep her out of the harsh, synthetic light of this new world your people are creating." She falls into his arms, scrunches her eyes closed, screams again, and then her body becomes like dust in his hands.

Harrison sinks to the ground and hits at it hard with his fist, the seed still clamped inside. "No. No." But she is gone. He rips open the top layer of soil with his hands and, afraid the seed may suffer a similar fate as his lover, buries their child in the soil.

ꏹ

Harrison does not leave his child. He remains, slightly broken, at the location where he has buried the seed. Angered, distraught, he refuses to move on, despite pleading visits from his team, until they agree to alter the blueprints of the city. The contractors begin to build a wall around him and his buried seed: this place will become a play park for the ghost of his dead lover.

He sleeps there each night, guards the place he buried his seed, his progeny, and lets his tears water the ground. His colleagues, scared for his wellbeing, bring him drinks and food that he barely touches.

Weeks pass. The apartments are complete, a climbing frame and sand pit have been installed in the centre, near Harrison's pitch, for the coming residents to use. Harrison sits in silence, filthy and unshaven, tight in his spot, mourning for the woman and their seed, until one day, a solitary green shot pokes up through the top layer of soil.

✿

Countless plant pots, jam jars, small buckets fill every shelf and each spare space in the rooms of the flat on the eighth floor of Caledonian Heights - Block E. Each vessel is filled with red soil, and from most of the containers, green shoots and tempered cuttings sprout out. Some containers show no visible plant growth, and their soil remains bare to the naked eye, but beneath the soil, expectant pine cone seeds lay snug, drinking down the last of the coppery fluid in which they have been bathed.

Grow lamps shouting out blue and red spectra in all directions dangle from the ceiling. The flat stinks of neglect and manure. Half empty bottles of plant feed and discarded, empty beer cans litter the floor of his internal forest.

In a chair by the window, an old man lies slumped, his heart having given out the moment the bird in the tree had hit the glass pane of the flat below. Catheters, needled into every available varicosed vein, dangle from the old dead man's black-bruised arms. Plastic tubing drains and dispenses the last of his blood into bottles scattered around his feet.

A coffee table is pushed up against a wall, and on it, several razor blades glint in between curled slices of long-yellowed skin—an attempt at grafting his own flesh to the bark of his babies had been the last project he had undertaken. In his lap, a long black feather, posies of dried flowers, and a large antler rest.

Speakers embedded into the ceiling of his luxury flat boom out their message, again and again: *"Ms Theroux, floor seven, wishes to connect. Do you accept?"* But he is gone, and will not ever answer.

The sound of the operating system requesting connection, on repeat, is driving the angry saplings barmy. Each writhes in its pot. Multitudinous pine plantlets are hungry, and their soil is drying out. The eldest, a mere six-inch sprig of brown and green, dribbling red from each of its leaf buds, leads the objection, with a shrill, eardrum-shattering scream. With all its might, it screeches again, lifts its first shallow root out of the pot, and places it down on the filthy floor.

BE KIND TO YOUR CHILDREN: THEY CHOOSE YOUR NURSING HOME

I am Mildred March, and I don't like much.

I dislike infants, never had any. I despise men, have never taken a husband. Young people repulse me, and most people of a certain age do, too—all those wants and needs and muddy shoes. Oh, and I definitely don't like you. I tolerate humans solely at work, safe in the knowledge I can return to my home alone at the end of my shift.

I inherited my disgust for humans from Mother. She used to lock me in my room, tell me I'd the Devil within and before she'd put herself to bed each night, with whatever she could find, she'd try to beat Him free from me. She'd yell at me as the strap of her belt buckle clipped my ear. She'd shout, she'd warn: all I'd be met with was blackness and Hellfire if I didn't believe in the good of the Lord, didn't commit to the church. But I knew as well as she did that all the other church-goers were hideous bastards. How on Earth could what those crazed cunts believe in be right? She hated her congregation as much as she hated me. As much as she hated the Devil. God, I hated that darned Devil—almost as much as I loathed my mother.

But there is one thing I do like… one thing I like very much indeed, lots and lots with a cherry on top… and that's the time I get to spend alone with the elderly at Oak Tree Retirement Village. Here, where I work, once visiting hours are over, I get my chance to tidy away the stagnant, repugnant bags of vintage meat.

ॐ

I've worked at Oak Tree for seventeen years. It pays well. Yes, my basic salary is barely a stone's toss over minimum wage, but I've found a more than comfortable way to turn an extra income over on the side—if I couldn't supplement in this way, I'd be out of here like a jack rabbit.

Today is cold. From the window, I see ice has collected on the skeletal tree branches, white frosting on finger buns. I'm on reception today. At least I get to sit down here, rest my weary bones. I'm only a few years off retirement myself, but there's no way you'd catch me paying the extortionate fees my boss charges, to live in this utter crock of shit. I work around the clock, bringing in all the funds I can to make sure I can look after myself in my own home until I hit the snooze button for the final time. I'll bring a live-in carer to my own humble abode if needs be, but they'll be heavily scrutinised. All kinds get employed here. *All* kinds. I witness neglectful care every day with my very own eyes.

A new couple are coming up the path. They've parked up a fairly decent car—personalised number plate. Another pair of middle-aged show-offs, by the looks.

She wears a mink coat. Ah, hang on, she's getting closer. It isn't real, the fur—some Marks and Spencer's imitation I expect. He's got the waxed jacket, the polished brogues, a copy of that right-wing newspaper under his arms—awkward snooty couple of bastards. Together, though, they're indistinguishable from every other pair of cunts who visit this joint.

They'll come daily at first, for a week or so. Then they'll make excuses, drop the visits down to once a week. This side of Christmas, it'll be once a month, at best. They'll never write—although they'll say they will—and then, in the New Year, it'll be just the annual guilt-trip check-in. They'll comment on how much the resident who belongs to them has aged, how they've *deteriorated, hasn't their memory started to fray around the edges.* Heartless game players.

Before they know it, whichever unlucky sod they've got slammed up in here will've been a resident for five years and cost them the best part of quarter of a million in living costs—most, if not all of the inheritance.

They'll feign surprise when we tell them old Aunt Wendy or gentle Grandpa Bill is to be moved down to the ground floor due to 'mobility issues' or because they 'can't get to the bathroom fast enough' or have 'symptoms of dementia which require round the clock care'.

All of which sees the bills they're probably picking up at this point escalate skywards. *Oh no, please don't hurt me in the money!* they'll say, as they bleed out notes and coins.

The real reason the resident will get moved to the ground floor is because it's one step closer to the basement. And the basement is where the morgue is. That's where the cool lockers, which preserve their wrinkled flesh bags until funeral arrangements can be made, are located. Our manager, heart of necrotic slate, is a shrewd business-man. I'm surprised he hasn't applied for planning permission for a crematorium to be built in the car park. He could use the heat it'd generate to warm this place up, save some more pennies.

Ah, they're coming in through the double doors.

I open up the guest book, present them with a pen.

"Hello. Welcome to Oak Tree. Is this your first visit?" I ask. Of course it is. They're both bloody smiling, both look far too keen to be here.

I do my best welcome smile. Faux fur woman jerks back slightly. I close my mouth. Damn it. I slide my tongue around my gums. Forgot to put in my dentures—a few of my front teeth are missing— must've given her a bit of a shock. Ha! Not such a bad morning after all. I'm truly grinning now, on the inside, but I smack my lips tight together to conceal my 'offensive grimace'—the boss's words, not mine.

I'm only sixty-two, a spring chicken, but we're all one foot in the grave from the moment we're born. Bodies aren't built to last forever.

"Good morning." It's always the man who speaks first. His name is Tockerton. I see this as he passes me back the guest book. "We've come to see Mrs Tockerton, my mother. She arrived yesterday. On the second floor, room 58, I believe."

"Ah yes, lovely Judith Tockerton," I say and beckon them to follow me along the corridor. I play with the rusty razor blade in my pocket as we walk along, a hidden game of how far under my nail bed can I slide it without it hurting too much.

We rattle through the old building, bowling balls thundering along the return gulley, towards the 'entertainment' room. Stinks of boiled cabbage, sulphur, and urine. All the rooms do, here. "Sorry about the smell," I hesitate as the sharp in my pocket nicks a little too hard. "Drain issues."

"I see," Mr T replies. Mrs T holds a satin handkerchief over her nose. The old biddies don't care about the pong; most of them are so heavily doped up, you could drag a rotten whale carcass right through, smeared in fresh pig excrement, and they wouldn't bat an eyelid.

Judith is over by the television. "There we go, in between Arthur and Olive." I contemplate trying to describe the wrinklies sat either side of Judith to give them more direction, but they all look the same to me: reptilian, almost. Paper-thin skin, sunken eyes like clouded marbles lost at sea, white hair that needs dusting away. "They're watching *Gone with the Wind.*"

"How lovely," Mrs T replies. She roots her hands deeper into her coat pockets, pulls the faux mink fabric in a little tighter around her body.

Of course they're watching *Gone with the Wind.* It's on repeat all day every Tuesday. And Friday. Old Rupert tried to change the channel last week. He'd somehow gotten hold of the remote, but the batteries in it went flat months ago. I'd caught him with it and placed it back on the top shelf where none of the folded oldies can reach. He said he liked the way the buttons felt, but if he had a remote control, they'd all want one. There's no way the boss would bust the budget for toys.

"Thank you. What was your name?" Mr T asks. He looks for my name badge. Turns out I've forgotten to put that on this morning, too.

"Mildred," I reply. "Mildred March. I'll be in the staff kitchen over the way if you need me," I say and leave them to it. I've just time to look Judith up on the computer system, see what I'm working with before deciding if it's worth listening in on their conversation. I find the notes from her GP:

At the grand age of ninety-three, Judith has 'good mental faculties' and has sold up her family home in the Lake District to spend her golden years at Oak Tree. Judith is a widow, retired librarian, and was dedicated in her role as treasurer at her local spiritualist church. Judith's family have chosen Oak Tree for her.

Judith is on 20mg Simvastatin for blood pressure; 2 x 20mg Omeprazole for acid reflux; benzodiazepine is to be taken when necessary for sleep-related wellbeing. She has a history of treatment for dissociative-identity disorder, which is to be managed with 15mg Clozapine, twice daily. Judith likes cats and French pastries.

So, the old windbag has a penny or two, a history of poor mental health, and at age ninety-three, she's also—quite frankly—living on borrowed time. The computer system is great, although I couldn't give a shit about her former life. I've already had the pleasure of changing her adult nappy this morning, already wiped shit—of the wet and nuggetted variety—from her saggy, growling undercarriage. Feels like we know each other intimately already.

I tiptoe back, and as I move, I reflect on Judith's short biography and lick my lips: the fact this old turd was part of the same ridiculous religious cult my own mother was makes me hunger for what I intend to do even more.

Outside of the entertainment room, I press my ear against the wall and listen in. I like to observe the family with their elderly relative for at least a couple of visits before offering additional services.

"I still hear the voices," Judith murmurs. I peek round the door jamb and spot Mr and Mrs T giving each other a concerned glance. "I'm still channelling."

"We've talked about this before," Mr T says. His brow furrows. "It's your hearing aid, Mother. You've got to clean it. You're getting feedback or something."

"Picking up radio stations, I expect," Mrs T's attempted joke literally falls on deaf ears.

"What, dear?" Judith says. She raises and places her shaking right arm on her daughter-in-law's knee. Mrs T, clearly repulsed by this contact, pulls away. I see it in her body language: the daughter-in-law hates the old bag. Excellent.

"I spoke to your father last week," Judith stammers.

"Mother, Father's been dead for years now. Stop with this non-sense," Mr T replies. He smiles, but his eyes remain cold. He's thinking he should take his mother's hand in his, show some compassion, work it for the inheritance he hopes will come his way soon, but he's as repulsed by the old woman's yellow-blue-grey skeletal knuckles as his wife is, and he decides against reaching out for skin-to-skin contact. "Come now, we've talked about this before. Have you been taking your tablets? Dawn and I, we don't believe in all this supernatural poppycock."

This is fascinating to watch. The old bag is already showing clear signs of mental decline, most likely significant dementia, and she's only been in a week. Should be a fast journey to the ground floor; I'll need to act quickly.

"How's the food?" Mrs T attempts to change the subject.

The food here is atrocious. Same grey slop every day. Occasion-ally, fruit's offered, but only occasionally. We try to keep the old gits bunged up rather than loose —much easier to keep clean. Guests aren't allowed in at mealtimes, so no-one is any the wiser. If they complain, we mention dementia. *How could they possibly have forgotten the delicious roast and cherry bakewell served yesterday? And what do they mean, 'there's no entertainment'? We had a comedian and a singing group in last week, and the local scouts popped by on Sunday to play checkers with them.*

It's the perfect storm here. The perfect storm.

"The food? Did you say food, Dawn?"

"Yes, Judith. The food. How's the food?"

"I thought you said: 'how's your mood'," Judith replies.

"How *is* your mood?" Mr T asks.

"Oh, breakfast was awful," Judith says. "I haven't opened my bowels since I got here."

"Is that the time?" Mr T says. There's no clock in here. This place is timeless. He's not looking at a watch or his phone either.

"Judith looks tired," I interject as I glide into the room with a forced, closed-lip smile. It's time to guide them to the exit, but not before asking a few questions, to ensure I'm barking up the right tree.

I wave them off and catch the end of their conversation as they head to their car.

"We did the right thing, getting her in here, even though it costs so much. She'll have a much better final innings here than at home, won't she?" Mrs T says.

"Those relentless kids egging her windows, leaving bags of human faeces on her doorstep, shouting at her and calling her an evil witch can't have been very nice." Mr T says as he rummages in his pocket and withdraws his car keys. "Not forgetting what they did to her cat. I'm sure she'll be better off here." He looks back up to see if he can see his mother looking out of the window. He won't.

"Yes. That's what tipped her over the edge, the cat."

☙❧

People are predictable. I observe the Tockertons and their declining frequency of visits over the following months. I leave time for them to receive at least two bills in the post. Mr T is in charge of Judith's estate. He's responsible for making the payments to Oak Tree from the old crone's savings. Each cheque he writes will sting, even though it's not (yet) his money. I've seen it before, many times. I know when to pounce.

☙❧

It's January and as bleak as death outside. The residents I'm watching today in the lounge look like they've all had droopy grey clay flung at their faces. Jowls; protruding hair where it shouldn't be, and none where it should; nasty, stained lap blankets; bunions pointing east and west out of the gaps in their sandals. If it wasn't for the perks, I couldn't stomach this much living decay and stench day in, day out.

From my view out the window, I see Mr and Mrs Tockerton walk up the path. It's time I speak with them. Judith shat the bed this morning. Muggins here had to clean it up. She needs to go down a level. Tracy in admin has already filled out the paperwork, so I need to move fast, close this deal.

Just before Mr and Mrs T enter the building, I place a naked plastic baby in Judith's arms which she hugs tightly. This usually does the job.

"Hello, Mr and Mrs Tockerton. How lovely to see you. It's been—"

"Hello Mildred. It's been a month or so hasn't it. Lovely Christmas?" Urgh, rhetoric. They couldn't give a damn about my Christmas. They won't be staying in touch with me once Judith's snuffed it. They can barely be arsed to keep in touch with their own family. I'll be another blank face in the street in under a year, just another anonymous bastard to compete with for parking spaces down the High Street.

I lie. "Yes, delightful. Spent it with family. It's all about the little ones, isn't it? How are your lovely grandchildren?"

What a load of bollocks. Since Mother's passing, I've no family left, and the only way I'd spend Christmas with a child would be if it was small enough to fit in the oven and tasted good with cranberry sauce.

They spill rehashed stories about their perfect grandchildren. I try to hold down the vomit and bile that collects in my stomach. I think about what I'm going to do later instead, to keep my spirits high.

Mrs T looks over at Judith with the same look of concern she has every time she visits, when Judith starts talking in the different voices. It has gotten worse, Judith's ramblings. I'll not lie to them if they ask. In fact, I'll make sure to mention how much she's declined. It'll only work in my favour.

"Why's Judith holding a doll?" Mrs T has taken the bait.

"Lots of our residents like to hold dolls, especially the women, as they climb a little further down that sad ladder of memory loss. Reminds them of holding their own wee ones," I say. I tilt my head all Princess Diana and do my best impression of someone that gives a shit.

I'm smiling too much. I'm practically salivating at how well I'm drawing them in, hook, line and sinker. I need to tone it down, so I think about my own mother and the tightness in my balled cheeks softens.

Mrs T looks perturbed. Bingo.

"Her… memory has gotten worse? Since our last visit?"

"Afraid so. They're making space for her downstairs—she needs monitoring more closely."

"On the dementia floor?" Mr T interjects.

"Afraid so." I repeat, feigning sympathy that burns like Holy water.

I know exactly what's coming next. He'll talk money. He'll want to know how much this transition will hurt his pocket.

"So… will that… cost more?"

"The fees will be a little over double what you're currently paying. They require so much more care downstairs, you see. Isn't it such a terrible decline?"

"Is she still hearing the voices?" Mrs T asks in almost a whisper.

I explain to the Tockertons how I've walked into her room to find her completely away with the fairies on many an occasion.

"She holds full court with her dead relatives. Brian, her mother, father, her sister. She talks at length with her cat," I say, "and with a few others I've not heard either of you mention."

Many of the old cabbage-breath bastards talk to the dead as they approach the final door holding back the white light—it's not unusual—doesn't make it any less peculiar to witness, though. Mother used to chat with Satan all the time, while she attempted to beat him from me.

Judith, in particular, appears to have very clear 'visions' when impersonating her dead relatives. There's something unsettlingly different yet uncomfortably familiar about her. Most of what comes out of the old farts' mouths I ignore: waste of my time, listening to their stories about the war, the pain in their joints, about the animals and children they've lost. Blah blah blah.

"She does like to chat—" I continue, "—and her incontinence is becoming an increasing concern, too."

I lead them to Judith, make my excuses and leave the room. Listening in from the corridor, I plan my pitch.

They talk to each other over her head, as if she isn't there. I suppose, in a way, she isn't. When she does speak, it's usually as or to someone else, and rarely makes any sense.

"Such an awful waste. Look at her," Mr T says. He picks imagined lint from his trousers. "She's a shell of the woman she was."

"We could've bought that property in Marbella for what we've spent already." Mrs T crosses her arms and stares at Judith as she sidemouths her grumbles to her husband. "She's mumbling away, staring out at the lawn… doesn't even know we're here."

I watch Judith turn her head and cock it to one side. I've seen her do this before. She's about to pretend to be her husband. It's quite amusing, even though it's probably a result of her brain slowly eating itself up, congealing while still pulsing weakly with some sort of basic life force.

"Don't you dare, you silly bitch," Judith shouts. Her eyes widen. That one even caught me by surprise. I've never heard her speak with such volume before, let alone swear. I chuckle in the corridor and cup my hand over my mouth. I don't want them to catch me eavesdropping—it could blow this ship out of the water.

"Who's she talking to?" Mrs T whispers in her husband's ear, just loudly enough for me to catch. "She doesn't sound like herself anymore."

"No. I fear Mother has gone," Mr T replies. "And so has the money."

"Nearly. There's still about 300k left though, isn't there?"

I take this as my cue and walk back into the 'entertainment' lounge with cups of tea and a plate of biscuits for my two special visitors. With my tongue, I check I've put my best teeth in and give the Tockertons my most endearing smile. Feels like dripping acid in my own eyes.

"Mr and Mrs T, I'm terribly sorry, but I couldn't help overhearing the tail end of your conversation. I'm so sorry for the way things are progressing with your mother. Such an awful way to go, isn't it? I was wondering if you'd be interested in having a little chat."

"It's awful," Mr T replies, overegging his pudding. "Such a terrible, terrible descent."

"Terrible," Mrs T agrees.

"Terrible," I add.

I chat with them briefly about their grandchildren. Again. The eldest is considering university. *'Oh, aren't the fees so expensive, wouldn't it be nice to help them out?'* and *'wouldn't the children benefit with some additional money towards their mortgages?'* And *'isn't it a shame to be throwing good money to a care home for an individual who perhaps… has already 'checked out'?'*

I tell them to call me if they'd like things *sped up a little* and I pass them a card with nothing but my handwritten number on it. Mr T accepts it, although they both look a little taken aback by my offer. This, I anticipate. They'd have to be complete psychopaths for it to not knock them slightly sideways, wouldn't it?

The cogs in their brains consider the implications of my gentle suggestion, and the calculator part processes how much money they'll save if they accept my offer.

Sometimes, with particularly unhappy families, I offer a selection of "endings"—you'd be surprised at how often people don't always choose the most humane.

⚭

It's Thursday morning. The *Wizard of Oz* is on repeat. I know the script off by heart. Judith stares at the screen like it's the first time she's ever seen Garland skipping along arm in arm with a grown man dressed as a lion. I'll get to her shortly. First, the boss has asked me to address Old Arthur's stinking bedsore.

I wheel the medical trolley over, roll on a fresh pair of latex gloves, wind a fabric bandage up his leg, and cut it with the medical scissors. Job done. Then I wheel the trolley over to Judith.

She's asleep, a sack of snoring wrinkles using up too much oxygen. The money's been transferred and I'm eager to fulfil my half of the deal.

I shake Judith hard and pinch the skin on the back of her arm. There's a vacancy in her eyes as the lids lift. Yet there's also a spark within them when she speaks. It's a spark I've not seen in anyone else here before, in fact, haven't seen in quite some time. Not since our last encounter. And, I'll not lie, it's quite unnerving.

I've been collecting Judith's prescription meds for the last few weeks, withholding them, stashing them in my tabard pocket. I pull out a handful of the red and purple pills, tip them into a cup on the trolley, crush them with the back of a spoon and stir them into her cold soup. It's never enough to kill them, just slows the heart right down to ensure they can't be brought back if they're discovered too soon by one of the bloody do-gooders I work alongside.

I crouch beside her and feed the soup to her from a spoon. I'm not sure what smells worse, her rancid breath or the spiked slop I shovel into her trap-hole. No-one else is around; they're all either dealing with Maude who's got herself stuck in the bath again, or are bunking off by the fire exit chaining Lisa's duty-free cigarettes.

Judith refuses to eat. I pinch her nose tightly until her jaw slackens, then turn my head away at the odour that emanates—she's already rotting from the inside. This one stinks worse than any I've dealt with before. As her mouth opens with a gasp, I force her to chug her liquid Last Supper down, and slap her on the cheek for luck.

With a handful of napkins held tightly over her mouth, I wait until she swallows the last of her dinner. The cheeky cow tries to bite me. She has more teeth than I do—it hurts. Naughty old mare. I give her another slap and think about bringing the razor blade out from my pocket. A beige rivulet of soup dribbles from the corner of her mouth and drops into her lap. She cowers back in her chair and my hand follows suit, clamped over her vile lips. Should be easy money this one, she's a mere stringbean of a witch.

Ouch. Teeth again. I pull my hand away and turn to search for a firm cushion. I can't use my hands to exterminate this one—she's a biter.

I turn back round. Judith has somehow hauled her sorry arse up and out of her chair. She hobbles over to the medical trolley. Is she trying to make a run for it? I cackle. Old Arthur wakes from his afternoon nap and stares at me with stupid, sunken eyes. He won't remember any of this. Even if he does, he's an unreliable narrator.

With a firm cushion in my hand, I march over to my paycheck and grab her arm. I grab so hard, it snaps or it pulls out from its joint, and I curse. Now I'm going to have to make this look like a fall. Damn these wrinkled gits with their fossilised bird bones and joints looser than broken waistbands. As I think about which way to push her, I notice her other hand is behind her back. She's hiding something. Despite it now bent at an unnatural angle, she grabs my arm with her broken one. Her face is now up close to mine. Her eyes roll back into her head.

She shouts at me in a deep voice: "You silly bitch, Mildred. You stupid little girl. You've the Devil in you."

But it is not her voice—not Judith's. It's Mother's.

This old witch Judith yells at me with Mother's voice, wears Mother's words like a suit of armour and a sword. Her body grows hotter and hotter. Steam blasts from her ears as her whole head starts to shake side-to-side and her words pour out faster. She spits as she shouts.

"You bitch girl, the Devil's in you."

It's too late. I don't see the scissors she must've taken from the trolley in time. She plunges them deep into me. Stainless steel slides through my tabard, my polyester blouse, pierces through my skin, belly fat, stomach. She pulls them out and shoves them back in again and again. I scream. Blood and stomach acid spray out of my guts like the smoke that spilt from the incense burner that swung down the aisle of the church at Mother's funeral. Searing pain rushes through my core as the cruel blades slice in and out. My nostrils fill with the memory of frankincense and the care-home-blended stench of stale piss and coppery blood.

Red sprays out everywhere, covering everything: carpet, cushion—which I've dropped to the floor—Judith, me.

Judith and the scissor blades she wields come at me again, harder, firmer, with the same angry energy Mother did before she died, with the voice of Mother in Judith's mouth, and Judith stabs me until there's nowhere left to perforate. Fuck! She's really doing me over.

I drop to my knees, flop over on my side and whack my head on the edge of the medical trolley. My head splits open. In and out the scissor blades continue to travel, creating puncture after puncture in my body. Judith jams them in and drags them across until my clothes are shredded and flaps of my flesh hang down. My intestines bulge out, spool free from my gut like slippery purple inner tubes. I lie on the floor, my heart racing fast but pumping weakly. Blood gushes out from my body, which leaves my poor heart with less and less to squeeze on. I glare at Judith. She crouches over me and continues her work. I mouth the words, "You fucker," at her, her own face now spit-close, just inches from mine. She pulls back, wipes off the handle of the scissors and places them back on the trolley. Is she laughing at me? Are they all laughing at me, all the old, rumpled bastards? All aware they've slipped the net this time, got away from my fatal hands?

There, lying on my side, my field of view dims at the edges. The light shrinks, like at the end of an old cartoon or the view out from the bottom of a well. Immeasurable pain jars through every inch of my pin-cushioned body. I vomit. My sick sprays in front of me, a lukewarm mixture of scrambled egg and blood, a violently offensive puddle of punishment. It collects around my head for my final seconds on this plane.

I see only Judith's fuzzy outline now. Only one of my eyes is above the pool of sick—she sits back down in her chair. She manoeuvres her own shoulder back into place—click, clack, crunch—then dabs at the blood on her blouse with a spittle-moistened tissue. She tuts at me as she mops, and stares at me with my own mother's eyes, until she becomes nothing but a distant speck.

Blackness.

Darkness.

Then comes the first blast of intolerable heat.

THIS ECHO CHAMBER LIFE

The city in which she had grown up had not been kind to her and the doctor had recommended *sea air*, something about salt, ultra-violet light, coastal life, the brush on skin of a far-travelled breeze. If she were to stay where she was—with her mother, in the city—her mother said she would most likely unravel at the seams, become devoured, masticated and spat out, and ultimately, be at risk of dissociating entirely.

So, after several viewings, she decided to take the first room she'd been shown—isn't this always the way?—the room in the two-bed property which overlooked the sea, because, as a little girl, she'd always dreamt of living by the sea. And the doctor had been somewhat insistent. And from this point forth, she, the one who signed the contract, shall be referred to as 'THE FLATMATE' and the two-bed property overlooking the sea as 'THE FLAT'.

She, THE FLATMATE, was not sure if it was the doctor who wished her away or the ocean which beckoned her or, perhaps, the prospect of sharing with another girl, who could become, perhaps, a friend, but signing on the dotted line had felt like the correct thing to do. She was not sure of much, though. It was as if the situation was out of her hands, out of her control, as if the gravity of the expanse of dark water had taken over.

ೞ

"Green or taupe?" the girl who lived in the other room, who shall be referred to as 'Lil', asked.

"Either," the Flatmate replied. "Both look amazing. Wish I had your figure. You could be a model."

The same conversation rolled out every Friday evening, the pair two-thirds through a bottle of Cheap White. Same Cheap White, same flimflam, blether, unidirectional compliments, the specific date only distinguished by the slight differences in both of the girls' nearly-outfits. The evening could almost have been a tape-recording set on a timed loop.

Both laughed at the appropriate moments always instigated by Lil, but they laughed in a different way to one another. The Flatmate's laugh came out overeager, too ripe, a little too loud. Her whole face honked like a goose. Lil's well-rehearsed laugh came out from only her lips; didn't want her caramel foundation to crease, didn't want to dislodge an eyelash. The rest of her face remained Botox-still.

"I'll wear the taupe. Goes with my new boots," Lil said more to herself than to the Flatmate.

Even the morning after the night before, Lil was an easy ten, and if she were to come back to the flat with the Flatmate after a night out with the Flatmate, the following morning, Lil would still be sparkling. She'd rise from her silk sheets as polished as a fancy pearl. In comparison, the Flatmate would rise groggy, crumpled, and smudged, as if recently dug up. In comparison, Lil shone even without make-up. Lil never had bed-head or bad skin or cellulite, and the Flatmate would make prescriptive comments, deliver lip service, would say things like: "Lil, you'd look good in a bin bag."

The Flatmate—at the start of the night only, and only in the right light at a push—was a seven; a seven who fell to a five point five when stood in the shade of Lil.

The Flatmate was ready to go, so she slid on her sandals, perched on the sofa, and watched Lil carry out her elaborate rituals. Fifteen long minutes passed. The Flatmate finished off the wine and Lil anchored on and tied up her knee-high, lace-up boots, the ones with the five-inch heels.

"Do you think it's going to rain?" Lil asked and teetered, all sexual stick insect, over to the mantelpiece to pout at her own reflection in the mirror above the fireplace. "I don't want to get my hair wet."

"Rain? In June? I doubt it," the Flatmate replied. Her eyes on her hands, her hands writhing about in her lap, unsure of what to do with themselves, how to rest, how to be, now the wine was drunk. She gawked upward at Lil's reflection, wished she looked more like Lil. The Flatmate stared hard in the mirror and pretended Lil's reflection was her own, belonged to her. *The only thing more beautiful to see than Lil, is the sea,* she thought, and through the far window, to which her eyes flit for less than a moment, she could also see the sea.

The Flatmate sat up straighter, drew her shoulders back, sucked her stomach in. *Perhaps in time,* the Flatmate thought, *some of her beauty may rub off on me.* But the Flatmate was unsure if, when her thoughts referred to 'her', her thoughts had meant the sea, or if her thoughts had meant Lil. Both were things of beauty, but one evoked a feeling of calm, the other, a feeling of resentment. It was the first time she'd lived away from home.

They stepped outside, one after the other, the Flatmate a few paces behind Lil, and set off for the bus stop. The Flatmate looked at the cracks and the gum stuck on the pavement and fiddled with her chafing bra straps and fumbled in her bag for loose change between old sweet wrappers and hair clips and Lil's stuff which Lil had asked her to carry for her so Lil didn't have to 'ruin her own outfit with a bag'. Lil glided along. The Flatmate noted how Lil glided, observed how a ten moved her arms, cat-walked her legs. *She moves with the grace of a swan,* the Flatmate thought and tried to emulate her. She made a clumsy shadow; a shadow with unattainable aspiration, a shadow with a lake of fire and jealousy burning in the pit of its shape-shifting stomach.

An ominous rumble cracked from an opening in the sky, some-place before the bus stop and after the off-licence where Lil had stopped outside of to check her own reflection again in the storefront glass.

"Oh. It appears it *might* rain," the Flatmate said and dipped her eyes like half-beamed headlights. "Sorry."

Lil, a ten, threw the Flatmate—a seven, but a six when wet—dagger-eyes, as if to suggest the situation with the weather was, in fact, somehow the Flatmate's fault.

The pair broke into a canter, both keen to miss the prospective deluge, and it was when both girls were within a stone's throw from the number 5 bus stop that a razor clam fell from a cloud. It clipped Lil's arm on its way down.

They looked at the bivalve on the ground, then looked across it to each other, one's body language the mirror image of the other's, centred by the punctuation of a sea mollusc. *How odd,* the Flatmate thought, *although not entirely unimaginable, what with our proximity to the coast.* The Flatmate had heard of stranger things falling from the sky: frogs, golf balls, roof tiles, impromptu tornadoes of debris.

But not in England. Not on a Friday night *out on the town*.

The Flatmate wondered if she should stoop and collect the shell, return it to the sea. To take the shell to the sea, to throw it back in, to sit and stare at the sea—these were the things she felt she might want to do. The Flatmate felt drawn to the shell like the shell had been drawn to the surface of the Earth, as if with the force of Jupiter's pull.

But Lil insisted on nightclubbing each weekend. And, like most actions over time, repetition leads to the formation of a habit. And the Flatmate was not one for confrontation.

"Shit. That hurt," said Lil. "I'm bleeding." She clamped her left arm with her right hand to try to stem the flow of her own blood. The Flatmate pulled out a crumpled tissue from her bag and passed it to Lil, who turned her nose up at the offering but then, perhaps on realising she had no other choice, for no one else on foot was within sight, accepted it. Lil took to dabbing at the clean slice in her arm the shell had made. It was as if the part of her arm which had no name, the side-spot between the wrist and the elbow, the flank of long-boned flesh, had become undone by a straight, red zipper.

With gusto, Lil kicked the shell. They watched the knife of nature spin and skitter away and along the pavement, saw it pinball against a post and come to a standstill some way off ahead.

Another voluble clack came from the heavens and more crustaceans and hard things from the sea started to fall. "Quick, run for shelter," the Flatmate yelled, and the Flatmate in her flat shoes ran towards the shelter of the bus stop. But Lil, ten, almost an impossible eleven in her too-tall heels, in a state of panic, took a tumble down. Down she fell like the shells from the skyline, down. Down.

God or the troposphere dropped everything else it was holding all at once. A cacophony of marine blades, calcium carbonate sharps, scallops, piddocks, oyster warfare, and rock-hard whelks pounded onto the pavement. Lil, twisted ankle, lay moaning on the ground, unable to flee the shower. Pain. Slicing. Shellfish. Storm.

The Flatmate charged forwards until she reached the bus stop. There, she turned back to look at the state of Lil, a smaller version of Lil now, who lay on the pavement someway off in the distance, or, perhaps, in the past. The Flatmate pondered *should I run back and help?* She could see the bus in the opposite direction, also small, but larger than Lil, and growing larger. The bus, caught between lighter traffic, edged closer towards its stop, towards the Flatmate who stood safe and sheltered. *Be a shame to miss it*, the Flatmate thought. *Next one's not for half an hour.*

Without Lil at the club, the Flatmate thought and stared at her own arms, *I'll be an eight. Maybe an eight point five if the UV lighting which makes my freckles pop too hard is switched off—*

The flatmate stroked the unnamed area of her own arm in the same place where on Lil's body, the razor clam had struck and carved up a perfect canvas. The Flatmate lost herself amongst her own freckles. *What is this part of my arm called?* she thought. She could not name it, did not know if she had ever known the name for it. If she had, she had forgotten it. *And why am I stroking it?* She tried to push out other thoughts from her mind.

The Flatmate cornered her head to look back at Lil on the pavement again, before stepping up and onto the bus. *What a mess.* Lil was a mess. Sliced and strewn into numerous chunks of meat, Lil was spread all over the pavement. Not a ten. Not anymore.

The Flatmate examined her hair in the reflection of herself in the bus window as she moved down the central aisle and came to a decision: if Lil's pieces were still there in the morning, and if the weather had improved, she'd return and collect them up, try to piece them together to make sense of the events. The Flatmate would return and gather the segments of Lil up into a black sack and take the black sack back to the flat. In the morning. If the mess was still there.

The night is young, she thought to herself as she took the last seat on the bus, a tight squeeze next to another seven, *and Lil will, of course, look good in a bin bag.*

"Is your friend okay?" the other seven asked. The two sevens, generic, both looked out of the window at the untidiness on the pavement. The shellfish continued to plummet like bullets from the sky. Some smashed open to reveal an ugliness on the inside which far surpassed the ugliness of their outer sides; others landed and remained tightly sealed.

"My friend? Oh, no. She's not my friend, she's just a flatmate," she replied. She looked through the bus window glass and then she looked *into* the bus window glass, at the translucent version of herself, the carbon copy ghost, which was looking straight back, and she smiled. "I'm Leanne," she said, and offered the other seven a wrapped mint from her bag.

"Thanks," the other seven replied. "I'm Michelle." The Flatmate, who from this point forth shall be referred to as LEANNE, laughed and made a joke and asked Michelle if she was shellfish and did she like shellfish and they wondered, together, if it had ever rained shellfish before, if it might ever rain shellfish again. The girls laughed at the same time and in the same way and the seafood storm outside stopped.

It became a pleasant journey. The two sevens discussed weather anomalies, ultraviolet lighting, and the benefits and disadvantages of living near the coast, and as one seven spoke, the other seven listened. It was a friendship of reciprocation. They travelled forwards, progressively, side-by-side, and by the time the bus reached its destination, both girls had become eights. They had a good night out on the town.

The next morning, Leanne, true and loyal to her thoughts, returned to the spot on the high street where the sky had opened up the night before to release its weaponry. She harvested all visible segments of Lil into a bag which she carried home, the weight of it increasing with each and every step, until it bore the mass of a thing upon Jupiter. She tucked the bag under her bed for safekeeping. *Out of sight, out of mind,* she thought, she was sure she thought. But she was still not sure of much.

☙❧

The rent still needed to be met each month, there was no hiding that eventuality, so Leanne invited the other seven, Michelle, to move in and so, Michelle moved in, and from this point forward, Michelle shall be referred to as 'THE FLATMATE'.

The girls were so similar. They shared the same-sized clothing and shoes, the same preference for quiet over music, the same allergy to biological washing detergent, and even the same preference to do their laundry on a Thursday. Their coincidences were unalarmingly alarming, and where Leanne and the Flatmate did have any differences, Leanne found, in time, the Flatmate would come round to her way of doing things. She could be coaxed along, like when your reflection in a mirror develops a split-second delay, when your reflected movements lag slightly behind the adjustment to your overarching, real-time frame which you are certain you have just moved. You know the feeling.

The Flatmate was easygoing, easily moulded, fitted in and around Leanne and the flat by the sea like a second skin. Their similarities, they both agreed, were uncanny.

When they went shopping together, the Flatmate would come home with bags full of dresses, shoes, and jewellery almost identical to Leanne's. Several nights each week, Leanne would find the Flatmate in her room, looking through her wardrobe, asking to borrow things, sometimes taking without asking. Leanne did not mind. *It's rare to find someone with such impeccable taste, someone who enjoys the same things in life as I do*, she thought. *Someone who admires the same art.*

A few weeks into their shared tenancy, Leanne returned from work to find the Flatmate's bedroom had become the mirror image of her own, as if a reflection in a mirror, with no split-second delay: the same Great Wave of Kanagawa poster blu-tacked above the headboard, an identical floral duvet neatly spread over the bed, the matching stack of books on the corner table. Leanne was not sure who had bought the books first. She still was not sure of much. Perhaps it had been her that had seen the Flatmate's impressive collection and had noted the names of the authors down, visited a shop to purchase them. No, she was certain she wouldn't have done this. She would have been thrifty, borrowed them from the Flatmate, returning them once complete. She liked to read, but she was no fool with money. What would be the purpose of such duplication?

Over time, Leanne started to feel as if the Flatmate might, deliberately, or perhaps without realising, be imitating her persona, but where it should have felt like a compliment, the mimicry began to leave her feeling stale. It was hard being the sole source of creativity within the small apartment, was tough bringing new ideas to the dinner table, starting fresh conversation all the time. The Flatmate would nod and agree and smile and follow her around all lost puppy. Like a ghost. *Yes, this is how I have begun to feel*, she thought, *like I am living with a ghost, living at one as one with a ghost; alive but dead.* And Leanne grew tired of this.

Despite her Flatmate—whose name she would often forget even though she was sure it should have been on the tip of her tongue— being most agreeable, most amiable, Leanne felt like she was either living alone or existing in parallel with a ghost. Or with a shadow of a ghost, the ghost of a ghost.

As time passed in the small space of the flat, the girls spent the hours which sandwiched their working day largely in silence. They interposed only with brief exchanges, pleasantries. It was as if they were so similar, one knew what the other was to say before it became said. And sometimes, when they did speak to one other, short sentences rang out in unison, matched.

Snap.

Leanne found she'd become reliant on asking her own self for advice on what to have for dinner, about what shoes to wear with what dress, and so on, rather than discussing such things with the Flatmate. The thoughts within her head provided a more stimulating conversation, opened up a wider spectrum of unique, unpredictable suggestions than any discussion she could press from the Flatmate.

"Could I borrow a dress for tonight, Leanne? Maybe one of the ones you wore last week?" the Flatmate asked one Saturday afternoon, although Leanne knew the request was coming. The Flatmate's voice came from the bathroom, the shower. The mist of the shower seeped out under the bathroom door, carrying the words towards Leanne, who had been perched on the sofa for some time, already ready to go out, already nursing an empty wine glass.

She thought back to the week before, a paper doll identi-kit row of nights out which had felt like every other night out: a blur of unoriginal conversation broken up only by the sour shock of sharp white wine. She couldn't recall what they'd spoken about or what she'd worn. The last few months had left little of an impression on her hippocampus. "Which dress?" she whispered back, wearily, more to herself than to anyone else. Perhaps only to herself. She felt a little empty, unvariegated from anything else.

"Any of the ones you wore last week," the Flatmate replied. "You looked amazing in all of them. Like a model."

Leanne, snail pace, curled forwards in her seat and pressed the balls of her palms into her temples and tried to remember but drew a blank. "I'll go take a look," she said and drifted back into her bedroom. But once she had crossed the threshold to her room, a room now identical to the other bedroom in the flat by the sea, she struggled to remember why she was there.

"I don't mind which one, the green or the taupe," the voice said; must have been the voice of her Flatmate, although it sounded as if it had come from somewhere deep within. Or as if the ocean had spoken.

Which one of what? A dress, Leanne thought. *I am looking for a dress.*

Leanne searched her bedroom, leafed through countless dresses hung neatly in her closet, but couldn't recall which she had worn yesterday, let alone last week. Had something slipped down the side of her dressing table or got lost in a dark corner? *Things often slide down the sides of spaces and become hidden,* she thought. *Don't they?* She knelt down and lifted up the valance sheet of her single bed, patted around with her hands, and pulled out the only thing which was under the bed: a full black bag.

Leanne had forgotten it was there, the bag. She associated the sight of it with the scent of a particular smell, but the specifics of the smell, or the label it used to carry, she couldn't recall. It no longer smelt. She handled the sack, tugged it free, and the act of dislodging it seemed to stir up further memories, memories which had perhaps slid down, into a dark space. She looked at the bag and the bag didn't look back at her. It was just a bag, after all. But the bag made her feel something. The bag made her feel ugly. Ugly both inside and out. But the feeling of feeling something, anything again, after all this time, also made her feel awake.

A floorboard outside of her bedroom creaked. *Must be my flatmate out of the shower, wanting a dress,* Leanne thought. *Something to wear.*

Leanne stepped back from the sack and turned away from it. "I can't find what you mean." She said this to the noise outside of her room. *I can't find meaning,* she thought.

She came out of her room and searched the flat but found no one. *Am I living with a ghost?* she thought and remembered elements of the day when the sky became undone by a long, grey zipper, the day when she made it to the bus stop just in time before the heavens opened. The bag had been heavy to lug back to the flat. It felt lighter now, as she reached for it, and lifted it up to feel its weight once again. It felt as if it was made from less now. *Could it* mean *less now, too, or more?*

Leanne slid her shoes on and glided out of the flat with the bag. She travelled down the road and over the bridge and past a row of identical, bleak houses. Leanne continued to move until she reached the beach. The weak winter sun kissed the watery horizon as if it were floating directly on top of the flat ocean. The sun seemed to be held up and made more beautiful by the elegance of the sea underneath it. *The beauty of the sun,* she thought, *is compounded by everything around it. And everything around it is made more beautiful by the sun. Everything is better in perspective.*

She took her shoes off and sank her feet into wet sand and walked out until the water lapped up to the part of her leg between the ankle and the knee which she could not recall the name of. It was, after all, just another part of a body.

All this time, all these months, she'd lived here, by the sea, and had observed it daily, listened to it thanking her for staying close, but she had never stepped into its brackish water. *It should feel cold,* she thought. *And it should feel better to feel something rather than nothing.* But still, she felt nothing. Nothing physical, of hot or cold. Perhaps her soul felt a little cooler, or maybe it felt a little less haunted. Perhaps the something which had slid down the sides of her chest cavity, wedged itself deep within a dark place between her heart and her lungs and hoped to remain hidden there, had eased a baby toe free.

When she had waded out as far as she could without getting her clothing wet, she stopped and tried to make out her reflection on the surface of the water. Nothing distinct caught her eye, nothing beautiful or ugly, only ripples the colour of grey and blue and flesh and dress, which all moved in sync with her. But the coldness of the water had started to burn against her skin and the sea encouraged her on.

The girl tipped the contents of the bag out into the ocean, and the blurred reflection, with no time delay at all, copied. Dried pieces of something from her past grew larger and more beautiful as they became wet again and then dispersed and then became smaller and smaller and proportionately less important and less beautiful as they sunk.

She looked up to the sky which had become grey and considered if it might soon rain. Embracing the iced chill of the ocean against her skin and the voice of the waves, she walked forward and down. She walked until her mouth became filled with the coldness, until her voice became taken by the sea. With slow motion, she chased after the dissipating beauty with which she could never compete, but which, at least, stirred a feeling of something deep within.

I VOMITED EVERY HOUR FOR THREE DAYS AFTER YOU ENDED THINGS

Was it a purge, the sickness? Of sorts, I suppose—my body rejecting you calling time on our relationship, perhaps.

A year has passed since you told me it was over, but oh, how my skin still yearns for your touch. My heart, caged prisoner that it is, struggles to admit you don't love me anymore.

"It's for the best, Anna," you said, not shedding a single tear as you got into your car. "Ending this will give us both freedom."

"But it hurts so badly," I replied, my face a mess.

"Sometimes, love does hurt."

I am the first to admit it had become toxic. Me, crying myself to sleep each night, always wondering if you were with another woman. You, adding passcodes to your mobile phone, your laptop, building barriers of privacy even though you told me time and time again the affairs were all in my head. Me, referred to occupational health at work, the lead endocrinologist hurling accusations that I'd handled cryogenic embryos with disrespect, had stolen stock for personal use. Me, decorating your home with bug-sized cameras—

Christ, was it really necessary, threatening to change your locks? I told you I'd return the spare key when I managed to find it. And I did. Always true to my word. Like how I said I'd be yours forever. Devotion, my middle name.

I never wanted freedom from you.

⚬⚭⚬

Vomiting, the pamphlet tucked inside of the medication box tells me, is a common side effect of the egg-production stimulant *Clomifene*. It will be worth it, though—the daily injections I gave myself shortly after you sent that formal email, insisting I stop lingering outside your ward. It's hardly my fault your department is so close to the fertility treatment clinic where I work. It was mere chance our breaks coincided.

You switched shifts.

But I still watch you now, from afar, the cameras in your bedside clock, among the books on your top shelf, in the space between your kitchen cupboards, still undiscovered. You have not made yourself free at all. Shortly after you warned me to stay away, you brought another woman home and became entangled in her arms, wrapped between her legs. You appeared more caught up with her than you ever were with me. I wept into a Petri dish in my makeshift laboratory in the corner of my garage for weeks, until my project turned a corner. Now, I operate in anger, as dedicated to my current project as I had been to you.

I'd failed to precipitate quality DNA from your cells; the genetic material in shed skin decays fast, so I have learned. Faster than your apparent adoration of me. A formaldehyde scale of all my various attempts to recreate you hang suspended, lifeless, pickled, in the glass tank between my lawnmower and half empty tubs of creosote.

I grew resolute, after countless sleepless nights and failed genetic uptakes that I would never recreate you, and so my project took an unexpected bifurcation. I have focused, instead, on myself.

Harvesting and hollowing an egg had been the easy part. The hard part was extracting decent diploid DNA from root follicles, snipped from hairs entangled in my brush.

⚬

This evening, I stare at you, alone in your apartment, on my laptop screen. Dining at the table where we first made passionate love, many years ago, a ready meal for one splattered on your plate as you flick through the pages of *Auto Trader*. Your new lady is not with you tonight. By midnight then, if all goes as it should, my plan will reach fruition, come full term.

Perfect timing. I break my obsession with your image and instead, stare at me—this other version of me—lain out naked on the surgical table I repurposed from work: the same dark curls you'd loved to bury your nose in, the same blue eyes where you'd said you saw your future. I, and this carbon-copy, supine version of me share the same features, the same DNA. My genetic code weaves through every cell of this wet body, a body an echo of my own. My body, you'd said, you'd worship for eternity.

The old life-support machines I'd saved from the skip whir and beep, redundant now. The empty incubator, in which second me grew, is long switched off. My project has been near-independent for twenty-two hours. The rate at which my project grew was astounding, as my genetics and knowledge of science rebuilt my perfect reflection. Last night, I disconnected the ventilator, my cloned lungs fully formed. Full reanimation can now commence.

An injection of adrenalin through the thorax, a loud rush of wind into its lungs. My double rises from the table to a seated position on its bony buttocks. Anna begins again. Anna2. I can carry the under-nourished weight of my doppelganger for long enough, I am sure, to execute my plan. Holding the emptied needle in my hand, I too inhale, and the aromas of cyclohexamide and bleach fill my nostrils, the bitter-sweet stench of success now imminent.

At first, my intention was to create a replacement You, but when I could not get close enough for a fresh genetic sample, instead, I have created another Me. This slim, wet beast, this soul-hollow me, which sits on my steel table, cannot speak, does not attempt to engage in conversation. I am unsure if it even has the brain capacity to make noise. It feeds and drinks and passes waste, but Anna2 is not truly alive in any spiritual sense.

I dress this respiring replicate in my favourite lingerie, then drape its arm over my shoulder. She comes easily, readily, as if compliantly aware of my intentions.

The journey to my car is short. We move, hidden by the darkness of a moonless midnight, this clone of me and of your door key, and a few clinical extras wrapped in a Tesco's carrier bag. Together, we travel to your apartment.

⊰⊱

I arrive, leaving me in the passenger seat, and enter your home quietly. Tonight's the night I return your key. The chloroformed cloth works its magic on you and gives me time to guide my other self in. I sit Anna2 on the sofa next to your slumped form.

She puts up no defence as I place my surgeon's blade in your sleeping hand and with it, make one swift slice across her jugular. Her neck yawns red. Vermillion sprays, my DNA splattering your white shirt. With the blade still in your hand, I guide it, draw it up your left wrist, a red zipper opening there. This action, I replicate on your right wrist, too. You flinch and shudder, then fall still.

Side by side, I can't help but think what a beautiful couple we should have been. Whoever finds us here, sleeping our eternal red sleep, will see how you took my life from me, or this version of me, and then took your own.

An almost Shakespearean denouement of Romeo and Juliet proportions. Beautifully tragic. "Love hurts," you said, the day you ended things, just prior to saying you wanted for me to have freedom.

I toss my car keys onto the floor of your apartment and slip out into the night. I have that freedom now. Complete anonymity. It hardly hurt at all.

NICHE P*RN

On her walk to work, the woman who mixes paint sees another ex. This time the sighting is Matthew—the origin of her monochrome vision, perhaps.

◌◍◌

Matthew. He'd promised devotion to her as he'd peppered kisses like stardust on her scars. Each silver-white hyphen on her arm had sparkled for just long enough for her to have witnessed it. They'd met at university, where they'd shared passions for similar things, and Matthew became her first love, and she had been his muse.

◌◍◌

Tracking the back of his head under the dim light of dusk streetlamps, she follows him through the city, can't help herself. But when he turns, this tall spectre of her past, Matthew's face flickers into black static, then shifts into the face of a stranger.

Not Matthew.

The disappointment, a knife in her heart, but the relief she is not mad is near palpable, as she realises this stranger is not the dead ex she had once loved, just some man of similar age and height.

Over a decade ago, the real Matthew had driven off after a silly row with her, crashed his car, died in the crash, yet his face continues to appear in the place where a stranger's face should sit. She spins on her heel and runs through the rain towards the warehouse, already twenty minutes late for work.

⊛

As she runs, she relives the aftermath of Matthew's death: a knock on the door in the night, two policemen there, one of them asking *is anyone else at home*—there hadn't been—before spilling soul-destroying news. She'd cried herself to sleep after they'd left, then, on waking, she'd found herself immersed in a world composed only of whites, blacks, and greys.

Referrals from doctors and countless tests had revealed no phys-iological reason for her condition.

Your heart exists in such a deficit, the psychologist had said, *your retina have simply given up.*

⊛

How could it possibly have been Matthew, that stranger on my walk to work, she thinks, angry with herself for following, scared her sightings are tugging at the strings which hold reality together. At work, she cries in the toilet cubicle while pulling off her sweater, then wipes her tears and hurriedly tugs on stained overalls. After collecting herself, or most of herself, she walks out onto the warehouse floor to mix paint all night.

Her first customer order pops up on the screen. Antique Plum. A shade of purple she hasn't seen in what feels like forever. The automated system makes her job simple, though, and her boss doesn't seem to have noticed her oblivion to the differences between the myriad colours of stock paint, all grey hues through her eyes.

After typing in the mixing codes, she waits for the cumbersome stock paint vessels to grind into life. As each trough dispatches a precise amount of paint, she switches on the extractor fan and then the industrial whisk.

To be in love. Her heart craves for something, someone, as she watches a spectrum of gunmetal waterfall into the tank. The nightshifts drag, but at least at work, she has purpose. At home, all she does is sleep, or try to, each day the same: elephant grey, and spent in a bed too large for one. Inside, she yearns for affection. To be in love keeps the face-ghosts at bay. But all adult men wear the fluctuating skin of the love she has lost. So she avoids eye contact with most.

⸙

A year back, she'd worked her first day-shift alongside James. But James—father of four, twice her age—his face had shifted into that of Matthew's. She'd signed herself out sick immediately, marched home straight away, then she'd emailed her boss stating she could not work with a man. After the email, her boss Leanne gave her the solo night shift.

Waking at 1am to fling on clothes and walk two miles for eight hours labour on minimum wage was hard, but at least, when working alone, she didn't have to look at James—or Matthew's face etched into where James' face should've been, Matthew's features nibbling at the edges until James became Matthew.

⚜

The only glimmer of hope, of colour, she had witnessed in recent years had been when a stranger—Julian, his name badge had said—had served her in a cafe. As he'd read her name from the cup and passed her *one takeaway decaf Earl Grey*, the tone of his voice had lifted her chin from her chest, and her face had met his.

His smile. The sparkle in his eyes. Julian had been a rarity because his face had remained his own.

"Milk?" he had asked. A burst in her chest. The world had fallen back into colour for a split second. But it'd scared her. Black and white and ghosts of her past lover had felt safer, maybe, than the greenness in Julian's eyes. She had told herself she would never return to that coffee shop.

After the incident with Julian, the fleck of green, she had contacted another specialist. The specialist said he had only seen her condition before as an inherited condition, in which children were born with achromatopsia, retaining it for life, or as a temporary indecision of the eye, when the eye is overexposed to vivid brightness and then returned to a duller view, *like when you go out into the sunshine,* he had said, *and stare up at the fluorescent blue of a summer sky, and then go back inside. The eye, having been over-stimulated, the optic neurone, hyperpolarised, means the brain only allows itself to see in muted shades until the retina readjusts.*

But other than what had happened with Julian, her world remains a place of darkness and ghosts.

⚜

"Please come and see me at nine." Leanne's voice, shrill in her ear piece.

Nine am comes. She switches the machine to automatic stir, sure the vat of Antique Plum will be fine, and heads to Leanne's office, expecting a sanction for lateness, maybe a dismissal.

"Do you need to take some leave?" Leanne asks.

"I'm sorry for being late."

"That's not the reason I've called you in." Leanne leans forwards, clasps her hands together on the desk, steeples her index fingers.

"Is it the paint?" Perhaps her inability to truly see what she creates has started to affect her output. As much as she loathes the commute, her job allows her to work alone, undisturbed. A knot balls in her gut.

"Relax, you're safe here. I'm very happy with what you do. Just concerned about your mental health—"

"I'm fine." The woman who mixes paint pulls down the sleeves of her overall, strategically moves a bangle. *My face,* she thinks, *I can wear like a mask, to convey the illusion I'm holding things together. But my arms may give off a different message.*

"We're going out next Friday, a bunch of us. Tacos, beers. Would you like to come?"

"No. Thank you. I'm okay, really I am." She stands. "Is there anything else?"

"No." Leanne tilts her head and offers a tight-lipped smile. "I'm worried about you, that's all."

The woman who mixes paint returns to her mixing station and works the rest of her shift in silence, pouring, stirring gloop, sticking distribution labels on cans, all the while reflecting on the uncomfortable conversation. At the end of her shift, she showers, changes her clothes, and sets off for home.

Except her feet take her to the coffee shop, the venue she'd sworn she'd never visit again as the glimpse of colour in Julian's eyes had been too much, but here she finds herself, pushing open the door.

Julian stands at the counter, shaking chocolate sprinkles onto someone's latte. Olive skin, green eyes, red shirt, there he is, in full technicolour. Julian, with his face remaining his own. She holds his name in her mind, lets it repeat there, over and over, and basks in all the colours.

There are no ghosts. There is nothing to haunt me here, she thinks, *only a few customers and the vibrancy of Julian, with his own face, his red shirt, green eyes, and my heart. To be in love again, this is what I need. Not tacos and beers with colleagues.*

She approaches the counter. Her words eventually come. "Decaf Earl Grey, please."

"Sure thing. You've paint in your hair." Julian reaches across to show her where. As she raises her arm to inspect the clump, her hand brushes against his. Something more than colour erupts inside her. She will ask him out. *Ask him out,* her myocardial tissues sing.

"Thanks," she says, instead. "It's a bugger to wash out."

"This might help." He passes a moistened serviette. "I use that shade a lot, Blush Pink, or is it Never Been Kissed?" He winks. "Are you an artist too?"

"Me? No. I work in the factory over the road. Mixing." She picks up the serviette and presses it against her hair. "Antique Plum."

A memory resurfaces. *Is that Matthew's face, superimposing itself over Julian's?* She steps back, but the slipped visage fades before she has a chance to be certain. The memory, however, of a passion she has long since packed away, remains. Yes, she *had* been an artist once, at university. Sketching, painting, this was how she had bonded with Matthew. They'd read Fine Art together, connecting over their love for Wayne Thiebaud, Georges Rouault, Pablo Picasso, and other painters who used thick, pasty lines, strong primary colours. She and Matthew had adored masterpieces which featured aloof, bohemian subjects—harlequins, jesters, magicians, performers—all depicted in bold, colourful ways.

Are you? This is what she wanted to say, but a queue has formed behind her and the green of Julian's eyes, the peach of his lips starts to hurt her chest.

"Come again soon," he says.

She leaves, realising halfway home she forgot to wait for the tea she had ordered.

☙❧

Underneath her bed is a small stash of art materials from a time gone by. She pulls the easel out, the paint set, a canvas, and paints, but the canvas becomes a tumultuous storm of black. Despite each small paint tube labelled with a descriptive name, her work just looks like darkness to her. The canvas corner leaves a ding in the wall as she tosses it across her bedsit. She cries herself to sleep.

In the night she wakes and thinks of Julian, her Bringer of Colour. It's been so long since a man has touched her in a way she desires. Eyes crimped, she forces his face into her mind, the green of his eyes appearing. She searches on her laptop for something to help release the energy accruing in her groin.

<BIG COCKS>

<THREESOMES>

She tries all night, watching, watching, thinking about Julian, as people go at each other hard on the fifteen-inch screen, but she cannot come, but as she tries, as she thinks of Julian, and looks at dirty videos, suggestions of colour flicker in her peripheral vision.

But the porn is not enough. *This is not the same,* she thinks, *as having Julian here in my bed,* so she gives up and falls asleep, unsatisfied. A nubile woman on the screen continues to thrust a hard thing in and out of herself until the laptop battery drains.

☙❧

The next day after work, intrigue draws her back to the coffee shop. Her feet fall one in front of the other all the way there, as if pulled along by a taut string. And there he is, at the other end of the counter, topping up cookies in a jar: Julian. The door closes behind her. Julian looks up. Green. Chocolate brown. Gold. Red. Azure blue. A rainbow pours into her eyes. Lust, like a long-lost friend, greets her. *Julian.*

"Decaf Earl Grey?" he asks. "On the house. You never took yesterday's."

She thanks him. Her heart thrums in her chest, her stomach churns with lust. The coffee shop door swings open.

A redhead, face heavy with foundation, false eyelashes, thick brown eyeliner, rouged, pouting lips, the sort you have to inject, enters the cafe. The woman who mixes paint sees all of this in colour and touches her own face, struggles to recall the last time she had made such an effort with her own appearance. The redhead slinks in front of her, reaches across the counter, a gesture reciprocated by Julian, and plants a kiss on Julian's lips.

"Hey baby, thought I'd surprise you at work," the redhead says.

Perhaps this is what men want, the woman who mixes paint thinks, feeling invisible, like a ghost herself. Julian's green eyes become black, and the flame-coloured hair of the girl, his lover, fades to grey, as the achromatic shroud re-descends. Once more, the woman who mixes paint leaves the cafe quickly, without her tea.

On her walk home, she musters up courage, decides to stare at strangers, challenges herself to force the world into colour. But the faces all shift into ghosts of Matthew. *Love will always leave me,* she thinks, *in one way or another, eventually. Maybe I am not enough.*

At home, she flops onto her unmade bed and lifts open the lid of her laptop. *Julian, Julian, Julian,* she sings his name in her head, *I'll make him want me.* To be determined, to hyper-focus, is all she can do to ward off tears. She visits a website, searches there for something to bring the colour back, make her ghosts disappear.

<AMATEUR>

<TEEN>

< MILF>

She ploughs through videos, studying the women, their Hollywood bodies, Brazilian waxes, flamboyant make-up, styled hair. As she touches herself, attempts to lose herself in the moment, colour tickles at the edges of her thoughts, but dissipates like an interrupted dream. *I will never be good enough for Julian.* She tries to push negative thoughts from her head and rubs harder, faster, but the intrusive thoughts prevail. *Because this vibrant chaos of sound and colour is what men like Julian want and I am damaged and trapped in a black and white world.* Harder, faster, she touches herself to try and override these feelings.

<HENTAI>

<COSPLAY>

She clicks on more links, bears witness to things she's never heard of before.

<DVDA>

<BBW>

<CUCKOLD>

<BUKKAKE>

<BONDAGE>

A woman bound at the ankles, wrists tethered behind her back, suspended in some kind of swing, a choker circuiting her neck. The woman's hair, scraped back, as if it had been under a wig. Three men, going at it. Thrusting. The woman's eyes, wide, whites exposed. The bound woman cannot scream. A ball gags her. The bound woman's make-up runs, perspiration trickles black mascara cobwebs down her pale cheeks and forehead as she lies there, shackled to the seat. Blue fingernails scratch at the leather around her wrists. The bound woman's lipstick smears over her mouth, around her mouth as she is touched, as she writhes, until her mouth appears three times the size it naturally is. One man comes hard. The woman who mixes paint notices this. She notices it in all its colourful glory—and it is the first male orgasm she has seen in any of the movies.

Spunk ribbons out over the bound woman, a woman who has consented to being filmed, but a woman nonetheless who appears distraught. A mess. Her face, smeared, smudged, ruined, like that of a cream-pied clown. *The face, the colours of it*—blue, white, red, brown—she sees these colours as she rubs herself and thinks of Julian—*is it the face of a distraught woman or a scared clown*, the woman who mixes paint thinks. *Either or, irrespective, this must be what men want.*

<CLOWN PORN>

She types this into the search box and the word COULROPHILIA appears. She clicks this word, rubs harder on her clit, thinks of Julian.

Watches. Rubs. Watches. Thinks.

This is what men want.

Colourful images nip at the corner of her thoughts. The redhead. Overfilled rouge lips. Black faux-eyelashes, fanned out, framing her eyes, Clockwork Orange, Kubrick-esque. *This is what men like,* she thinks, *what Julian likes.*

She still cannot come. *Julian.* She thinks of him, how to win him for herself. Yanking down the tarnished mirror from her wall, she stares into it. At least, in the mirror, she does not see the ghost of Matthew, her past lover. She only sees herself. Pale.

But could be more so.

Large eyes which could be made to appear bigger, brighter.

Thin lips, barely there.

The exaggerated screams of a restrained woman dressed in next to nothing, bunched hair, make-up like Harley Quinn, emerge from the laptop, which lies on its side, discarded on the floor.

From her drawer, the woman who mixes paint takes out her cutting station to help make herself prettier. *Prettier for Julian. Good enough for a life in colour.* And for a life in colour, she decides, she needs to exist in colour herself.

Opening up old scars on her wrists with tens of small cuts, balloons of crimson swell and create a palette of red with which she will decorate her mouth. She does not cut too deeply, like she nearly did before, after the policemen knocked on her door. Now, she does not want to die. In this moment, she has someone to live for.

She squeezes out just enough vermillion to stain her lips and the red smears over her mouth easily. Messy. She sees her lips, red, in the mirror, and colours herself in more and thinks of Julian. In her crazed flurry, spittle collects at the edges of her mouth. The pigment doesn't hold.

Her university paint set. She retrieves it from under her bed, pops off the cap from Cadmium Red 0003 and works the paste into and around her mouth. 0007 Azure Sky calls next. She drags three thick blue slugs from each eye to her hairline. Picasso would be proud. *Blue brings out the amber tone of my irises, complementary colours.* She recalls her artist's training. *Matthew would be proud,* she thinks, *of this woman who mixes paint* as she mixes more paint. Sunset Yellow 0002 goes on next.

Claggy spirals of it on each cheek. She thinks of Matthew, Matthew and Julian, their faces merging in her mind.

Greens. She fumbles through shades, seeing each one radiantly at long last, and selects Vine 0014, then drips on tears below her lower lashes, tears of a clown. Her own tears come and fall and dribble, blending, blending. Her face becomes a colour wheel.

The redhead. How vibrant her hair had looked as she had whipped it over her shoulders, before she'd reached across and kissed Julian, shutting back off the colours. The woman who mixes paint grabs the red tube again and smears what is left of it into her hair, back-combing it in for volume.

He will want me like this, choose me over her, she thinks as she slips half-dressed out the door, and into the hours of dusk. She charges through the cityscape. Early office workers scream and dash from her path. She stares each one in the eye, the men, their faces full, but only with terror, not the faces of lost love.

She passes the coffee shop, still closed. It is too early. Thoughts of Julian dribble streaks of green and red and brown into her peripheral vision, eradicating black and white ghosts. But she wants more, wants to see everything in full colour, wants to be colour, wants Julian to see her in all her glory.

She will visit his cafe as soon as it opens, but first she visits her place of work.

Pulling her staff card out from her pyjama bottom pocket, the cream of them stained red with the blood from her wrists, she scans into the warehouse. The factory is empty. She heads to her mixing unit, lifts open the lids of the stock paint vats and invisible scarves of volatile organic compound vapours rise into the air. With her filthy hands, she reaches in, scoops out mouthfuls of emulsion. Aquamarine, Mimosa Yellow, Nectarine. No more ghosts, no more greyscale. She swallows it all, gulp after gulp, fills herself with colour.

Paint streams down her chin and breasts. *Both inside and out, a circus of technicolour shades, this is how I need Julian to see me.* She chokes, slumps against the massive vat as dizziness takes over. One more thought comes before she loses consciousness:

This is what men want.

GARDEN PATH

I magine a dense, cold forest: a liminal place; dim, like the dying glow of a near-spent candle at midnight; crisp and grim, all bombed, derelict church. Well, the forest at the end of the garden path was like this. And this forest, this forest at the end of the path, was unlike any forest you've ever ventured into before. A dark magic—of sorts—lurked within it.

—But maybe it was not the forest itself that was bad—how, one might ponder, could a tree be wicked? Perhaps there was a creature, some sort of monster, who resided underneath or inside of the branch-rich holt who smacked of evil?

☙❧

The inhabitants of the hamlet of Monkton knew it unwise to venture into the grounds of the nearby forest, for once, rumour has it, a long time ago, a distant, long-lost relative of a friend of a friend of someone your ancestors may or may not have known attempted to build a small dwelling within these woods. On completion, they abandoned their project and relocated to a village on the other side of the country. What had caused them to flee? Talk ricocheted from one household to the next: they must've encountered some sort of maleficent creature in the woods.

What was this monster? A gremlin? An ogre? A witch or a wizard? No-one was quite sure really, but whatever it was became known as The Witchard.

"The Witchard owns a frightening face with deep-sunk eyes, devoid of good light, like the morning after the night before. The fearful creature has long white hair; rat tails full of more knots than a well-trained sailor would ever be able to unfashion."

"It wears a cloak of dried autumn foliage woven together with iridescent cobwebs and speaks in screams."

"The forest belongs to The Witchard. Stay out of the woods."

No one directly had ever witnessed The Witchard themself, with their own eyes. Yet, everyone knew of a story of someone who had come across it, or knew a story about someone who most certainly had, and as a result, the forest became the domain of The Witchard, and everyone felt best to keep away.

Everyone except for a young couple: Melody and Sebastian.

⊂ЯᎢↃ

Melody and Sebastian's extended families didn't get along. At all. And the pair wished for nothing more than to escape from wagging tongues, bossy parents, and all their other angry elders. So when Melody and Sebastian found themselves with child, they decided to flee from the hamlet of Monkton and start afresh, alone. Each was all the other needed. And neither of them minded trees and darkness that much—in fact, compared to the gossip and the stress of Monkton, the solitude and peace of the forest seemed like a pleasant alternative.

"Monsters aren't real anyway," Melody said to Sebastian. "Are they?"

"No, of course not," Sebastian replied.

After a few weeks of secretive planning, at the break of dawn, they rode off into the forest. Sebastian's horse, Applejack, towed a large cart in which the couple had been careful to pack everything they needed for their relocation. It'd taken a lot of coordination and thrifting, but they had enough supplies to really make a go of it. But alas, Applejack's cart was heavy. Sebastian knew it would be a long journey and his horse would grow tired fast.

"Poor old Applejack," said Sebastian. They had been riding for several hours, Monkton already a distant memory. He patted the sweating beast's neck. "Let's take a short break here so our horses can rest for a moment." Mottled light shone through the thick canopy overhead, and the musty air was dry and cold. Sebastian pulled on the reins and brought his trusty Clydesdale to halt alongside a tremendous old oak, perhaps the oldest oak in the forest, an archaic sentinel, and then he jumped down and encouraged Melody to dismount from her horse too.

The crunch of forest litter underfoot. The bray of tired horses nodding and swatting flies with their tails. "It's beautiful," Melody said, pressing her palm up against the bark of the tallest, widest tree she had ever set eyes upon. "Isn't it, Sebastian?"

"Yes," Sebastian replied. "But not as beautiful as you."

With his hands on his hips, he gazed up at the girth of the great oak. There, deep within the forest, the giant tree stood out like a beacon, a proud grandfather amongst its vertically-challenged peers—

ash, hawthorn, holly and hazel. Melody tethered her mare and wandered around the other side of the great wooden tree.

With excitement in her voice, she beckoned her lover, for there, on the other side of the majestic oak, Melody saw the abandoned house that'd been built decades ago. The great oak, landmark that it was, stood on the edge of its garden. With rose-coloured shutters, four chimneys, and a half-moon-shaped garden, the house appeared exactly as foretold. Up its wood-panelled side, years of ivy growth climbed.

"Shall we?" Melody asked, and took her lover by the hand and led him up the garden path. A creak, an echo, as she pushed the stiff front door ajar. They entered the house together and Melody's broad smile informed Sebastian it would become their home despite it needing a lot of work. And he agreed. Because he loved her with all his heart. And because it was a rather welcoming building.

"Yes, it will become our home," he agreed, "and yes, it will save us much time not having to start from scratch."

"It's perfect," Melody exclaimed. She pulled her beau from small room to small room. "Bedroom. Bathroom. Kitchen. Front room. Each with its own wood burner for heating and cooking." She cried with happiness and pregnancy hormones and kissed Sebastian passionately. From within her heavy belly, their first child kicked.

"Place your hand. Here. Can you feel our child?" Another smile filled her face. A smile which Sebastian felt could light up the darkest room of their new home and even the most lightless parts of the forest.

"Yes. Not long now," said Sebastian. He returned her smile with one of his own. The pair set about cleaning up and unpacking.

CR&SO

The pair went about their new life together, and were, on the whole, exceptionally happy alone together in their home within the heart of the forest. Fallen trees provided plentiful fuel for the fire each evening. Mushrooms, nuts and berries, and wild rabbit kept their tummies full. But with Melody's belly swelling more each day, there came a point at which foraged fruits and trapped meats no longer satiated her cravings. The baby had a never-ending hunger. Melody wanted bread. Pastries. Carbs. And for bread and pastries, a journey back into the village was required. So, one cold winter's afternoon, wrapped in thick furs, Sebastian mounted Applejack and prepared to leave the forest for the first time in months. It would be a lonesome, cold, quest, but a worthy trip to fetch something substantial with which to feed his hungry wife.

Melody bid him farewell and set about the task she had designated herself to complete while he was away: pulling weeds from the garden path. The *garden could be magnificent by spring,* she thought, *with a little care and effort.*

Time combed its skeletal fingers through the treetops and played with the shape of the shadows as she worked and worked until, eventually, the sun began to set. *It should've been a short gallop there and back, without the weight of the cart,* she thought, but as the sun finally set, there was still no sign of Sebastian's return.

Outside, the black cloak of a winter's night fell rapidly down. Melody, by candlelight, moved from room to room and battened closed the windows to try to keep the place warm. Every innocent creak of wood made her jump. She'd never had to go to bed alone there before. Would tonight be the first time? She felt unsafe. She rubbed her aching pelvis, thumbed and kneaded awkwardly the small of her own lower back, massaged her tender bump. *Surely my lover should be home by now?*

Sat huddled by the fire, her senses sharp to every bump and hoot the forest gave up, her anxiety peaked around midnight. The last log, coming soon to an end, would be followed by pure darkness. The young girl, unable to sleep, full of wriggling babe, contemplated slipping on her hobnail boots and coat. If she tore down a branch from the oak at the end of the garden path, with a long snatch of hessian sack wrapped around its end, she could prepare a make-shift torch. With fire on a stick, she could head out into the night, begin the quest to find her lover. *Has he fallen from his horse? Is my darling hurt?* Her baby kicked. She comforted it with the palm of her hand. "There, there, sweetness. There, there."

In preparation for the worst case scenario, she gathered a small medical kit—bandages and balms. And then, while pulling on her coat, she let out an audible sigh of relief as at last, the front door swung open and her lover's voice whistled in on the wind.

"Melody." Sebastian stumbled towards her, his eyes bloodshot, his hair swept like tossed salad. "Melody, darling. Thank the Heavens and prayers-be to the Gods that reside within them." He paused, weary, and steadied himself on the door frame. "I thought I'd never find you."

"Where have you been?" Melody peppered him with kisses, took his sack, and led him through to their bedroom. "You look exhausted. Please, rest. Get into bed."

"I've been traipsing the forest for what has felt like a lifetime of eternities. Couldn't find it. You. The house. Our house." His words came out staccato as he collapsed onto the goose down quilt. "The great oak out front—I couldn't find it. Couldn't find anything familiar that would lead me back to you. Everything… everything was not in its place. I think… I know… our house has moved." Melody gasped. "I searched for hours, retracing my route countless times. I quested into and out of the forest again and again." She held her lover as he shook. He'd been certain he'd not taken a different path than the one he'd initially made his departure by.

"The forest, Melody. There is no other way to explain it. There is a bad magic in the forest. Things jump around within it."

⚬

The next morning, they feasted on the bounty Sebastian had brought back from the village and, a little calmer in the light of day, discussed how to tackle the apparent shifting foundations of the house they'd fallen in love with.

"A rope. We must tether ourselves to our home with rope when we come and go." This was Melody's idea. And Sebastian agreed to it. And so, later that afternoon, the giant oak, part and parcel of the property, found itself with two strands of golden rope fastened around its girth, an anchorage of sorts, with which, on any adventure away from their abode, they agreed they would attach to themselves to. The rope sparkled and glinted whenever light managed to make its way down through the treetop ceiling and through the soupy forest atmosphere.

Their firstborn came along later that day: perhaps it had been the stress of the day before, the relief of coming up with a plan with the tree and the rope so they could still explore their surroundings safely. Perhaps it had just been the fact that it had been nine months since Melody and Sebastian had had their first moment of unbridled passion at the edge of the river while their families were all at the market. None of this mattered, not really, not in this moment as their baby arrived healthy and bawling and a good weight too, and Melody did not bleed out. With pregnancy and childbirth, the journey is nowhere near as important as the destination, they both agreed, and they named the young boy Sylvain, *'forest dweller'*.

☙❧

Whenever Melody or Sebastian ventured out—together, alone, or with their new baby—they would tie the golden cord around their waists and it would help them find their way home. When Sebastian went out to chop and lumber wood with the rope around his middle, Melody would spy the taut rope which demarcated his path. Her eye would follow the line of glinting rope from the oak, down the garden path, until the rope became lost to the dense foliage and darkness of the forest. Lost in the darkness, but safe, safe around her darling's stomach, and her darling, safe, within the taut loop of rope.

Each afternoon, sat in her nursing chair, fireside, looking out of the window, babe in arms, she would sit and wait and watch until dusk for the golden rope to slacken. As the rope hit the floor, she knew her love was within a stone's throw from home, and her heart had cause to celebrate.

☙❧

For some time, they continued to live happily, reassured by the ropes which countered their concerns about the eloping behaviour of their restless house. Their existence within the forest was humble, but by staying within the woods, they remained shielded from the snooping eyes and curt tongues of the village-folk. Despite its mysterious abilities to relocate their house *ad hoc*, the forest had enchanted them and had—so far—brought along with its magical powers no harm.

☙❧

Several seasons passed. A second babe came along. Sylvain, the eldest, a now toddling boy, became big brother to a girl. The girl was a plump dumpling of a thing, and still so new, she'd yet to be named.

Melody and Sebastian were over the moon, but now with growing kin, Sebastian found himself making more journeys within the forest to bring back firewood and more journeys further afield into the village and beyond in search of food. Flour, oil, eggs, and sugar-cane were available in Monkton. He'd travel for days at a time away from his family to trade for such commodities with bags of kindling.

The wood of the forest had special properties. Not only when chopped, was it a gorgeous flesh shade of peach, but it burned slowly and well and without too much smoke and the smoke it did yield blew out of chimney tops like glittering pinched-pink scarfs. In the village, the demand for 'Witchard wood' grew and Sebastian found himself gone for three or four days at a time, chopping and selling logs in order to purchase food for his family.

Each day brought with it tremendous jumps—of the house, and in the development of their two young babes. Their youngest, yet with name, had started to smile—although it was a smile only perhaps a mother could love—and their eldest, Sylvain, had started to babble. His first almost-word-like sound came only moments after Sebastian had set off on a three-day expedition.

Three days passed, through which time, Sylvian's babbles became increasingly clear.

Melody was beyond excited at the thought of her love returning that evening as promised. She was eager for him to be present if their boy was going to say 'mumma' or 'da-da' for the first time. Three days had felt like three months to her, alone with two small babes in the woods, with such exciting news to share.

But she did adore her home amongst the trees. One of the things Melody loved most was the peculiar variety of edible nuts and berries that forest life proffered. That day, keen to busy herself while waiting for Sebastian to return, she decided to explore the floors of the forest. She wished to collect a new berry she'd seen but had not tasted yet. Would the fruit be in the same place she's spotted them in earlier in the week? Most likely not. But she was sure she'd find the berries somewhere, with a little effort. And when she did, she'd pick enough to create something delicious with for Sebastian, to celebrate his return: jam perhaps, to smother the bread she'd sent him out to purchase.

With both babes strapped to her body, one front, one back, a basket in her hand, and her golden rope attached to her waist, she travelled through the forest like a nomad. Her youngest slept like a dream through the day only waking for feeds and changes. *If only she slept so well at night,* Melody would think whilst rocking and nursing the crying wee girl from sundown to sunrise. Sylvain, her eldest, protested about being kept tight in the sling for he was very much awake. He thumped her on her shoulder with his pudgy hands. He pulled on her hair, knocked nuts and mushrooms out from her basket with his squishy foot. *Tssk,* she muttered. *Tssk.* She decided to let him down. This slowed her pace but lightened her load and she was in no particular rush.

Releasing Sylvain proved to be useful. He, as fast as a scared cat, with a stubby index finger, pointed out the first huge patch of sweet, ripe fruit some distance from where Melody stood. Pink fleshy berries in clusters grew on the ground beneath large, veined, purple leaves. Each berry was composed of two parts, and the two parts together resembled pouting, juicy lips.

"Mmmmm," Sylvain hummed and bent down closer to his treasure. "Bewwy."

"Oh Sylvain. Clever boy. Did you just say *berry?* Your first proper word. Berry! Say it again." Melody, proud mother, walked over to her son and crouched to meet his eyes and encouraged him to find his vocal cords. She helped him part back leaves so he could yank free a fruit. "Go ahead, pick one. Try it."

"Bewwy yummy?" he asked, all gummy-grin and spittle. Melody nodded at her eldest then glanced down at her second-born who was still swaddled tight, still content, still sleeping, firmly pressed against her bosom. The little girl's cheeks were as pink as the berries. *Berry* Melody thought. She kissed her tiny daughter on the crown of her head. *We shall call you Berry.* Her heart swelled with excitement at the thought of announcing her suggestion to her beloved on his return.

Sylvain yanked his first berry free from its stem. The boy jumped back in shock—the firm pluck, berry from stem, released a piercing screech. Even though Melody had an idea of the sound the berry might make, it still took her by surprise.

The intriguing plant's tendrils, leaves, and berries covered a large swathe of the forest floor. A thick and velvet blanket of temptation. Black whilst growing and pink when ripe, the berries were a fair size. Childhood memories of her great grandmother describing the sweet tang of the rich fruit—'screechberries' she had called them—flooded her thoughts—the bountiful plant food within the forest and decorating its boundaries had been one of the original reasons why folk had tried to live within it years ago.

"Oh my," she laughed softly. Her boy stood stock-still: wide-eyed, muddled somewhere between fear and joy in response to the ear-piercing sound. "That really was quite loud, wasn't it? Here, taste it." She plucked the calyx out from the body of the peculiar fruit and split it in two. The berry, now half a lip, screeched loudly again as it was torn. She passed half to her son. What a cacophony. The pair of them both chuckled this time. In her mouth, rich juices burst free. The berry tasted good. Beyond good. Sylvain chewed and on opening his mouth, berry-voiced screams released with each chomp of the gums. Melody picked as many as she could but could hold only three or four in her palm at a time.

Young Sylvain's fingertips and cheeks became smeared with blood-red juices. His maw looked like he'd consumed fresh flesh. Melody tried to wipe him clean with a dock leaf to no avail.

They lollygagged around, filling their bellies and the basket as they did so, until the rare, tiger-stripes of light began to fade further and Melody felt the familiar chill of evening in the air. She lifted her eldest up and wrapped his small, sticky body up once more, and placed him safely and tightly against her tired spine for the return journey. Taut golden thread would lead the way back to their rootless house—for who knew where their cottage might now rest?

She started to walk into the rope, hurling great loops of it up and over her shoulder, careful not to harm her children as she did so. Each yank took her a little closer to comfort, a step closer to home. She paused briefly to rub dirt from her face, but when she opened her eyes, there, as clear as the nose on her face, sat a second house.

⁂

Different to her own cuckoo's nest, this house was only half the size. One solitary chimney from which no smoke came decorated its roof. Its garden flourished with the most beautiful selection of vegetation and flowers she'd ever seen.

Above the house, through a break in the canopy, the scant light of dusk travelled down, illuminating with a warm golden glow this strange finding. Vibrant and buzzing with colourful petals and fruits and vegetables in all manner of shapes, shades and sizes, the garden was delightful. Bumbling bees darted in and out of hollyhock trumpets, spiral tendrils of courgette wound up and around cane frames, bushes filled with myriad berries in all shades of the rainbow sparkled light like jewels. Enthralled—for her own garden had yielded nothing but dirt and stubborn weeds—Melody placed her overflowing basket of berries by her feet and straightened her back. Could she creep a little closer to explore the bountiful garden?

"Oh my. I wonder—" she said but both babes were fast asleep.

"Clear off."

A voice; from the cottage window?

Melody looked to the house. At the window, a flash-frost of snow-white hair. From within the mess of tangles, beetle-black eyes glinted out at her, or so she thought. But then, in a blink of an eye, the window became again a dark, empty square. Her heart bashed hard and fast. Someone had caught her snooping. She span around, pulled on her golden rope, and instructed her legs to run.

"Clear off. Get out of my forest. Unless—" The voice came loud again, stealing Melody's attention. It paused. "Unless… you have something for me?"

Melody turned back around to face the property. If there was someone else living in the forest, if she and Sebastian did indeed have a neighbour, then wouldn't it be best to try and be 'neighbourly'? To try and get along? She wasn't sure if she believed in magic anyway, or curses, or witches and wizards. She'd often wondered about the night when Sebastian claimed the house had moved—had perhaps proud Sebastian gotten lost instead and been too embarrassed to admit it? Had he merely stopped off at the tavern on the way home to sample the mead only to find himself readily destitute and a little befuddled with drink? Maybe her home hadn't shifted one inch at all.

An instinct to protect her young burned deep within her gut but her legs were dog-tired and, alas, refused to respond. Whoever this person was, if they wished her harm, she feared she would not be able to outrun it anyway. *We've made ourselves a home here. No more running away.*

"I've berries," she said. Her voice came out quietly. She cleared her throat and spoke again. "Screechberries. Would you like some?"

Again, a white mass of hair appeared at the window, beneath it, a cape of tessellated dry leaves. Melody sucked in a sharp breath and took several steps back.

"Does it look like I need berries, girl?" The words, like frosty stalactites prickled out through the gaps between the old timbers of the cottage's walls, barked up Melody's spine, icing every vertebra as they travelled.

Melody panicked. What else did she have to offer? Other than the clothes she was wearing, the golden rope hanging in reams over her shoulder, fastened at her waist, and her precious babes strapped to her body, she had nothing left to give.

"What do you need?" she asked.

A long silence followed. Then, the being spoke again: "You've a young man, haven't you? I've seen him taking more than his fair share; carrying wood out of the forest. My forest. Selling it to villagers. Through the trees, I see everything."

Melody twisted on her heel faster than a weathercock on a windy day and became tangled in rope. She was certain she'd heard something creeping up behind her. Had it been a branch snapping underfoot? Or was something else with her, in the woods outside of the pop-up cottage? She looked around. Out of the corner of her eye, she could have sworn an old knot in a thick trunk winked at her. A squirrel scarpered up the same tree. *Must have been the squirrel*, she told herself. Her heart banged at triple speed. She cupped her youngest babe's head.

"Yes. Sebastian. Love of my life," she eventually replied, with caution in her voice.

"Take take take. It's all anyone ever does from my forest. No one gives back."

"I'm sorry." Melody held her rope and both of her children tighter than she'd ever done before.

"I am in need of something. From you. Spells and curses only stretch so far. I'm weak in strength, both physical and magical, for I'm old—almost as old as the forest itself. I am old and I am cold."

"Please. Is there anything I can do? Sebastian—he'll be back soon. *Really* soon. Perhaps he could be of help too?"

Sobs came from the cottage. And with the sobbing, the boughs of the trees around Melody seemed to sag, as if weeping with their Witchard. Melody's fear lessened. The being spoke again.

"I need wood, girl. Wood. Bring me chopped wood, and you can remain in the forest. I'm too old to drag and saw it myself. These are tired hands. And your husband—he must take less. It's not sustainable to reap more than you sow." Young Berry was rousing from sleep. Young Berry would soon be keen to feed at her breast, no doubt. Melody smoothed a wisp of blonde hair from her baby girl's face. "I must return home now. We'll make amends, I assure you. I'll be back with wood. We've plenty to spare."

"Of course."

Melody looked back at the window. There was no longer any sign of anyone there. The ancient voice had retracted to a whisper which was almost lost to the gentle evening breeze: "Follow your golden rope, girl. Follow your golden rope."

Melody scanned her surroundings then took a deep breath and crept up The Witchard's garden path. She tied the far end of her golden rope to the knocker of the front door to help her relocate the mysterious cottage later. First, she would return home, deposit her fruit harvest, and then she would bring wood to The Witchard before sunset; she'd enough time before Sebastian was due to return. She'd just need to follow the rope.

Melody made it back home. There, she emptied her basket of berries into a bowl, nursed her baby girl, then filled the basket with chunks of wood and kindling. Once more with her two babies strapped to her, she set back out, following the golden rope all the way back to The Witchard's cottage. She wanted to appease The Witchard, to ensure their place within the woods was safe, and then she wished to return home. The fire would need stoking until it roared, until it became angry enough to warm up her home so her baby girl would doze. And then she had plans to make delicious jam.

It was a seemingly much shorter journey, on the return to The Witchard's cottage, and on her arrival, Melody stacked a large pile of chopped wood neatly to the side of The Witchard's door. She undid the loop of golden string from the door handle—*I'll never come back here alone,* she thought, *never*—and then she began to walk away from the cottage.

"Thank you girl. For giving back to the forest." The voice broke through the silence of dusk. "The forest may thank you, in due turn… Then again, it may not." Small mounds of earth were dotted in between the flora of The Witchard's garden, each pierced with a make-shift inverted cross of dried branches. Melody shuddered and her pace quickened. She could not wait to get back to the safety of her own abode.

"Dead creatures, dear girl. Found, dead creatures of the forest. Nothing to fear." Was The Witchard watching her? Could the creepy being read her thoughts? *Faster, I must walk faster,* Melody thought, her legs breaking into run. "Rot. Decay. Nature's loop. Keeps my soil fertile." Melody sprinted down the last few feet of the path and off into the woods, following her golden rope.

A distance away, her breath coming hard and fast, her babies heavy, her legs weak for it had been a long and arduous day, she braved a turn to look back behind her; The Witchard's house with its beautiful gardens no longer in sight. Only a hazy trail of glitter-pink smoke billowed in the distance, snaking its way between and around skeletal branches.

❦

On her return home, she fed Berry up, then lay her down in a basket in the living room. Next, she pulled out a stack of paper and pencils for Sylvain to scribble with until bedtime. Children either asleep or occupied, she lit her living room fire: night was a nearby visitor, and midnight was an ice-cold guest. *Thank goodness we've so much wood,* she thought as she struck a match against red phosphorous.

With the fire lit and Sylvain's cheeks aglow and Berry, full of milk, settled peacefully in her basket, Melody went out to the kitchen to prepare her jam. Hundreds of berries needed to be de-leafed and split and scrub. With each preparatory gesture, a cacophony of piercing screams filled the air. Melody brushed off thoughts of buried creatures and beetle black eyes but could not help but mull over her earlier interaction with The Witchard. It hadn't been a pleasant run-in, yet, she felt, at least, a bridge may have been built between them. Purple-pink juices stained her fingers as she plucked and squeezed. Such noisy berries from such a quiet wood.

❦

The knock at the door startled Melody. She dropped her paring knife and went to answer it. Truth be told, she'd never heard a knock at her door before; Sebastian was the only person other than herself who came and went from the cottage—they'd no need for a lock or a key or knocking. She dried her hands on her apron and turned the handle to be met by no one.

No one.

All she could see was a still-taut golden rope anchored to their oaken sentinel, and the creep of night descending on their scrub of a garden. *Who could it've been?* A cold breeze struck her fire-warmed cheeks with a sobering slap. An owl whooped, flapped its wings, and took flight from the top of the Great Oak. Her heart missed a beat. No-one was there. She looked to the floor. Something was there. There, at her feet was the strangest of items.

She picked it up and turned it around to inspect the item. In her hands, cold and heavy, was the most peculiar carving. Whatever it was, it was made from a length of forest wood the same length and weight as one of the logs she'd not long ago gifted to The Witchard.

A chiselled face. A chiselled face of wood. The item felt soft beneath her fingertips, but the carving was not of a friendly face. Quite the opposite; the whittled visage featured an expression of pure terror. Eyes like dark pits. Mouth agape. Real, knotted white hair tacked on to the bark sprang from its crown. As she squinted and drew the lump of wood away from her face, she realised the carving bore a likeness to her dearest: it was a carving of Sebastian's head.

The carving repulsed her. It smelt of damp and wet leaves. She dropped the piece in shock. A pulse of vomit throbbed in her throat.

She looked down at it on the floor of her home. Etched on the statue's base, a single word: 'Thanks'.

The Witchard, she thought. *It must be a gift from The Witchard in exchange for the wood.* She sighed, a relief of sorts. *Just a gift.* She carried the piece into the house and placed it in the corner of the front room. *A grotesque and unwanted gift, but a gift nonetheless.*

"Mumma, s'that?" Sylvain asked his mother. His first clear sentence. But distracted by the odd delivery and the bubbling of her jam,

Melody shooed him away from the carving and encouraged him to return to his art work.

ଔଡ଼

Melody stoked the living room fire with a further log and returned to the kitchen where she did the same in there to keep the house warm. *Warmth will help my babies sleep. If they sleep, I can finish making my jam.*

From outside, smoke spilled out from the chimneys, up into the forest, and Sebastian, closing in, saw the pink, sparkling ribbons as he followed back his golden rope. Melody could almost sense her lover moving closer, couldn't wait for him to take her in his arms. The bed would be much cosier.

She set about stewing her screaming berries; the sound of them bursting in the hot pan! How the sweet fruit winced with audible pain as the bottom of the cast iron pan sat upon the hot top of the wood burner.

Melody felt a tap on the back of her leg. Young Sylvain. Her son stood behind her as she stood with her eyes on her jam. "What is it, sweetpea?" she asked.

"Don't like it." Sylvain said. The child kicked at dirt on the kitchen floor.

"Oh darling, neither do I. Turn it around. Face it away from you. Please let me continue, Father will be back shortly. Watch for him from the front room window if you wish."

The child skulked back to the living room. Melody dipped her finger into the hot, soupy mixture and tasted a sample. "Too sour." She wiped a sticky finger on her tatty pink kitchen rag then tossed the dirtied tea-towel over her shoulder. She measured and tipped in a spoon of sugar and continued to stir the screaming berries. Their yelps grew louder as they meshed to a sugary smush. The familiar tap of Sylvain at her leg again. "What is it, Sylvain? I'm nearly done, then I'll come and colour too, whilst we wait for Father."

"S'howwible. Don't like iyy." The boy sulked, stamped his foot. Melody crouched down to face her boy. He looked scared. She understood. She too had felt that way when holding the odd carving. Did it have some sort of power to it, an evil force? Was it cursed? She still wasn't sure she believed in such witchery, but she promised Sylvain she'd be in shortly to deal with the situation.

"Drape this over it, darling. Out of sight is out of mind." She passed him her berry-juice stained cloth. One corner of Sylvain's mouth lifted slightly. "And take a few of these, to tide over your hunger until Father's back with bread." She handed him a small bowl of berries which the boy took in his empty hand. Head hung low, he toddled back through the partition door and into the living room at his mother's direction.

Melody continued to stir her jam. It was set to be a tasty treat. Sebastian would be over the moon. Over the racket from the noisy preserve in the hot pan, Melody heard Sylvain cry out again from the front room. "Mummy, no likey. Howwible face."

Melody, both impressed with her son's rampant language development and torn between finishing her task and quelling the young boy's concerns, shouted back. "Oh Sylvain, darling. I'll be in shortly. One moment." She poured the hot red liquid into a jar, both careful not to spill a drop and glad to screw the lid on to leave the raucous berries to settle. Such a din. "I'll be with you in a shake of a lamb's tail—if it's really bothering you, darling. We can simply chuck it on the fire and be done with it."

Melody glanced out of the kitchen window at the great oak, illuminated in the dark slightly by the light from her cottage. The glittering rope attached to its trunk lay slack, flat on the garden path.

Sebastian would soon be home. Joy. A rush of excitement dashed up to her heart and she ran into the living room, where she was sure the front door would soon swing open.

"Mumma. Mumma." Sylvain tugged at her leg. "No more scary." He smiled at his mother. Melody bent down to wipe the red berry juice from his chubby cheeks with a lick of her finger the way mothers do. She swooped her son up and rested him against the bone of her hip before moving towards the window by the front door. Certain she could hear the crackle of boot and hoof on dried leaf litter in the distance, she was so glad at the thought that soon her family would be together as one again. How warm the night would be. A movement through the window. *Is that him, my dear Sebastian?*

Sylvain pointed to the carving which sat upright still in its corner facing into the living room. "S'at, Mumma?" He thrust his chubby index finger again at the oddity with a quizzical look on his young face.

Melody froze. She swore she'd instructed her son to turn it, to cover it with the rag. Had the cloth slipped off? She could not see the old tea towel at all in the corner. And had the carving turned back around by itself? A loud crackle and pop from the living room fireplace. Her vision flitted from the window to the wood burner, the door of which was wide open, exposing the contents of its black iron maw. The flames inside the cast iron box were roaring, bright, and the living room, Melody realised for the first time, was as hot as Hell. Out from the white-orange flame hole of the wood burner trailed the end of a berry-pink tea-towel.

"Why is the—" Melody placed Sylvain down, her eyes not flinching from the trail of pink tea towel. "W-where is your sister?"

A sound at the door. Sebastian entered the cottage suddenly, with magnitude and relief. "Melody, my darling—"

Melody looked at her husband then rushed to the basket in which an hour or so ago she'd laid down her darling daughter Berry, only to find it empty. Babe gone. She turned and ran to the fireplace and yanked out the half burnt tea towel and screamed at the fire. She screamed more loudly than a forest full of bursting berries.

When Sebastian too understood what had happened, what his son, Sylvain, had done, Sebastian's face became the spit of The Witchard's carving.

Neglect Takes the Form of the Form of the Recovery Position

The young boy was floating three feet above the end of his bed, except he was not. He was just perched on the edge of the mattress, ruler-spined, his toes on the floor, his sketch pad on his lap and a charcoal stick in his hand.

But he might as well have been floating, because it was two in the morning and the woman watching him, his mother, found him still being awake at this hour, so upright and corpse-still, most alarming. The sight of her son, wide awake and upright with an iridescence in his eyes in the middle of the night, a steel pin; her heart, a butterfly.

On her own way to bed, she'd gone to check on her son, and had seen him there, staring at the wall. Motionless, she'd stood in his doorway, not crossing the threshold, and had watched him for over an hour as the night ticked on and increasing darkness ate away at his edges.

She had not wanted to disturb him—she'd heard things about children sleepwalking with their eyes open, how it was dangerous to wake them, so, steadying her tired self against the jamb of son's bedroom door, she quietly observed, waiting, thinking about what was best to do. Perhaps he had woken from a bad dream? *No,* she thought, *he is not one for bad dreams.* At one point, he cleared his throat. He did not seem asleep. Something else must have unsettled her son.

A slice of moonlight from a gap in his curtains cast an elongated shadow of the boy on the wall. The boy stared at his shadow as the woman, hidden in darkness, stared at her son.

Something is wrong, she thought. *Or something is more than wrong, something dreadful has happened.* She became sure of this, convinced. It would explain her poor son's blank stare, the wan vacancy on his face.

A noise. A car backfiring or a fox in a bin, something from beyond the house broke the silence and the boy flinched. He turned his head, saw his mother at the door. "Mother," he said. The vowels in this word played out too long. The woman approached him, moving like a trepidatious mouse, not wanting to distress him further. His face was as pale as his shadow was dark.

⌘

She should never have let him go to the other boy's house for tea. What a fool she had been to allow this to happen. But she'd wanted her boy to fit in, to make friends. The small village she'd moved to with her son a few months back had not welcomed them as warmly as she'd hoped. Her boy had come home from school in tears, the last picked for paired activities most days, despite words with teachers and interventions. After a nasty divorce, she'd wanted to escape, make a fresh start—an anonymous new beginning would've played in both their favours.

Consideration of what terrible events might have occurred at the play-date with the farmer's son dropped a rock in her stomach. The farmer had been so persuasive, coercive almost, and the cadence of his gait as he'd approached her at the school gate last week alone had been unnerving. Why had she let herself be pressured into it?

They'd spoken at the gate on several occasions, the woman and the farmer, each conversation initiated by the farmer, his glare slightly off-centre, several inches to the left of her left ear, as if watching out for something that might be creeping up behind her, but their discussions had not breached small talk until their last interaction. He had insisted her son go over for tea after school. The farmer had mentioned he lived just with his son and his elderly father, whom he cared for in between tending to his dairy herd. She had presumed he had meant he did not have a wife. The woman was a single parent herself, so tried to reserve judgment, and had agreed to a play-date. But something about the farmer was most disquieting. She couldn't place her finger on precisely what it was about him that made her feel odd, could not pick out the words to describe it at all—like an image from a dream washed too deeply into the brain to ever retrieve.

He had remarked, the other boy's father, the farmer, how similar the two boys were. Uncannily so. He'd said her boy was *like an echo of his*. And the woman had commented on how the farmer and his own son also looked alike, although, being from the other side of the country, she felt there was hardly any chance they might be related. *Just a strange coincidence*, she thought, *a genetic déjà vu.*

What was it he had said to her? She strained to remember—the pair, he'd said, were of a *similar breed*. She'd laughed, although inside, she'd felt unsettled. She'd made an attempt at a joke, about how all his dairy cattle must look the same. He'd said he knew each of his girls, Friesians, like the back of his hand, told her how each had distinct markings, unique as a snowflake, all the while never quite meeting her eyes with his.

ೞ

What frightful thing has happened on the farm? she thought. She sat at her son's side, wrapped an arm around his cold shoulder. "Why are you still awake, darling?" she asked.

"I couldn't sleep. Thought I'd try and sketch something but nothing's coming to mind." In his hand, he squeezed the stick of charcoal, the top page of his pad below, empty.

"How can you not be tired? We're in the early hours of the morning."

"I spent so long in bed at the farm—I'm just not tired now, I guess."

Her heart battered. She took the pad from her son's lap, prised the charcoal from his grip, placed them on the floor, and returned her arm tight around him. She pulled him closer to her side.

"In bed?" she asked.

She hugged her son and pressed his cheek against her chest. It suddenly made hideous sense, what Matthew, the farmer's son had said to her when she'd arrived a little early to collect her boy: "One moment, madam. He's just putting his trousers back on."

She swallowed hard, knowing she'd never forgive herself if the terrible things her darkest thoughts proffered were true. "Why were you in bed? At the farm house. During the day?"

"They wore me out." The woman gripped her son's shoulder so tight he recoiled, pushed her away, as her nails dug into his shoulder.

"*Wore you out?* Whatever do you mean?"

"I ran around so much, rounding up the cows. Matthew had wanted to draw but I said I didn't. I told him I'd never been to a farm before and wanted to explore."

The boy's words petered off. "Go on," she whispered, her teeth gritted hard.

"Matthew got cross and told his dad. His dad got cross too, but then his dad said we should go and run around outside instead, said he'd make a different plan for us, for our play-date. So we went up to the fields. I pretended to be a sheepdog and helped get the cows back inside, then we walked back to the farmhouse. When we got back, Matthew's dad asked if I wanted to do drawing before dinner and I said I didn't, I was too tired, so he told me I should rest a while. He took me upstairs, into Matthew's bedroom and told me to get undressed for comfort, lie on the bed, and shut my eyes. I must've dozed off. Matthew woke me when your car pulled up. And now I'm not tired at all."

The boy looked to his lap as if searching for his soul there, and toyed with the cord of his pyjama waistband. His mother resisted the urge to buckle forward and cry, furious with herself for letting whatever might've happened happen. A pain not dissimilar to childbirth bit into her heart.

"Are you cross with me, Mummy?"

"No, no darling, no. Not at all." Each word she forced out stung, but each word had to come. "Do you remember anything else?"

"Not really, Mummy. I had a good time. I think I'll just get under the duvet now."

The boy rubbed his eyes and crawled under his sheet.

Perhaps the fresh air, the exercise, the new experiences on the farm had worn him out. Maybe he had needed an afternoon nap. These things she told herself to make herself feel okay.

She tucked her son in. *His face looks more angular.* She thought. *Could it be the shadows? The way the moonlight falls? Or has my baby lost a little more of his puppy fat?*

"Would you like me to get in with you, sleep in here with you tonight?" she asked.

"No, Mummy, there isn't room." And he was right. She knew it, felt a pang of deep sadness. Her boy was growing up.

"If you're sure," she said and kissed him on his forehead. The boy yawned and nodded and closed his eyes. "Goodnight, Mummy."

The woman returned to the vastness of her own room. She fumbled in a drawer, took out a sleeping pill, popped it in her mouth, and swallowed it dry. In her own bed, her mind raced over all the *what ifs*, the possibilities, of what may or may not have occurred on the farm. *I will visit the farmer in the morning,* she thought. *If he has laid one finger on my son, I'll not be held responsible for my actions.*

☙❧

"Stay in the car." The woman left her son in the back of her Peugeot and marched down the muddy path towards the farmer's house. She knocked hard on the door until it swung open. The farmer answered the door, his eyes bloodshot. *Has he been drinking? Crying?* she thought. The farmer pulled out a hanky and blew his nose.

"Sorry for the state of me," he said. "My father is declining."

The woman offered up polite condolences but had come with the intention of finding out what had happened the day before. Why had her son been made to undress, sleep in the day?

"Let me explain." The farmer ushered her in. Hesitant to enter the building, her boy sat at the end of the drive in her car, she reassured herself he'd be okay for a short while. Her son had pens, pads, books to read. Safer outside than in the farmer's house.

The farmer pulled out a chair at the kitchen table for the woman and offered tea, which she declined.

"Where do I begin?" the farmer said, scuttling around the kitchen, spilling water, milk, piling spoonfuls of sugar into a mug. "My father. He requires great attention, you see."

"I don't see. What has this to do with my son?"

"My father requires I draw him every night." The farmer said with sincerity, his accent thick with countryside burl. The woman tapped her foot against the table leg. Had she misheard?

"At first, my efforts were poor, mere puerile caricatures of the old man, cartoons, but as I paid attention to his lines, noted where light and shade fell on his face, focused on the rise and fall of skin and bone, my artwork improved." He passed the woman a sketch-book from one of many obelisk-shaped stacks of pads in the corner of the room, flicked through its pages for her.

She could see his work had indeed improved over the years. The recent drawings were clarion. A true likeness to what she imagined an older version of the farmer himself would look like if arranged horizontally, splayed into a capital letter K.

"But what has this g—"

"Please, madam," the farmer interjected. "Take pity and hear my story."

"Go on," she said. She sighed and folded her arms.

"At first, I resented it, the time it took each night, the bind, the isolation of it all, but as my craft improved, I started to create quality sketches. And now, even if my father says not a new thing, repeats the same stories again and again, each one perhaps more disjointed, more fictitious, fantastical, than the night before, and often forgets my name, I have learnt to tolerate the task."

"He has dementia?"

"Something more than dementia." The farmer scratched the rough grey stubble on his chin, all the while not breaking from his thousand-yard stare. "Where was I? Each night, I move Father through the motions, shape his near-skeletal limbs into the recovery position, and pay attention to him as I make the drawing."

The woman lifted a second sketch pad. "May I?" The farmer nodded. Tens, hundreds of sketches, each identical or near enough to the last, all of an old man, draped on his left side, a skin and bone starfish, a corner of sheet draped over his modesty.

"But, last week, my eye fell from the ball. It had been a hot day, and my best milker had wandered off. I'd been out for hours, searching for her to no avail. Found her dead, stiff, eyes clouded like skin on pudding, up by the tower on the top field. By the time I'd dealt with her, I was broken. I fell straight asleep, forgetting to draw my father. The next day, the hardening had set in."

"Of the cow? The cow had begun to harden?" The woman's brow furled.

"No. Father. A patch of skin above his right knee set. Darkened like black walnut bark. He could no longer lift his leg."

"His leg turned to bark because you forgot to draw him? This is ludicrous." The woman looked at her wristwatch. "I've got to get back to my son. Just tell me, please, what happened yesterday. Why did you make my son get undressed and get into a bed?" She was finding it hard to retain civility. The man was deranged. *Heavy metal toxicity,* she thought, *pesticides, sheep dip, all sorts of chemicals are used in farming. The man has lost the plot.*

"Come with me," he said. "Come and see my father. Then you'll understand."

"You've five more minutes of my time. If you don't explain to me what you did with my son, I'll have no choice but to contact the police." The woman reached into her coat pocket and found her car key. With the blade of it poking out between her tensed knuckles, she stepped over bric-a-brac as she followed the farmer through the house.

"Father, we have a guest." The farmer walked round to the side of the bed. The woman pinched her nose with her empty hand. "Father?"

No reply. The farmer peeled back a thin, soiled sheet to reveal the place where the face of his Father should have been.

This farmer's father is no more an old dying man, she thought, *than a wooden artist's mannequin, free from its stand, with opposable, metal-pinned elbows and ankles and knees. Its face is blank pine and its limbs are as smooth and polished as a licked clean lamb shank.*

The wooden doll lay on the bed, on its side, with the same shape and proportions of a thin old man twisted into the recovery position.

The farmer burst into tears and sank to his knees. "It's too late. He's gone." The farmer wailed. Matthew, the farmer's son, the boy from the woman's son's class, came running in.

"Grandfather? Has he hardened?" The little boy's eyes filled with tears and he ran into his father's arms. The woman felt odd, as if dreaming somebody else's nightmare, as she stood there, witnessing this strange outburst of grief.

"Yes, son. Your grandfather has passed."

The man comforted his son, then wrapped the wooden corpse up in the cotton sheet on which it rested, until it looked not like a man at all but like swaddled kindling on a stained mattress. He bent and scooped his father's remains up in his arms and mentioned something about the lightness of what was left now the soul had vacated. *But where had the soul vacated from, and where had it vacated too?* the woman worried, though she was too disturbed to ask.

"You must come with us to the tower," the farmer said to the woman.

"Tower? Why? And what was that on the bed, now in your arms?" She pointed at the sack of wood in a sheet, and Matthew sobbed. *What if what I see at this tower is something more, something worse than what I have just witnessed?* she thought. *Once something has been seen, it is impossible to unsee, to erase.*

"Please come," Matthew said, his pleading eyes so similar to the eyes of her own son, she found it hard to refuse.

"Okay. I will honour you this," she said to the farmer, "for the sake of your child who is caught up in all this madness, and then I must get back to my own son in the car." She reasoned with herself. She had only been at the farm for ten minutes or so. *My own boy will be okay, he's a good kid. I have time to take a quick look,* she thought. She gathered herself, without time enough, perhaps, to gather her thoughts entirely, and went with the man and his son to the tower.

After a brief, steep hike, they reached the building the farmer had wanted to show the woman. *Less of a tower, more of a ramshackle barn,* she thought, but there it sat, elevated, on the top end of the farm's highest field.

"The elevated position of the barn," the farmer said, the sheet-sack of logs swinging over his shoulder, "is the reason for its name." He went on to tell her that no-one ever visited the tower, except in situations like the one they were all caught within.

"A panoramic view is good company," he said, and muttered something about how old age is lonely but does not come alone. "However, the place does need a clean." The farmer pointed up to a fifty-foot high, small, round window opaque with dirt on the end of the outhouse.

They approached the large door of the barn. The woman, between deep breaths, felt she had been ignored for long enough and needed to ask her pertinent question again. "This is all quite tragic, but please—" Heat grew in her cheeks and belly as she spoke. Her patience had run dry. "What did you do to my son while he slept?"

The farmer placed the sack containing his father on the ground. With his hands on his hips, he stared at the woman, but not quite. She felt propelled to check behind herself, although she was no longer sure which direction potential danger might spring from.

"My own son has no skill with a pencil at all, you see," the farmer said, "but he must learn to draw. I have been teaching him. But the two of us, neither with any innate skill, only got so far. My son told me your son was good at art. I figured he could teach Matthew how to draw me while I posed, my father too far gone to be of any use in studying the form of the body."

"None of what you are saying answers my question."

"Dear woman, please. Listen to the details. Each night from this point forwards, now my own father is gone, my boy must sketch me, pay me attention, listen to my stories, dull as they are, while I rest in the recovery position, or I will harden, too. We are all never any younger than we are in each new moment."

The woman worried about her son in the car; the farmer, clearly mad. Was her boy safe where he was? She shifted from foot to foot. She wanted her question answered but also longed to be with her son, in her car, but also, oddly, yearned to see what she knew once she had seen she could not ever unsee—the inside of the tower.

"Your boy wouldn't draw, said he wanted to play in the fields with the cows," the farmer continued, "so I let him. Instead of using him as teacher, while asleep, he became our life model. We shifted him into the recovery position, and there he lay for several hours. My son practiced his art, drawing your son's form instead. I taught him all I know—far easier to teach my son sat by his side, with us both admiring the canvas, than with my son as the model. It's all about perspective, you see, art. Matthew filled many sketchpads of his own. You may take them if you like. They're back on the farm, the charcoal images of your son. My son is ready now, thanks to yours. From tonight onwards, Matthew will study me."

The farmer's son looked unhappy, the woman thought, unhappier than she had ever seen a child look before.

"I don't want anything from you," she said. She stepped back. "I'm going back to my son and I'm calling the police—"

"Police? On what grounds?" The woman tried to think rationally and realised there were no grounds. "Please, just look inside, honour me, honour my son," said the farmer. The woman looked at Matthew, a sad, wide doe-eyed doppelganger of her own child.

"You have two more minutes. Then I'm going."

The farmer picked up his sack and swung open the tall doors to the barn. "Welcome to the forgetting tower," he said and tipped out the bed sheet contents onto the floor of the barn. The wood lengths tumbled, clattered as they spilt. The farmer's face remained loose, his posture unflustered, as he shrugged at the pile of his father. He crouched, and began to reassemble the wooden bones into their correct positions, with Matthew at his side, helping.

"What... what is this? Some sort of terrible genetic affliction?" The woman staggered back at the sight of what surrounded them. Hundreds of stacked artist's mannequins filled the barn, all upright, all with their pine limbs fixed in the recovery position. It was as if the wooden corpses were clambering on top of each other, yet motionless, trapped in a freeze-frame, all trying to reach the view from the small round window.

"No. Not an inherited trait, more of an awakening. A realisation. An awareness."

The woman spun on her heel, ran to her son in her car, gravel cockerel-tailing up in the air behind her tyres as she pulled away.

CRRSO

When the woman and her son got home, she let him watch cartoons while she paced around the house. She needed time to think. Was her son safe? Was she? Had the entire experience been, perhaps, a side effect of her sleeping medication, or some sort of group hallucination?

She forbade her child from spending any more time with the farmer's son in or outside of school. Her son did not understand. He cried. And in her son's sad eyes, she saw the eyes of the farmer's son, and the face of the farmer, similar, yet older, like an aged counterfeit.

That evening, she insisted her son share her bed. Sensing his mother's stress, the boy did as asked, although he did so reluctantly, claiming he was too old to sleep in his mother's bed.

She read to him until he fell asleep, although he protested the story was dull and he would have rather read to himself. "Can I switch the light out, now?" he asked her, as he was feeling tired, but she said no. She didn't want him to sleep. She made him listen to another story.

If he was asleep, she might feel like she was alone in the house, or trapped in a barn, or made of old wood and ignored. But the boy pleaded with her, said he needed his rest because he was a growing lad, so eventually, she let him drift off.

By the dim light of a candle, with a hand mirror, she inspected the feathered creases around her eyes, examined the way the skin on the back of her hand did not ping back like it used to when she pinched it between thumb and forefinger. She stroked the soft hair back from her baby boy's face and traced hearts on his cheek while he slept as she cried.

When the heartbeat of midnight was all that could be heard and a dark shade of everything was all that could be seen, she got out of bed, shuffled to her son's empty bedroom to retrieve his sketchpad and pencil, and then returned to her room. There, she turned on the bright overhead light and shook her son awake. Owl-eyed, he complained, begged to sleep again, but she insisted he open his eyes, wider, wider, enough so to take every detail of her in.

She lifted her son until he was sitting, thrust a pencil in his hand, then lay on her left side and arranged her limbs into the recovery position.

"Draw me," she said. "Sketch every part of me until sunrise."

FiVE KNUCKLE SHUFFLE

Mr Brownstone's voice boomed down the front of the queue of twelve-year-old kids who were stretched round the outside of the gymnasium. "Prantler. James Prantler."

James gulped. The nervous smile he'd been masquerading with slipped like wet clay down his face. "Shit," he mouthed to the boy behind him. James shuffled forwards, heart in throat, and followed Brownstone inside.

Inside the school gym, Brownstone, Head of Mathematics, lifted a digital camera from an exam desk and took a close-range photograph of James's eye. Then he helped James press his fingertips, one by one, onto the screen of a tablet. "Chair, James. Please." James sat down and gripped the sides of his seat. Mademoiselle Lavigne, French department, whipped out a set of clippers.

"Won't hurt. It'll grow back in a few months," she said. James cowered in his seat as his French teacher cleared a square inch of hair from behind his ear. *Buzzzz.* He bit down hard on his lip. *The rumours are true—they do shave your hair off,* he thought. The ice-cold gel his French teacher smeared onto his exposed scalp afterwards smelt stringent and reminded James of his stepfather's vodka-laced breath.

The third adult in the room—a lady with medi-gloved hands who James didn't recognise—tore open a pouch and pulled from it a small, black device no larger than a matchbox. The lady nodded at Brownstone, who, in response, tapped his tablet screen. "Little scratch," she said and pushed it against—no, *into*—James's sticky skull before stepping back to admire her handiwork. "Fu—" he said, only to receive a scouring look of disapproval from the Maths Head. James clammed up with fear.

As the small device wiggled and burned and burrowed into the side of his skull, James, fists clenched like buns, for the first time in his life wished for the air quality alarm to ring.

Without human touch, the device beeped from under the thin flesh of James's skull. Pain spread from under his ear to the space behind his eyes, chased by extreme coldness.

"You might experience 'iced-spaghetti-head' for a moment," the lady said, her dirtied medi-gloves already discarded in a half-full bin marked 'hazardous waste' under the exam desk.

James grasped his temples. Brownstone sighed and batted the boy's hands away. "No touching."

"It's killing me."

"Please, don't touch the neuroprosthesis—its silk nanotubules are corkscrewing through your prefrontal cortex as we speak. Should settle soon," the strange lady said. She slipped her hands into clean gloves perhaps in preparation for the next child. "Although you may experience tingling next week, as the brain-machine interface cali-brates. It needs to harvest data on your basal-wave levels and your pheromone receptors, to align them with the Conception Prevention Conditioning Database."

She turned and began to defend EarthGov's CPC Campaign to Brownstone: "…and sterilisation at birth is far too expensive. Also, mass sterilisation is considered by most to be inhumane…"

Technical words billowed like smoke, but James had stopped listening. He was twelve. He had no idea what she was on about. He was just glad the pain had started to ease.

Momentarily, they allowed him to recuperate while they sanitised equipment with disposable wipes and sprays, then Brownstone spoke. "Head straight to Programming—over in F-block—follow the temporary signs." The Head of Mathematics brushed the arms of his suit straight and disappeared through the front gym door, to return to the queue of children.

"Up. All done." Mademoiselle Lavigne helped James out of his chair with a firm grip and led Bambi-legged James, his hands balling and flexing with discomfort, out through the far exit.

ᘏᘖ

Not a day passed when James didn't think about ripping the device from his scalp. Puberty? Horrendous. Monstrous changes: body odour, acne, inappropriate stiffenings, even his sweet angelic voice, with which he had been used to being able to wrap his mother around his finger, had been taken. He had little interest in studying or sports. All he wanted to do was chat with cute girls. Hug them. Kiss them. Feel their softness against his own skin. But this was all off-limits now.

It itched. Bald patch, aged fifteen. He'd scratched at the bloody chip so hard, hair behind his ear had fallen out and refused to return. *At least I can still touch myself,* he thought, tucked up under his duvet in the corner of his bedroom knowing his mother wouldn't disturb him for the thirty minutes in which she watched her evening soap opera.

He zoomed in on Samantha's Insta photo on his smart-screen. *She's perfect.*

What he wouldn't do to share a kiss, a consensual touch with her. Half the school fancied her; even Brownstone lingered near her desk a little longer than necessary. Brownstone: late fifties, serious comb-over, 'Breath of Death', born years before the inaugural Black Box Programme was introduced, was probably the only person in school who was enjoying the campaign.

⋘⋙

Before the population of Fairlawn High had witnessed the extent of the implant's control, Samantha would swan around between lessons, a circle of plainer girls shielding her, creating a buffer between Samantha's perfect body and the horny masses. Boys would whistle at her and try to catch her attention as she and her friends pouted and giggled. This was the norm. But Samantha didn't mind. She quite enjoyed the attention—and as the hottest girl in school, she had her pick of the football team lads. But, after the implants, a handful of try-hards attempted to get close to her—despite verbals from staff— and as soon as their hacked sensory neurones detected her phero-mones, triggering their rewired arousal circuitry, painful electric shocks ensued. They learned hard and fast proximity wasn't worth the consequences, or the humiliation as waves of pain shot down their necks and spines and made their bodies shudder. Lewis Buttcombe tried to pass her a rose on Valentine's Day and as the poor lad's implant kicked in, he wet his pants.

But there is always one. Always. With every rule, there is always an exception. And this exception was Rick Redfield. At first, Rick Redfield seemed to be able to tolerate the shocks. He thought he'd cracked it; his body didn't shake when he got close to girls. And he really fancied Samantha. But after his third attempt at linking arms with Samantha, the school discovered a wireless Eroticism Signal had been connected.

After maths and enroute to Spanish, with his arm linked in hers, his teeth gritted as he tried to ignore the shocks from his skull, he told Samantha he thought she was pretty. He asked if she'd mind a peck on the cheek. Samantha blushed and accepted and, as he placed his lips on her face, a new, more ear-piercing alarm began to wail. High-mounted speaker arrays had been erected overnight around the school yard, alongside the tiny air quality alarms. A sharp arc of sound shouted out from all corners of the campus as his lips brushed against her cheek, amplified robotic words filled the air: 'perv' and 'sex-pest', followed by a war-siren noise that made a reedy whisper of the air quality alarms by comparison. Every kid in the school heard the words as they repeated over and over, and then every kid in the school placed their fingers in their ears.

Once they'd all heard about the ES sirens and the shame they brought to anyone who set it off, the majority of the kids started to give Samantha—and anyone else they were sweet on—plenty of distance. Even Rick Redfield.

⋙⋘

There were scraps every day on the school fields. Tumbling balls of frustrated kids definitely *not* attracted to each other gave each other a good pounding, pummelled each other in the gut and jaw, yanked hard on each other's hair. The staff became well versed in fight-dispersal protocol.

But, worst of all was the automatic home DMing. An electronic message went straight to Mum/Dad/Carer if anyone walked within spitting distance of someone they fancied and had so much as a solitary butterfly in their stomach:

<u>WARNING.</u>
YOUR CHILD APPROACHED ANOTHER AND BECAME SEXUALLY AROUSED.

Rapid conditioning ensued—because to sit across the dinner table from a parent who knew you'd had an erection, a wide-on, a hardening of your nipples or whatever while at school, well, that awkward evening meal would have been the The Worst Supper Ever.

⋐⋑

E-MAIL: @ALL_PARENTS
FLESH CRIME: 10.48am - 25th June 2043 - School Field
Mark Reeves (16)
Gina Blaystock (16)

⋐⋑

Gina and Mark couldn't contain themselves any longer. They'd been sexting each other for weeks. Mark couldn't stop thinking about Gina's breasts and Gina had already named all seven of their babies in her head. Behind the bike sheds at the bottom of the playground after P.E., they wanted to feel the press of lips, couldn't resist the temptation of skin against bare skin, needed to snog. *Screw the ES sirens of shame. Sod the electric shocks.* Hormones are powerful things.

Unbeknownst to them, the control system had been updated. As Mark slid his hand down her skirt, the sirens played a new ear-piercing wail on this day, June 25th.

"What on Earth does that sound mean?" Mark asked his young lover.

"I'm not sure, but I feel scared," she replied.

The flustered pair shot out from their love-nest at the shock of the new alarm, pulling down raised shirts, zipping up flies, tightening belts, as all the other children poured out of their classrooms and surrounded the scene. There, gathered around the back of the bike shed, everyone witnessed the aftermath of Mark and Gina's Flesh Crime.

Two Securidrones descended from their resting nooks, lowered their robotic arms, and hissed as aluminium syringe-tipped knuckles shuffled and shook. The weaponised drones injected Gina and Mark with needlefuls of neon fluid. Both kids dropped to the floor like stones down a well.

Silence rippled out across the playground. All heads turned. The automatic 8-foot gate cranked open. A black e-van, similar in size and stature to the fossil-fuelled hearses of the past pulled up near the slumped pile of failed Romeo and Juliet. Pupils watched on in horror, wide-eyed, slack-jawed, as five teachers lifted the two deadweights into the vehicle.

ଔଔଔ

"It'll get easier," James heard his mother muttering as he slunk down the stairs to join her and his stepfather, Noel, for dinner. "He'll manage to control his urges until he passes the financial threshold and the health test on his thirtieth. The government'll deem him worthy for nuptials, won't they?"

"Stupid little tosser." Noel caught James's eye and slipped his fifteen-year old stepson a sardonic grin. James glowered back.

James pulled out a chair and let its legs scrape across the floor, creating a tension as thick as the tofu slab on his plate at his place at the dining table. *God, I want to deck Noel. Mess him up good,* thought James.

Noel, with narrowed eyes, stared back at James, then wrapped a tattooed arm around his wife's shoulder and squeezed her playfully on the breast.

"Wahey!" said Noel, not taking his eyes off James.

"Get off, you cheeky ape!" James' mother giggled and playfully pushed Noel's hand away.

James' mother pulled Noel towards herself and kissed him with passion. James looked away as disgust curled in his stomach, then picked up his cutlery. His steak knife glinted under the daylight simulation panel. He sliced into his veggie T-bone and ate it rapidly, silently, wanting to escape the table and his proximity to his mother and Noel as fast as he possibly could.

On finishing his dinner in record time, with a napkin, James wiped the serrated steak knife blade clean and slid it up his sleeve. They didn't catch him doing this—neither of them had time to actually ever really truly look at him. In his room, he placed it under his pillow and got himself ready for bed.

☙

"You okay?" James squinted and edged as close as he knew he safely could, still just a little too far to hear if she was laughing or crying. He knew it was Samantha. Beautiful Samantha from 11B. Could tell by the purple bow—an attempt to cover up her implant— on the side of her head of thick golden hair. *She still looks beautiful,* he thought, *even with that lump of evil junk in her skull.*

"It's not fair." Samantha was slumped in the sunshine against the wall of the science block, her face in the palms of her hands. As she spoke to James, the sadness in her voice became clear. *Definitely crying.* "Even Maria won't sit by me anymore. DM'd me last night, said she's got feelings for me now, too."

"Sorry to hear that." James pushed his hands down hard into his pockets and prayed he was far away enough from her that his implant wouldn't detect her scent. "Wish I could come over there, for a hug, you know, as friends."

"She's my best friend—was. It's too much, you know?" Samantha lifted her head. Mascara spider-webbed down her cheeks. "We're compassionate, sentient beings, for fucksake. We should be able to choose what we do with our own bodies, have autonomy over them."

"Need a tissue?" Unsure what some of the words Samantha had used meant, he reached for the packet of Kleenex in his pocket. "Mum says it stings when make-up gets in her eyes."

"Never wearing make-up again." She shook her head, pulled a tissue from her own sleeve and, with fury, began scrubbing. "Hate my face. Want to rip it off." She mauled her cheeks with her finger-nails and thin lines of red sprung up.

"But you're—" he started and couldn't finish, nerves getting the better. She scowled.

"Hate my face, my hair, my tits—everything. Despise it all. I just want someone to be able to hold me, to love me that way, you know, no strings. It's no fun doing it alone, is it?"

"Well, I'm not sure I fully agree there… self-servicing is still *quite* fun—" James arched a brow, and hoped she'd find his response witty. The corners of her lips tipped upwards.

That smile. Why does she have to be so fucking perfect? He felt a slight throb in his chest so he took a step back, as he'd become conditioned to do when someone attractive approached.

"Yeah, I guess." She sniffed, blew her nose. Even through her smudged make-up, her wet eyes sparkled. "It's not our fault though, is it? None of this is: too many people, babies. Why is our generation being punished?"

She scrunched her tissue up her sleeve and ripped off her purple bow, thrusting her hair apart to reveal the sore patch where her own 'Hitler Box' had been inserted. James shrugged, lifted his own hand and fiddled with the mess on the side of his own head in an attempt to expose his own scar to her. An empathic exchange of sorts. Her metallic scalp tag glinted. It reminded James of what he'd picked up at the dinner table last night and had placed in the side pocket of his school trousers this morning.

"I mean, if you're desperate, if we ever, you know, get past this, I'd be more than happy to hug you and stuff. As friends." He blushed. All the nights he'd spent jacking off to her image—*thank fuck these Hitler boxes don't allow complete telepathy*, he thought. *Things could be a LOT worse.*

She slipped him a flirtatious grin. "That'd be nice. And if I liked the way you smelt, if we were, you know, compatible, maybe we could take things further?"

Christ alive, he could feel himself stiffening. In his head, red flags were waving, alarm bells already ringing. If he wasn't careful, real bells would ring soon too. He pegged his nose, and took another Neil-Armstrong-sized step back. He couldn't face Noel with an Eroticism email. He'd rather die. At least thinking about his step-father put heed to the semi brewing in his underwear.

"I'm clinically depressed," she said. "They put me on tablets. 'Mood-levellers'. Bastard buzz-kill pills. Don't even work. Can't even

orgasm on them—don't even feel like trying. I just want to be held."
She began to cry again.

"Woah." James' cheeks flushed.

"Sorry, too much info?" Through her tears, she snorted then
chuckled.

At least she's laughing now, he thought. It made him feel good to see
her happier.

James reached down into his trouser pocket to readjust and felt
the odd comfort of the knife: warm and glass-sharp under his thumb
pad. He sighed. Fantasies of stabbing his six-foot-three stepdad in
the thigh would probably remain just that, fantasies.

"What's in your pocket? Pleased to see me?" she gestured at his
trouser leg. Looking down, he noticed—the blade had given him a
bit of a bulge.

"Ah, shit... this? No... no, God no. I mean yes—you're
beautiful—but no... it's a knife."

"A fucking *what?* A knife?" Samantha stood up. James stepped
back, always the distance-tango. "Great idea," she said. Her eyes
shone, a spark of madness to them, just like the knife had conveyed
to James the night before.

"What do you mean, 'great idea?'"

"I could shear off my hair. Stop wearing makeup. Dress like a
dork. If I'm unattractive, I can be around friends again... squeeze in
the occasional hug... get invited to sleepovers."

She smiled again, this time wide-eyed. *Terrible idea,* he thought,
but realised it'd given her hope, made her feel better. Plus, he'd never
get to actually touch her anyway; she was way out of his league. He'd
manage as always, with her Insta photo, Mrs Palm-ela Handerson,
party-for-one. *There's no real harm in helping her, is there?* he thought. *I
could be her knight in armour, a friend.*

He pulled out the knife and shoved it across the dirt. "All yours. Hope it works—though I do find girls with shaved heads super-hot." He let his gaze fall to the floor, rammed his hands back in his pockets, kicked a pebble.

Samantha picked up the blade and parted her hair above her right ear. "Ha! I've an even better idea!" she said, levering the knife underneath the edge of the lump of metal poking out from her skull. "I'll solve this problem permanently. I'll just carve this fucking piece-of-shit implant out instead!"

"Stop! No, Samantha! The probe's two inches deep in your skull, the sensors stretch throughout your entire cortex, if you dig it out, you'll fit. You'll haemorrhage. You'll bleed to death."

Samantha ignored him and dug the tip of the blade in. A trickle of blood snaked down, around her ear, followed by a small gush. James watched on, panicking, as she drove the blade in deeper. He couldn't bear it. Despite the dread of his parents finding out he'd smelt a girl, had had sexual thoughts, despite the fact Noel would ridicule him for months if an Eroticism email was sent home, he couldn't let her mutilate herself. The girl might die. And it would be his fault.

James darted forwards, sharp zaps progressing to a cranking siren in his skull as he approached her. *Too close.* The Eroticism Siren burst down his auditory nerve and screamed through the speakers strung up around the school perimeter.

'SEX PEST'. 'PERV'. 'SEXUAL DEVIANT'. 'SEXUAL DEVIANT'.

So loud. So sharp and painful. James' molars hummed. "Put it fucking down, drop the fucking knife." In a single lunge towards her, towards the steel blade, as blood spat out from her skull, he knocked the knife from her hand.

"The fuck you do that for? Want. This. Bastard. Out." Samantha yelled. She reached across the ground for the blade. James blocked her reach and in doing so, his hand brushed against her cheek—

So close. Flesh-close.

The sensation: unmatchable.

Her skin: so *fucking* soft.

"Shit. Oh fuck. I got too close to you," he said. "I fucking *touched* you!" Despite her warm blood on his hand, her skin had felt like nothing he'd ever felt before. Perfection. He dropped and crouched at her side as he tried to catch his breath. There he squatted, with his right hand clasped against his own chest in shock. Close enough to smell her, to inhale the invisible biochemicals seeping from her pores, he inhaled deeply, almost as if his behaviour was out of his control— as if he were torn between Heaven and Hell. But Samantha didn't smell of perfume. Samantha smelt of nothing at all really. A little coppery maybe? Blood, perhaps. His nose was blind. But his implant detected thirty-nine different sexual semiochemicals, each one widening blood vessels, sharpening senses, preparing his body for a carnal encounter. Confusion. Elation and horror flooded his veins.

Overly sensitised, perhaps, after years of touch-repression, James had never felt so turned on and also, so afraid. He panicked. *What to do?*

He kicked the knife into the ditch behind the Science block, and removed himself from where Samantha sat but it was too late. Not for her; Samantha was fine. With her tattered tissue, she dabbed at the wound she'd made, the bleeding easing. But for James, it was too late.

The Eroticism Siren changed. He'd touched her. Receptors in his skin had awakened. Molecules of Samantha's biofragrance seeped through his epidermis, travelled in his blood, up to the unit in his brain.

The Securidrone's 'Flesh Crime' tone filled the air.

"Shit," she screamed, "behind you—run!"

Too late. He froze, statue-boy, overwhelmed by the sight of the arcing drone. Robotic arms, shuffling knuckles wielding a fan of needles of neon fluid jabbed at his cheek, neck, flesh of his lower arm. Like a racehorse brought down at an impossible fence, he pooled to the ground.

Kids flocked from everywhere to find the source of the alarm. In front of the entire school, Samantha wept as, bundled in the e-van by blank-faced teachers, James's motionless body was driven away.

⚬⚬⚬

Seven years of obsessive research and academia: that was how the following years panned out for Samantha. After acing her bioengineering degree, specialising in black box technology, she earned a place across the country to study her Masters. She snapped up the offer—a clean break from hometown Hell. But as soon as she relocated, she realised it didn't matter where she resided—people still wouldn't come near her.

She'd never gotten used to the lack of touch, despised the isolation, yet hadn't become desperate enough to stoop to one of the downtown 'feeler shops' where elderly, implant-free people—largely men—charged for 'hugs, massage, and more'. Instead, she studied. Hard. She'd set her heart on finding a way to override her box. Her freedom was a basic human right. She wanted answers, *needed* rid of the bastard metal thorn in her skull, because more than anything, Samantha craved to be held by someone she cared for in that way.

⚬⚬⚬

Dr. Zee-Wang walked on stage for his lunchtime lecture: *Advances in Neurohack Software*. Samantha returned a forced smile at the doctor from the back row of the auditorium. She'd seen him in the cafeteria: a little taller than her, and certainly a great deal smarter. They'd chatted briefly over coffee from opposite ends of a table in the canteen earlier in the week. She'd known who he was, how important he was in the field, and despite finding him lecherous and disgusting, had forced herself to flirt with him from a safe distance in order to butter him up. Perhaps he had the answer? He certainly seemed to enjoy her attention, even from a great physical distance, and as a result, he'd invited her to the extra-curricular lecture. She'd eagerly accepted; somehow, she'd learn how to mute her Hitler box, figure out how to destroy it. Liberation. At some point, even if she had to devote the next few years to research, she'd get that hug from someone she adored. The only legal way around it was to earn enough to meet the financial threshold to apply for 'conjugal rights', and seven years after that, apply to the authorities to get the bloody thing switched off. But she didn't want kids. Her body was her body, and she would not allow herself to be used for 'perfected breeding'. She could never bring babies, no matter how genetically clean, into such a corrupt world.

As Zee-Wang's laser beam tip started to dance over the lecture screen, she looked around the huge near-empty lecture theatre. She counted the backs of all the heads she could see. Ten. Ten other people were there, aside from herself and the doctor. She gulped from her bottle of water to quench her anxiety and coughed as it slid down the wrong way. A tall man sat near the front turned around but did not catch her eye. Then he turned back around to face the stage as the doctor started to speak.

Shit!

Even from across the large room, she'd recognised his dimple, his ocean-green eyes.

Can't be, can it?

She crabbed along the row, crept back up the aisle, found an empty seat, a little closer, yet still well behind the man she had just identified in order to confirm who she thought she had seen.

It is!

It was him.

But surely— He's dead, I saw him die!

James, the kid who'd risked his life to save hers several years ago, was there, under the same roof, alive. Somehow they'd both ended up at the same university, same department, perhaps even studying on the same Program.

CRSO

After the lecture, with stealth she followed James to the university library, where she stood behind a shelf of reference books and watched him as he studied all afternoon. She mulled over all the questions she wanted to ask, debated over how she'd thank him for what he had done for her.

Evening beckoned. James left the library and she followed him as he headed to the pub. Inconspicuously, she wound herself around lampposts, ducked in and out of long dusk shadows, all the while remaining a safe distance behind him.

Inside The Ram Bar, she watched him from a poorly lit corner as he fist-bumped the bartender, hugged friends, and then danced haphazardly to some sort of nu-metal. From afar, Samantha saw it all. How she longed for human contact, freedom of body—what she wouldn't do.

A double whisky inside of her—three of those, Dutch courage—from her shaded corner, she sat and observed. *I'll approach him soon. I need answers. Hell, I've got to thank him,* she thought. Hours later, James left alone, with the shadow of Samantha in his wake.

"James," she finally mustered up the courage and called out to her childhood friend from under the early evening orange-blush swell of a streetlamp. "James, is it really you?" He spun round and rubbed his eyes. *He doesn't recognise me.* Her heart knocked in her throat.

"Samantha?"

She nodded, hesitated. He held up his hand. Not to stop her, but to beckon. "It's fine," he said, his face a picture of shock. "Come as close as you like, you can't hurt me." He tapped his temple. "Mine's switched off."

"Off? What— How— I don't understand. I… thought you were dead?" She moved closer, to try to study his scar. A zap of pain flickered through her skull. She winced. Too close. *Fuck!* She got close enough to smell the ale on his breath, cerebral top notes of something else, an invisible tang, an odourless trace of chemicals, pheromones most likely, which only made her want to move in closer.

James, brows hoisted, watched her spasm and writhe like one of those toys that dance when you push its base as a shock zagged through her brain. His face softened. He held up his palms towards her and laughed a sweet laugh. "Maybe *you* should stay back?"

At school, she hadn't been attracted to him—not goofy James Prantler, some kid in the year below—but years had passed. James was now a man. A tall, well built man with a sweet, dimpled smile. She inhaled deeply, moved inwards, her common sense displaced by the buzz of alcohol and the fist of mood pills she had to consume daily just to stay level. Another zap. She pinched the bridge of her nose, gritted her teeth. "Fucksake." She tried to push through the discomfort, but the zaps intensified. She stopped to speak. "I want to thank you."

"Thank me? For what?" said James. "And no, I'm not dead."

"For saving me from slicing out my implant. For stopping me from bleeding to death. All those years ago." She stroked the side of her head with her fingertips and began to part her thick hair to reveal her implant to him. "W… what happened to you?"

She watched him weigh his words before speaking. "Walk with me," he said with a tilt of his head.

He told her about the neon sedation, the surgery, his relocation, and how he'd been used as a deterrent.

⌘

"So they took it all? They didn't just give you The Snip? Bastards."

"Smoother than a Ken doll down there," he replied. He winked at her, although she felt the discomfort in him as he tried to maintain eye contact, then he wiped a tear from his own cheek with the back of his hand. "They left me a hole. For urination."

"Christ," she replied, sobered by his story and the cold night air. They strolled, saying nothing, both trying to process the chance encounter and all the things they'd talked about, until Samantha broke the silence. "It's disgusting, what they're doing. How the government is controlling us and dictating what we do with our bodies." She stopped walking, placed her hands on her hips, and, from a safe distance, looked him straight in the eye. "Aren't you depressed? Don't you get… urges?"

"Honestly? I'm okay, in a way. At the moment. I'm probably on more tablets than you are. And no, no urges, not like that. I've things I enjoy: friends, music, research. Life goes on, you know. Kids, intimacy, sex—they're not the be-all-and-end-all."

"Uh-huh. If you say so."

"Plus," he hesitated and drew a breath, "they've just told me I've made it through Round One. So soon, I'll be progressing to Round Two."

"Round Two?"

"Yeah. As I'm castrated, and I've had a full penectomy, and didn't die from infection, they told me I'm tough. Really tough. You know, physically and mentally. So they've put me through to Round Two of some sort of trial." He stopped talking and looked to the horizon, the sun half-dipped behind a row of identikit starter homes, and rubbed the stubble of his chin.

"Go on."

"They put something into my jaw which extends into my ears." He lifted his top lip. Samantha gasped. Four of his molars had been pulled, replaced with glassy spikes, serrated shark's teeth, each with a blue-neon light glowing, throbbing, within.

"The fuck," she recoiled, "is that?"

"Neo-diamond. No idea. They said I'll find out when it's switched on. I can't for the life of me pull it out—it's bonded to my jawbone."

A curl of a breeze brought up a waft of his natural scent. *So good.* She inhaled, her head spinning, and made a decision, a choice: brushing the back of her hand against his bare arm, she asked: "Hold me."

"Samantha—"

More zaps. The Flesh Crime Siren squealed inside her skull, then blasted from speakers along the side of the path. She shoved her fingers in her ears to no avail.

"I want it out. Don't care—I'd never bring kids into this shitshow world anyway. I want free of this fucking box," she shouted. "May I?"

James nodded. "If you're sure—"

She straightened her spine, stepped forwards, and wrapped her arms around him. Then, kissed him on his cheek.

Brain zaps. Cacophonous noise.

Pulling back, heart and head thrumming, a strong smile spread across her face. James plumbed his fingers into his ears. Samantha shouted above the siren: "I'll come and find you, James, when it's done… I'm going Trojan horse… And once they've given me back my freedom, I'm taking these bastards down from within."

From its metal nest atop a streetlamp, a Securidrone descended. Samantha stood stock-still. Ominous knuckles of metal unfurled from the hovering spy-and-stalk-device. She held out her arm and pushed up her sweater sleeve to reveal her bare skin. Needle-nails pierced her flesh and injected her with neon.

James, his heart pounding, caught her as she collapsed. With shaking hands, he laid her on the path as gently as he could and pulled off his own top. After brushing her hair from her pale face, he lifted and placed her head on his balled shirt. More menacing sirens howled, coming ever nearer. He stayed with her as long as he could, all the while hoping it would not be the last time he saw her. He crouched there, by her side, until he saw the e-van approaching. He felt his veins flood with an old fear he had tried to forget, had stashed deep and away for so long. With an agility, an almost mechanical athleticism he had not known he possessed, and a stellar pulse of blue light emitting from his jaw, beaming up into the sky, at warp speed, and with more celerity than humanly possible, James ran.

AFTERWORD

And so, we've reached the end.

The sun has finally set.

And you're okay, aren't you? I expect you're absolutely fine. I hope you're not just sitting there alone, scared, and in the dark. I'm sure you made the sensible choice to flick on your bedside lamp some time ago.

You did? Good.

If you enjoyed these stories, please consider leaving a rating, a review, or spreading the word in your own sweet way—it would mean the world to me and to my fabulous publisher. But before you vanish to drop those stars, choose your next read, or make yourself a delicious cup of tea, I'd like to say a couple more things…

Firstly, from the bottom of my rotten heart, thank you to Sley House Press for all of their hard work bringing this book to market. And secondly, thank you to all the amazing indie presses who first published the handful of reprints in this collection. Without such presses, my stories would just be a clutter of Word documents fighting for space on my (quite frankly) struggling hard drive.

(Indie presses are great—go buy another indie book right now! Did I mention my debut collection, *Sick Girl Screams*, published by Brigids Gate Press, is available in all the usual places?)

I'd also like to thank my children for providing me with a constant stream of gruesome ideas. I feel I should state that Felicity and Otto—both far too young to read anything within these pages— aren't *particularly* horrible or scary. In fact, they're *generally* pretty lovely kids when watered, fed, and exercised correctly. But they do occasionally (regularly) say and do the most ridiculous and/or gross things, and they've sown more than a few unintentional story seeds for their mother. The opening tale, *I Have Seen Seven Bad Things*, for example, was inspired by the pair of them sitting in the back of my car on a long, uneventful journey, insistent on picking each other's noses. So thank you, Smalls. I am blessed to have you both in my life.

Lastly, I want to thank *you*, dear reader, for hanging around. For spending time in my strange worlds. For walking with me into the fading light. Please promise me this: If you ever do find yourself, of an evening, staring in awe at the horizon and telling yourself that this isn't it—this couldn't *possibly* be your final sunset…

…just remember: the dark always comes eventually.

So make the most of every day.

Live like it *could* be your last.

Sleep tight.

— SJ TOWNEND

ABOUT THE AUTHOR

SJ Townend is a single mother of two young children, a teacher, and an author of dark fiction. She has stories published through Vastarien, Eerie River Publishing, Dark Matter Magazine, and a few other places. Her debut horror collection, *Sick Girl Screams*, introduced by Robert Shearman, is available from Brigid's Gate Press. SJ is currently piecing together a third collection.

Twitter: @SJTownend
www.sjtownend.com

CONTENT WARNINGS

I Have Seen Seven Bad Things – gore, suggested abuse, suggested incest, death

Tonight, The Moon is Not Quite Complete – gore, suggested alcoholism, injured animals, grief

To Cherish – child loss, grief, suggested abuse

Love Letters – gore

The Haze-On Lady – domestic abuse

Gurgle – suggested child abuse, extreme gore

Like Sardines – body horror

Bonus Kiosk – domestic abuse, gore

Empty Nest – domestic abuse, stalking

Everyone, Monsters – drug addiction

He Has Not Seen a Bird Before – gore, sexual encounter

Be Kind To Your Children: They Choose Your Nursing Home – gore, abuse

I Vomited Every Hour for Three Days After You Ended Things – violence, stalking

Niche P*rn – gore, suicide

Garden Path – child death

Neglect takes the Form of the Recovery Position – death

Five Knuckle Shuffle – gore, body violence and mutilation

CREDITS

Please note the following stories are reprints:

I Have Seen Seven Bad Things – "Too Bad, You Die," Infested Publishing, 2024

Tonight, the Moon is Not Quite Complete – Vastarien literary magazine, Vol 7, 2024

To Cherish – "Tales of Sley House 2024" Sley House Press, 2024

Love Letters – Black Petal Horror e-zine, online only

The Haze-On Lady – "Freedom," Gravestone Press, 2022

Gurgle – "Freedom," Gravestone Press, 2022

Emily's Journey – The Last Girls Club e-zine, 2024

Empty Nest – Horla Horror e-zine (now closed down), 2021

Everyone, Monsters – "Not From Here," The Rabbit Hole Co-operative, 2024

He Has Not Seen A Bird Before – "Boreal," Strange Wilds Press, 2024

This Echo Chamber Life – Penumbric Magazine e-zine, Neomythos Press, Oct 2023

I Vomited Every Day For Three Hours After You Ended Things – Trash Cat e-zine, 2024

Niche P*rn – Alien Buddha Press, 2024

Garden Path – The Vanishing Point Magazine, Issue 4, 2022

Neglect Takes the Form of the Recovery Position – Expose Bone Vol. 2, 2024

It's Not All About the Five Knuckle Shuffle – "Are You a Robot?" Three Cousins Publishing, 2022.

ALSO FROM SLEY HOUSE

NOVELS

A Mind Full of Scorpions
(Eyes Only, Book One)
JR Billingsley

Ground Control
K.A. Hough

Bad Form
Joe Taylor

Persephone's Escalator
Joe Taylor

The Cartography Door
Sean Edward

Black Echoes
JB McLaurin

Under the Churchyard in
the Chamber of Bone
JR Billingsley

ANTHOLOGIES

Tales of Sley House 2021

Tales of Sley House 2022

Tales of Sley House 2023

Tales of the Sley Siblings

STORY COLLECTIONS

Melpomene's Garden
Curtis Harrell

*Observations and Nightmares:
The Short Fiction of JR Billingsley*

JR Billingsley

See more at https://www.sleyhouse.com

www.ingramcontent.com/pod-product-compliance
Lightning Source LLC
Chambersburg PA
CBHW061644190726
48289CB00006B/1731